PRAISE FOR STEPHANIE ROWE AND *UNBECOMING BEHAVIOR!*

Stephanie Rowe "is a new voice to be reckoned with."
—The Press Enterprise

"*Unbecoming Behavior* is an uplifting story crafted for the true romantic. Ms. Rowe conveys a fresh outlook and an undying sense of humor."
—*Romance Reviews Today*

"Rowe has some serious things to say about love, work, family and expectations, but it's nicely coated with laughs and a frantic pacing."
—*Romantic Times*

STEPHANIE ROWE

UNBECOMING BEHAVIOR

MAKING IT®

December 2005

Published by

Dorchester Publishing Co., Inc.
200 Madison Avenue
New York, NY 10016

ISBN 0-505-52662-X

The name "Making It" and its logo are trademarks of Dorchester Publishing Co., Inc.

Printed in the United States of America.

Visit us on the web at www.dorchesterpub.com.

To my parents, for giving me the opportunities
to become a Boston attorney and acquire experiences
that were the inspiration for this story.
This is a work of fiction, however, and any similarities
to real-life people or situations are a coincidence.

To my fantastic and beloved agent, Michelle Grajkowski,
for encouraging me to write this story
and being a dear friend.

To my wonderful editor, Kate Seaver,
for supporting me and giving me great advice
as to where to take this story.

Thanks also to Leah Hultenschmidt and Rachel Granfield
for all your work behind the scenes.
Without you, none of this would be a reality.

And as always, thanks to my wonderful husband
for being so supportive and believing in me so completely.
Every woman needs one of you in her life!

UNBECOMING
BEHAVIOR

CHAPTER ONE

What in the world was a total hottie doing sitting in the office next to mine?

I barely caught a glimpse of dark hair and broad shoulders as I walked by. Was it too obvious to walk back by and take another look?

Probably. It was a law firm, after all. Must always be circumspect. Too bad being lawyerly and dignified wasn't my best attribute. Probably a good thing I wasn't actually a lawyer, huh? Much to my parents' dismay.

But hey, I was twenty-four. Hardly had to be living out my parents' dreams now, did I? Especially since I'd promised myself that I'd be pursuing my own dreams by the time I was twenty-five, which left me less than two months to figure out exactly what my dreams were. At least I'd finally broken up with Max. That was a start.

"Morning, Isabel." I nodded at my secretary as I walked by, then stopped and retraced my steps. Isabel would know. "Who's my next-door neighbor? Office was empty when I left on Friday."

Isabel looked a little frazzled, even for a Monday morning at seven thirty. "Blaine Hampton. New partner they hired from outside."

"Partner?" He'd looked way too young to be a partner. "Already?"

"Comes from money," she whispered. "Lots of connections."

Ah, excellent. Just my parents' type. Perhaps I should cozy up to him and make him my new boyfriend. Wouldn't that do a lot to get me back in the McCormick family's good graces? I had taken quite a hit when I dumped Max, who they all thought was my ticket to respectability. He had a good résumé and even better bloodlines. What more could a girl ask for?

"Bad news," Isabel continued. "Your event on Friday night? Canceled. Place had a fire on Saturday night."

"Canceled?" I felt my heart start to do weird little palpitations, as it always did when I felt an encounter with the firm's managing partner coming on. "I don't have an event for Friday?" The culmination of the first week of the summer interns. Always a huge event. Canceled? Visions of tearing out my hair and racing through the halls screaming and hurling things at random people popped into my head, but I immediately dismissed the idea as dangerously close to that "unbecoming behavior" standard the firm was always using to justify firing people. It was a nice, vague term, infinitely useful for tweaking to fit any situation the firm didn't think was up to par. Seeing as how I was but a lowly social director, I didn't bring enough value to the firm to be able to get away with any unbecoming behavior.

So instead of freaking out, I smiled and said, "Can you

make some calls and see if you can find another venue?"

Excellent, Shannon. Way to keep your voice calm. See? I could be a lawyer. Totally able to handle stress.

"Ahem."

Ahem? Who "ahems"? I turned around to find potential new boyfriend himself standing behind me. Early thirties at most. Kick-ass blue eyes. And to think I complained regularly about working in a law firm. I took it all back. "I'm Shannon McCormick. Your next-door neighbor."

He looked at me blankly. Okay, so he was a literal guy. He'd never get my oh-so-witty sense of humor. So I pointed to my office. "My office is next to yours."

"Oh. I'm Blaine Hampton."

"Nice to meet you." When I shook his hand, I actually felt my stomach do a little somersault. Blaine was totally hot. Terrible name, but very hot guy.

"Isabel is your secretary?" he asked.

"Yep."

"How much of her time do you usually take?"

Didn't like the attitude behind that question. Defenses: armed. "As much as I need."

Smokin'-hot next-door neighbor pursed his magnificent lips. "Well, I have a big deal I'm working on this week that will require pretty much all of her time. Can you try to limit your use of her?"

My mouth gaped open before I could stop it. "What?"

"My deal. I need Isabel."

I glanced at Isabel, who shrugged apologetically. "You two are my split."

Blaine turned to go back in his office, not even waiting for an answer. Yeah, right. Just because I didn't have a law

3

school degree on my office wall didn't mean I was some unworthy pond scum. "Excuse me? Blaine?"

He paused in his doorway. "Yes?"

"I have a lot going on this week. I run the intern program, and they arrive in a half hour. My event for Friday night got canceled, and I need Isabel's help to make all the arrangements for everything else this week. It's not like I can just *not* have these things done." My parents might think lawyers were better than social directors, but I sure as hell wasn't going to let some partner walk all over me, even if he was droolworthy.

He lifted an eyebrow. "You're welcome to take it up with Otto, but somehow I think he'll opine that a six-billion-dollar merger is more important than your interns' lunch plans. That's why I have you as my split. Because my work can take precedence."

Was he kidding? The pretentious beast who was no longer a boyfriend candidate wanted me to take it up with *Otto Nelson?* The managing partner. Seventy-three, totally old-school, believed it was a lawyer's prerogative to be an ass to every single person who worked for him, from junior partners all the way down to secretaries.

He scared the crap out of everyone. Including me. Oh, except, apparently, Blaine, who had somehow gotten Otto on his side. Blaine could probably indulge in all the unbecoming behavior he wanted and he'd never be held accountable. Jerk.

Blaine flashed me a dimpled smile that would have brought me to my knees if I didn't want to grab him by the neck and throw him out the window. Then he shut the door in my face.

I closed my eyes and pictured his head as a punching bag. Did a few quick jabs, then slammed my foot into it. Hah. *Not smiling so much now, are you, Blaine?*

"Shannon?"

Right. Standing there still facing a closed door with my eyes scrunched shut probably wasn't quite the professional and together look I usually strove for. I turned back to Isabel. "Okay, so can you help me find a place for Friday?"

She gave me an apologetic smile that sent waves of terror thudding through my body. "I'll try to find some time, I promise. Otto introduced him and told me his work took priority. You know I want to do your stuff, but . . ."

But Otto's a bastard who would think nothing of carving you up into little pieces, and you don't want to risk that kind of a miserable death by arranging for my event on Friday night. Totally understandable. I gritted my teeth and smiled. It wasn't Isabel's fault. "No problem. Just keep me posted on what you can do."

Isabel shot me a grateful smile, picked up a file that wasn't mine, and walked into Blaine's office.

Excellent.

Perhaps if I became some ornery bitch, then people would be afraid to piss me off, and then I might actually get some respect around here.

Yeah, right, the only way I could get away with being a bitch was if I had a law degree and brought in buckets of money, neither of which applied in my particular case. Besides, my job *was* about being fun and nice and approachable and beloved. Keep those interns well fed and pampered, and make sure their stories about their summer outshone the stories of all their classmates who interned somewhere else.

That was my job.

A professional entertainer. Swallow your pride. Keep everyone fat and happy, and you may survive to see another summer.

Not that I was bitter. Or insecure. Or had self-esteem issues. Never. I didn't have time for such ridiculous emotions. I had twenty-seven minutes to make sure the breakfast buffet was set up and the interns all had their name badges.

I dropped my briefcase on the floor of my office, glanced at the note from Isabel that Friday night's event was a bust, deleted three voice mails from Max-the-ex, tried not to wish I could crawl under my desk and hide, smoothed my bun, straightened my suit, and marched into the hall to put on the Shannon Show.

Some days I really *loved* my job.

"So then what happened?" My friend Emma Jansen kicked off her spiky sandals and propped her bare feet up on my desk. "Did you find an event for Friday?"

"Dog track." God. I was going to lose my job over this; I just knew it. I had to think gambling on dogs was at the top of the list for unbecoming behavior. Then again, so was a total failure to do my job, which would have happened if I hadn't found an event for Friday night. At least with the event, there was a chance I would escape unscathed.

It was almost ten o'clock on Monday night, and I was finally sitting down at my desk to return e-mails. Between the welcome breakfast, office assignments, lunch, dealing with crises, and the cocktail hour, I hadn't been at my desk to make phone calls until twenty minutes ago. The dog track was one of the only places open at this hour on a Monday night to take my reservation, so it won. "Isabel was occupied working for her new boss, so she wasn't able to make any phone calls."

Or track down the W-4 forms for the interns. Or copy the firm's handbook when we ran out of copies. Or anything else she would normally have done to keep me from completely losing my mind, going insane, and throwing myself down the elevator shaft. Good thing I hadn't been able to wedge the doors open.

And I had tried. Stuck the heel of my shoe in there about ten minutes ago, just to see. Not that I would actually have hurled myself down there, but . . . well, you know, it's always good to know your options. You never know. Maybe Blaine would accidentally tumble down the shaft instead of me, if only I could get those doors open. Terrible tragedy that would be.

"Dog track." Emma widened her eyes. "Really? That seems a little decadent for a stuffy place like this."

"Tell me about it." I picked up another slice of pizza Emma had been thoughtful enough to bring when she found out I was still at work. See? Who needed to have friends at work when I had real friends in my real life? "But it's not that easy to find a place that will take one hundred people for dinner in a private lounge with luxury accommodations on such short notice."

"And the dog track has those?"

"Apparently, yes." Heaven help me if the dog track's definition of *luxury* didn't fit in with Otto's. Dammit. There went that gut-gurgling thing again.

"God, you look sick. You thinking about Otto coming after you with a baseball bat again?"

"I only dreamed that once, and I won that battle by siccing a rabid pit bull on him, so obviously, in my subconscious, I realize that if it really came down to a battle, I'd win. So no, I'm fine."

Emma drummed her fingers on her desk. "So all this because some pretentious bastard usurped all of Isabel's time?"

"I'm a pretentious bastard? Is that what you've been telling people?"

Emma and I bolted upright in our chairs and looked toward the door.

Crap.

There was Blaine, sans the suit jacket and tie, but still looking sexy and arrogant. Typical of my life. A gorgeous guy who would actually help my cause with my parents, and he was a jerk.

Note to self: When you're insulting the person who occupies the next office, make sure he's gone home for the night before spouting off in loud tones with an open office door.
"My friend was talking about someone else," I said. Yes, that was a great cover-up. He'd be sure to believe that one.

Emma hopped to her feet and stuck out her hand. "Emma Jansen. Shannon's friend. No money, no contacts, not worth a lawyer's time."

Blaine grinned and shook her hand. "Blaine Hampton. Nice to meet you." I watched his eyes flit over her body. Cutoff denim shorts that showed off a daring amount of flesh, a tank top, bare feet with sparkly purple polish, and plenty of curves. Not exactly the type of outfit usually seen in a law firm, but apparently the type of outfit that caught the eye of Mr. Pretentious Bastard.

And no, that jab in my gut wasn't jealousy because he certainly hadn't looked at me that way. In fact, he'd barely looked at me at all. Just passed over me as some insignificant speck of dust in his way.

"So where are you from?" Emma asked.

Good question. If I'd had any sort of brain, I would have engaged him in some friendly conversation like that. Then maybe he wouldn't have been quite so ready to treat me like pond scum.

"New York."

New York. Figured. No wonder he was rich, with connections. Probably worked for some huge firm in New York and now was going to bring all that New York business to Miller & Shaw. If I weren't so tired, strung-out, and annoyed at how he was checking Emma out, I might have been mature enough to admit that perhaps he deserved to be partner and that it was a good move for the firm.

But as it was, I was way too far gone to generate that kind of dignified response.

"So you know anyone in town?" Emma asked.

Blaine raised an eyebrow. "Some business associates."

"Well, that's no fun. Come out with us on Thursday night. Shannon and I are meeting up with a couple of our friends at a fun bar."

What? That's exactly what I wanted, having one of my

work nightmares invading my inner sanctum of peace and tranquillity. Not. Emma knew that. What was she doing?

Blaine glanced at me, then at Emma's legs, then back at her face. "What time?"

"Oh, maybe nine thirty? Gives Shannon time to get through with work."

He nodded. "Sure."

Sure? What was that all about? Blaine coming out with us? To a bar? After work?

"Great. I'll be by to pick up Shannon. If you make sure you're clean and promise to stay ten feet behind us, you can walk over with us," Emma said.

Blaine grinned. A real grin. Not some boring, staid smile. A grin. His dimples looked damned cute. "It's a deal." He looked at me again, and some of the sparkle in his eyes faded. Not that I was taking personal offense to that little nugget or anything. "So I'm outta here. You guys okay to get home?"

I narrowed my eyes. "Is that why you came in here in the first place? To see if I was okay getting home?"

"Of course. It's after ten. If you want, we can share a cab."

Great. So he was rich, arrogant, connected, a secretary thief, totally hot, lusting after Emma, *and* he was enough of a gentleman to want to make sure I got home okay?

Bastard. What kind of a combination was that?

"I'm fine, but thanks for asking." Maybe it wasn't too late to salvage the situation. Maybe I could show a little cleavage on Thursday night at the bar and then he'd realize that he had a diva on the other side of his wall. And then he'd be treating me differently. Oh, yes, he'd be getting my coffee, making up excuses to talk to me, helping me with my work. Anything to get his hands on my body.

Ah. The beauty of being a woman in a world dominated by sex-crazed men. Breasts had all the power.

"See ya," Emma chirped, getting another smile in return.

I waited a full three minutes after I heard his feet walk down the hall, and then I turned to Emma. "What was that?"

"Oh, my God, Shannon. You didn't tell me he was *hot.*"

It was part of our code: Always alert each other to the presence of hot guys. "When he shut the door in my face, he lost some of his appeal."

"Wow. Rich, gorgeous, and lonely with no friends. He's just waiting for me to warm him up." Emma waggled her eyebrows. "Thursday night is looking mighty interesting. . . ."

"Emma! You can't sleep with him!"

"Why not?"

"Because I work with him." Duh.

"So?"

"What do you mean, so? He's a jerk, and I have to deal with him every day. Seeing him in his underwear in the middle of the night isn't exactly conducive to a great working relationship." The downside of Emma being my roommate: her sex life was my life too. "Besides, where's your support of me? He stole Isabel. Insulted me. Slammed the door in my face." Okay, so I was exaggerating. So what? To combat the pheromones he'd apparently been waving Emma's direction, I needed to play hardball.

"Shannon?"

11

Here we go. The apology. "Yes?"

"Did it ever occur to you that if you make nice with this guy outside of work and maybe be friends with him, he might become easier to work with?"

I hate it when I look like an idiot. "Perhaps."

Emma grinned. "Relax. It'll be fine. And I won't sleep with him. He's not my type anyway. You know how I feel about men in suits."

True. Emma's idea of a hot date was a guy with a Harley who was in serious need of a haircut and a shower. Which worked out perfectly. We never encroached upon each other's men. I always dated the suits.

Including Max. Two years of my life thrown away on him. Good thing women didn't reach their sexual prime until their late twenties or I'd be *really* mad. Assuming I was right to break up with him and that my true love lay somewhere in my future. Which I wasn't sure of at all. Scratch that. Yes, I was sure. It had been the right thing to do.

"So I have a new gig. Want to help?"

I eyed Emma. "You quit your job already? You've been there for what? Three months?"

"Wasn't for me." She perched on the edge of her chair. "I'm going to be a Bud Light girl."

"Interesting job title. What's it entail?"

"Going to bars in cute outfits and flirting with all the guys and giving away Bud Light stuff." She grinned, her eyes dancing. "Does that sound awesome or what?"

"It does sound fun," I admitted. Not that I'd ever quit my job to do that. My parents were barely surviving my lack of a graduate degree. Imagine if I said I was a Bud Light girl? They'd probably disown me and tell all their friends I was in prison for embezzling billions of dollars. At least that would be impressive because it would involve large sums of money.

"So, want to do it with me?"

"Can't. Already have a job, remember?"

"You don't have to quit your job, you dork. Just fill in with me sometimes. It's at night, so you can do it when you get off work. Like Saturday night. Got plans Saturday night?"

Other than dreading the pink slip I was sure to get Monday after Otto, managing partner from hell, got wind of the Friday-night outing to the dog track? No, not really. "I can't be a Bud Light girl."

"Sure you can. It'll be fun. It'll loosen you up. Take your mind off Blaine and Max."

"Max? Did he call again?"

"Well, actually, he was passed out in the hallway in front of our apartment when I left. I had to step over him. Hopefully he'll be gone by the time we get back."

And to think my parents were upset that I'd dumped him. "Excellent." And I refused to feel guilty about the fact that he'd drunk himself into oblivion, even though it was completely my fault for dumping him two weeks ago. Okay, so I felt guilty. How could I not? I'd gone out with him for two years and still loved him and had spent most of the last two weeks wondering whether I'd done the right thing by breaking up with him. There was nothing *wrong* with him, but . . . well, I don't know. I felt like there should be *more*. But what if I was wrong? What if Max was my best chance for happiness and I made the mistake of dumping him in hopes of that elusive man who would stir my soul?

Emma wrinkled her brows. "At least he's not violent or anything. I'm sure he'll get bored eventually and move on."

Move on? I didn't want him to move on. What if I changed my mind and he was already married to someone else? Then I'd spend the rest of my life alone and suffering because of my idiocy.

No, it was right to break up with him. I had to trust my gut.

Emma rubbed her chin. "Maybe we should invite him along on Thursday and try to set him up with someone else so he'll forget about you. . . ." She saw my face. "Or not."

"Appreciate the consideration for my feelings." Blaine and Max in one night? I'd have to make sure I got hit by a bus on the way to the bar so I wouldn't have to show up. A quick trip to the emergency room on life support would be preferable to Blaine and Max at one time. Nothing like being around an arrogant bastard who was too good for me to make me want to go crawling back to Max. I wasn't immune enough from Max yet, and I needed to avoid him. It was my only chance to break free and try life without him.

"So, you on for Saturday night? A little barhopping and flirting?"

Though totally undignified for a McCormick, it did sound like fun. . . . Oh, hell. "Wait a sec. The Bud Light girl thing is this Saturday night?"

"Yeah . . . why?"

I flopped back in my chair. Relieved that I couldn't go. Annoyed that I couldn't go. "My sister's engagement party."

"It is? This Saturday?" Emma looked startled. "Really?"

"Yes, really. You'll have to postpone starting your new

job, I guess." As a longtime friend, Emma was an automatic invite to my sister's engagement party.

She frowned. "I'll have to see if I can get out of the Bud Light thing for that night. Not sure, though."

I tightened my grip on my chair. "You're going to bail on me?"

"Well, I'll try to come. I've only had this job for six hours. I'm not ready to lose it yet." Emma stood up. "Come on. It's ten thirty. Give it up for tonight already."

Emma was right. I'd gotten the reservations for Friday night, had the major crises dealt with today, and no doubt needed some sleep to deal with the ones tomorrow. Gotta be bright-eyed and bushy-tailed for the interns, as my grandma used to say.

My grandma. The last member of my family (except for me) on either the McCormick or the Fischer side who didn't have a graduate degree. Too bad they killed her to protect the family name.

Oh, sure, they say she died of a heart attack, but I never believed that.

I figured it was just a matter of time until they did me in. Unless, of course, I landed a guy like Blaine, or took back Max. When they realized all hope of my redemption was lost, I'd have to institute a new policy of checking under my car before I started the ignition.

And to think it was only five days until my sister's engagement party, when every overachieving member of my family would be present. How would I ever survive the anticipation?

CHAPTER TWO

I followed Emma out of the elevators, then saw that my favorite security guard, Van Reinhart, was on duty. At twenty-six, he was one of only two security guards from the same generation I was. The rest were retired uniforms looking for some extra dough. But not Van. Van was cool, and he was my buddy. My respite. "Hey, Emma, let's stop and say hi to Van."

Emma checked out the security stand, then shook her head. "I'm going to hit the road. You can catch up." Emma was inspired to stop at the guard's booth for a little chitchat only when Van's hot counterpart, Fritz, was on duty.

"Fine." I waved her off and headed over to see the one normal, nonbaggage person in my life. Van was safe because he was outside of every part of my life. He didn't know my family, anyone at work, my friends, or even anything about being in a law firm. He was the antithesis of the world I was stuck in, and he was my oasis. No pressure, no deep relationship, just a friendship of convenience. It was perfect. I grinned and sat down next to Van behind the booth. "Hey, Van."

He doffed his navy-blue security cap. "Shannon. You're looking haggard and tired tonight. Good day at work?"

"Is that how you seduce all the ladies? Tell them how horrible they look?"

He shrugged. "Just you."

"I'm honored." I swiveled back and forth in my chair and said nothing.

And neither did he.

But I could tell he was watching me.

I decided to count to thirty, and if he didn't ask me what was wrong, then I'd tell him. But it would be so much easier if he'd ask, because I knew he could tell I was out of sorts.

I only got to seven.

"What's wrong with you?"

"Broke up with Max."

I heard Van make some sort of weird choking noise, so I looked up sharply. He was grinning at me, his green eyes open in astonishment behind his glasses. "You broke up with Max? Unheard-of. How could that be?"

I shoved him. "This time it's real."

"Like last time?"

"No, not like last time."

"Then like the time before? Because that was real too."

I frowned. "Did I say it was real each of those times?"

"Yep." Van pulled open a drawer and he handed me a Snickers. "Here."

"I'm on a diet." I took the candy bar and unwrapped it. "I don't eat junk food anymore." Then I took a big bite. Damn, it tasted good. Probably because it was contraband.

"Are you saying that just so I'll tell you that you're hot and you don't need to diet?"

I rolled my eyes at him. "Do you really think I'm that type?"

"No." Van leaned back in his chair and put his black boots up on the desk. "So, why is it real this time with Max?"

"Because it is." I licked the chocolate off my fingers and tossed the wrapper. "Do you have any more?"

He pulled the drawer open with his toe. "Help yourself."

Wow. What a selection. Twix, Butterfinger, M&M's. All my favorites. "I had no idea you ate this stuff."

"Only at night to keep me awake. I don't do coffee."

Wish I could have a body like Van's and eat chocolate every night. As it was, I'd have to eat rice cakes and water for the next few days if I wanted to fit into my engagement party dress this weekend. Though I suppose if part of my job were being fit enough to chase down and tackle intruders, I might go to the gym a little more often. As it was, I waved to the gym every morning on the way to work. That was about it, as least during the summer, when all the interns were sucking up my time.

I helped myself to a Twix.

"So, about Max?"

"Right." I copied Van's posture, crossing my ankles to make sure I didn't flash anyone. "He's not the one for me."

Van lifted a brow. "According to who?"

"Me." Okay, so I was having major déjà vu. Had I really had this exact conversation with Van every time I'd broken up with Max? "Sure, he's handsome and rich and success-ful and totally in love with me, but that's not enough."

"Not that you have high standards or anything."

I frowned. "Have you ever been totally in love with someone? So in love that you'd step in front of a truck to save them?"

"Only if the truck was parked."

"See? That's how I feel about Max!" Well, maybe not parked. I might venture out for five miles an hour, but nothing more. "That's not true love, and that's what I want. And I'm never going to find it if I keep hanging out with Max." Even as I said it, I got a little misty eyed. Max was my best friend. Why didn't he pass the truck test? I cleared my throat. "So, anyway, I wanted to ask you if you would please not let him upstairs if he comes to see me."

Van looked at me sharply. "You serious?"

"Yeah." Oh, God. This wasn't easy.

"You've never told me to do that before."

"See? I said this was for real." I was smart enough to know that if Max showed up with food when I was tired and crabby . . . well, my resistance would be down.

"You going to change your mind? Because I'll be pissed if I stop him, and then he calls you on his cell phone from the lobby and you change your mind and invite him up. Makes me lose credibility."

I frowned. Would I change my mind? No. For Van's sake, I couldn't. Excellent. Added motivation not to succumb. "I promise I won't change my mind. Your reputation is safe with me."

He eyed me for a while, then finally nodded. "I'll do it."

"Thanks."

He gave me a half smile, and we fell silent again. It wasn't an uncomfortable silence. It was a silence born because the two people barely knew each other, and yet didn't feel the need to dig further. He knew nothing about my life, other than what I complained to him about—which was mostly Max and some general miseries about my job. And I knew nothing about him, other than that he worked night security at my building and didn't drink coffee.

It was the perfect relationship for both of us.

"So I guess I'll head out."

"Want me to call a cab?"

I shook my head. "The T is still running. I'll just hop it and head home." I wasn't in the mood to have to make chitchat with a cabdriver, but it was impossible for me to take a cab without chatting. If I didn't make conversation, I felt like some pretentious bitch who was being escorted around. I felt like any other member of my family, all of whom I tried to distance myself from whenever possible. Why couldn't they have regular jobs, like Van? Then they'd probably be proud of me. Or maybe not. Well, we'd never know, would we? Because they weren't regular people.

"Shannon."

I turned just in time to catch another Twix from Van. "Thanks."

"Cheer up."

"Why?"

The corner of his mouth curled up. "Because you have a great body that a lot of women would pay good money for."

My cheeks flamed. "Shut up." But I grinned all the way to the corner. Every girl needs a Van in her life.

"Shannon? Do you have a minute?"

Do I look like I have a minute? It wasn't as if someone had just spilled wine all over the imported carpet in the conference room or anything. Or like Otto wasn't due to arrive in, like, one minute to meet the interns. But I looked up from the floor, where I was on my knees frantically scrubbing, and I smiled at the twenty-three-year-old Harvard Law student named Jessamee Bouchillion. "Yes, Jessamee?"

"You know how yesterday I volunteered for the office that's on the fourth floor of the firm?"

I sat back on my heels and pictured using Jessamee as target practice with Emma's new darts. Ah, so cathartic. "Yes, you said you wanted the biggest available office, so we agreed that space was a good choice for you."

"Well, I changed my mind."

"That you want a big office?"

"No, that I'll accept an office on that floor. It's way off in the corner. Away from all the action."

"Well, Jessamee, most of the offices have already been assigned. That's by far the largest, most comfortable one available right now. Plus it has more windows than any of the others. I really think it's your best option at this point." Most of the interns worked in glorified broom closets— and were just happy to have their own space—but as Jessamee had noted, this one was pretty isolated and therefore not particularly popular.

Jessamee folded her arms across her chest. "I don't care. I want an office that's next to a partner in corporate, not two floors down in bankruptcy. How am I going to impress the corporate partners if I'm off in bankruptcy?"

My knees were starting to throb. In case anyone was wondering, there wasn't a great deal of padding beneath the Oriental carpet in this conference room. "If you do good work and attend all the events, you'll meet everyone who has a stake in your future." That's me, all about giving basic advice to these kids who were younger than me and making more in their eight-week internship than I did practically all year.

Not that I was immature enough to keep track of those kinds of things. Or maybe I was. Just a little bit.

Jessamee scowled. "It's not enough. My professor told me office location was key. I need to be constantly visible so they can't forget me. I want an office in corporate, next to a partner."

"I understand, but I've already filled the open office in corporate."

Her beady little eyes narrowed. "How would your boss like it if he found out you weren't being nice to the interns? Isn't it your job to take care of us?"

She was threatening me? I couldn't believe it. "Jessamee—"

"I heard the managing partner is addressing us for lunch. Shall I tell him that I'm thinking of moving to another firm for the summer, since this firm doesn't take care of its interns?"

Bitch. If she weren't an overachieving superstar with serious family connections that Otto would die for, I'd totally get her fired. But Otto would pick her over me, and she knew it. Leaving me no choice but to grit my teeth. "I'll see what I can find." I wondered if the office next to Psychotic Otto was open. We seemed to have trouble keeping it occupied.

Jessamee immediately flashed me a brilliant smile. "Thanks so much, Shannon. I knew you'd help me."

"No problem." Yes, I was pretty sure the office next to Otto was open. And, of course, I'd have to switch her secretary split, because she was on a new floor. I wondered if

22

Otto had room. . . . Yeah, right. Otto never shared with anyone, let alone an intern. It definitely wasn't a good idea to bring myself to the forefront of Otto's radar by stealing valuable secretary time from him. Though it would be fun to see Jessamee fight over an assistant with Otto. Who knew? Maybe Jessamee would win.

Jessamee sauntered off to chitchat with more important people, while I resumed my floor scrubbing. And to think I'd pooh-poohed a job as a Bud Light girl. At least then people would be noticing me, even it was just for my boobs and my shwag.

I felt a hand grab my arm. "Shannon! Get up! Otto's on his way down the hall."

One of the few lawyers that I could actually see myself being friends with pulled me to my feet. Hildy Moss, a junior partner who was the nicest woman ever, grabbed the towel from my hand. "You'd better go. I'll pull a chair over this stain."

"Bless you." I handed over the towel, brushed the white fuzz off my navy skirt, tried to tuck some stray hairs back into my bun, and took a quick glance around the room.

Twenty-six interns present. Good.

Seventeen attorneys present. Not so good. Where was everyone else? I pulled out my cell phone and dialed Isabel. "Isabel. Shannon. Can you do a quick roundup and get some more attorneys in here? Otto's due here any minute and he's not going to be happy with the ratio." There went my stomach getting all queasy again. Why was I so afraid of him? The worst he could do was fire me. Actually, no. The worst he could do would be to totally humiliate me in front of a roomful of strangers, and then let me keep my job, so I had to face everyone daily for the rest of my life. "And can you make it fast?"

Isabel hesitated. "I'm in the middle of typing up a document for Blaine."

"Isabel! Please!" *Oh, don't let this happen to me now.*

"Well, he said it was urgent. . . ."

"Put him on the phone. Now." I wasn't heartless enough to make Isabel fight my fights, but this had gone too far.

"This is Blaine."

So Pretentious Bastard even had a sexy phone voice. Maybe he got all his connections by doing phone sex for rich women, then using blackmail to get their business. Excellent. It made me feel much better to think of Blaine as having a secret that could potentially destroy him professionally. "Blaine. Shannon. I need Isabel for ten minutes. Give her your permission."

"Why?"

Un-friggin'-believable. She'd been my secretary for three years; Blaine had been at the firm for three days, and I had to explain my requests to him? Like I wasn't sophisticated enough to assess on my own whether I was having a crisis? Then I recalled Emma's suggestion: Make nice, and maybe he'd be nice back. I refrained from educating him as to exactly how many swear words I knew, and said very calmly, "Blaine. I'm having a crisis. Otto is due in this conference room any minute and he expects at least thirty attorneys to be entertaining the interns. I have seventeen. I need fourteen more in about one minute. So give me a break and let Isabel help me."

"Thirteen."

"What?"

"Seventeen plus thirteen is thirty. Fourteen would be thirty-one."

And thank you for that. Exactly what I needed: yet another person trying to make me feel like an insignificant peon.

So I hung up. Then I paused for a moment to picture hanging him out his twenty-eighth-story window by his ankles and leaving him there all day. Even better, I'd pour water on him every five minutes to take advantage of the windchill. Nope, not enough. I'd also need a staple gun to shoot staples through the bottom of his feet. Must make the torture worthy of the crime.

"Ms. McCormick?"

Otto. Oh, God, I was going to throw up.

Instead, I turned toward the door and smiled. "Mr. Nelson. So nice to see you."

"Where are the rest of the attorneys?"

I would hate Blaine Hampton for the rest of my life.

"They're on their way."

Otto looked at his watch. "It's three minutes past noon."

"Right." And, of course, it was my fault that the attorneys weren't here. Like I could control them. "Don't worry, sir. They'll be here."

He didn't look pleased. "I'm going back to my office. Call me when you're ready."

And then he left.

I decided to quit, right then and there. If I didn't, I was going to have a bleeding ulcer just in time for my twenty-fifth birthday.

"I'll go find some folks," Hildy said. "You take care of the interns."

25

No need. I'm going to quit. "That would be awesome."

Hildy squeezed my arm, gave me a wink, then slipped out of the room. Did I mention that Hildy was the nicest woman ever? Couldn't imagine why she was a lawyer. A successful one too, from what I heard. A woman. And nice. And successful. And a partner at Miller & Shaw. Unbelievable.

I could almost hear my mother whispering, *That could be you, Shannon.*

Ack! Shut up, Mom! I'm in the middle of a crisis!

Trying not to think of Otto sitting at his desk, tapping his fingers, watching the clock, I circulated among the interns, making sure everyone was doing all right. Took notes on a faulty mouse, a conflict with the Red Sox game next Tuesday night, and a complaint that an attorney had told the intern she had to miss Friday night's event to work. How were these interns supposed to be blinded as to what life as an M&S lawyer was really like if they were forced to work nights and weekends?

Obviously I needed to do a little reminding.

Three attorneys walked into the room, and I saw Isabel hurry by the doorway. Isabel! Thank God!

Unless she was picking up dry cleaning for Blaine. That would probably be more important than my avoiding public humiliation by Otto, huh?

Another circuit of the room, during which seven more attorneys came in.

That had to be good enough, right? I mean, eight minutes had gone by since Otto left. It was almost twelve fifteen, and he was supposed to present at noon. Which was worse, making him wait longer, or inviting him back when his audience was still too small?

Hildy walked in with the entire family law group, which put me over my limit.

So, deep breath. I had to call Otto. I walked to the conference room phone and dialed the operator. "Kathy Michaels, please." Okay, so I was a wimp. I'll bet almost every person in the firm would call Otto's secretary instead of calling Otto himself. Besides, he preferred it that way. It was old-school never to take a phone call that hadn't been screened by his secretary, and as I said before, Otto was old-school.

"Kathy Michaels, can I help you?"

"Hi, Kathy. It's Shannon. I have thirty-six attorneys here now. Do you think Mr. Nelson would be available to return to the conference room?"

"I'll check." The phone went on hold, and I noticed that I'd dug deep crevices in the palms of my hands from my fingernails. How was I going to make it through the summer?

"Hi, Shannon. Mr. Nelson is on his way."

"Thanks." I hung up and walked over to the door to head off three attorneys who appeared to be sneaking out. "Hi. Sorry. You can't leave yet. Not until Mr. Nelson has given his speech." As much as I tended to dwell on my perceived inferiority toward the attorneys in the firm, bossing around people who had no reason to listen to me wasn't particularly daunting when faced with the alternative possibility of disappointing Otto again.

I literally blocked the door and gave them my sweetest smile. A few rolled their eyes, but at least they clumped next to the door and didn't try to run me over. Thank heavens they were weighed down with the burden of having to behave in ways "not unbecoming to the firm"—in this case, not trampling the social director.

I heard a throat clearing behind me, and I looked back. *Crap.* "Oh, hello, Mr. Nelson. Sorry to be in your way."

Otto said nothing, simply walked past me into the room, surveyed the crowd, then nodded at me.

Right. My cue. I clapped my hands and raised my voice. "Can I have your attention, everyone? I have a special guest. Mr. Otto Nelson, managing partner of Miller and Shaw." I then proceeded to give a glowing recitation of all of Otto's professional successes, and was exceedingly grateful for a few wide eyes and whispers. Feeding Otto's ego could only help my cause.

I finished with a plea for a rousing round of applause, which I got. Then I stepped aside and let Otto take over.

Damn. Someone had moved the chair. If he looked down and slightly to the right, he'd see the big wet spot on a very expensive carpet.

I spent the next twenty minutes cringing every time Otto's eyes wandered toward the spot, but he never looked down. He was too busy judging the worth of each intern according to their facial reactions to his brilliant prose.

He finished to another round of applause—thank God—then walked over to me.

I swallowed. What if he'd heard about the dog track already?

"So tell me about each intern, what college they went to, law school they are currently attending, and their GPA, law review status, any family connections, their work ethic, and what they bring to the table that no one else does. Go."

I went.

The first summer at M&S, I'd nearly passed out in terror when Otto had confronted me with the same questions, and I'd been totally unprepared. Now I mailed out a question-naire to the interns a month before they started and I had the results memorized by the time they walked in the door.

I was no fool. I wanted to avoid bleeding ulcers for as long as possible.

I got back to my desk and collapsed in my chair. I was still employed, Otto hadn't insulted me, and none of the interns had offended him. Lunch was a success. I rocked at my job.

My phone rang and I answered it without screening. Did I mention I was an idiot?

"Shannon. It's Mom."

Crud. There went my feeling of self-satisfaction. How long would it take for her to make me feel bad? I set the timer on my watch and hit start. "Hi, Mom. How are you?"

"Fine." She paused for a moment. "So, um, seen Max lately?"

I pressed my lips together. "We haven't gotten back together. We're not going to."

She let out an exasperated groan. "This is ridiculous, Shannon. He's smart, rich, successful, and he loves you. You aren't going to do better than him."

No way was I going to tell her I had that same paranoid thought every ten seconds. "He doesn't pass the truck test."

"The what?"

"Never mind." Then I tensed. "You aren't inviting him to

the party this weekend, are you?" That would be my sister's engagement party, which was already going to be stressful enough without adding Max to the scene.

"He's a family friend. Of course he's coming."

"Mom! Can't you have any respect for my feelings? I don't want him there." Why couldn't my family accept my decision to end things with Max? There was more to a good match than money and power, at least in my book. "Mom? Did you hear me?"

"I'm very disappointed in how you're handling this situation with Max."

"Yes, you've made that clear. Is there anything else you want?" I had to get her off the phone before she ruined me for the day.

She sighed with dismay that made my stomach curl. "What are you wearing to the party?"

"A dress." I frowned and tried not to pout.

"Did you buy a new one, I hope?"

"Yes." My sister was marrying a doctor and all of the crème de la crème of society would be at the engagement party. Mustn't let Shannon embarrass the family in public by being herself.

"Whose is it?"

"Mine."

"Shannon. You know what I mean. Who is the designer?" For those of us on a budget, buying clothes with designer tags wasn't an option. "I don't know. But it looks good on me. You'll like it."

Disapproving silence.

It took her less than a minute to make me feel bad about myself. She was quite the talent, wasn't she?

"Why don't you head over to Stacey's Boutique and pick something out? I'll have her put it on my tab. You do realize how important this event is, don't you?"

I ground my teeth and counted to ten. "Mom, I'm twenty-four and I work in a law firm. I know how to dress." And there was no way I was taking money from her. That would give her power over my life. "Give me a little credit."

Her voice was tight. "Fine."

"Fine."

"Don't disappoint me."

Yeah, we both knew there was no chance of my not doing that. My mere existence was a disappointment to her.

"Sit down, Shannon. Eat." My friend Dave Siegal grabbed my hand as I ran by him to check on the entrées.

"I can't. What if the food is late? The show starts at eight. We have to be there by quarter of, which means we have to leave here by seven thirty, which means the entrée has to be on the tables by six fifty-five, and it's already six forty-seven and I haven't seen it." I glanced around the room. Everyone was finished with their salads, yet the staff hadn't started clearing them. It was bad enough to have to manage dinner for all the attorneys and their interns, but this "spouse" night really killed me. Way too many people.

And figuring out the seating for the theater had been a nightmare. Nightmare! The seats were spread all over the theater and I'd spent all day with Hildy trying to figure out who should go where. Or rather, I'd spent a half hour with Hildy, and the rest of it crying alone in my office because I didn't want to put anyone together who hated each other, or who'd slept with the other's spouse, or usurped a client, or anything like that.

Isabel knew all that stuff. Too bad she'd been occupied with Blaine's stupid deal. Oh, sure, to him maybe a six-billion-dollar deal was more important than a social director's issues. I, however, felt that making sure I didn't wind up with a political crisis that made the firm explode, lose all its best clients and partners, and go bankrupt was pretty important too.

Too late now. I'd made my assignments. No going back.

"Shannon! Sit!" Dave pulled me down beside him. "You've been in that kitchen six times in the last twenty minutes. The staff knows what time we have to leave. If you bug them one more time they're going to spit in everyone's food and poison us."

I stared at Dave. "Have I been rude?" Dear God, don't tell me I'd been rude. I dealt with enough rude people all day—had it finally rubbed off on me? Was I treating people like I was the one with the graduate degree and so much money I used it to line my cat's litter box?

Dave laughed and rubbed my shoulder. "Shannon. You're fine. You just need to relax and enjoy."

"Ha!" I grabbed my water and chugged it down. Probably a bad move, because I'd have to pee right when I was trying to get everyone organized. Dehydration was definitely preferable to bolting for the bathroom. I should have worn Depends so I could just keep on powering. Of course, Depends probably wouldn't work with a thong, but hey, I could adjust. There was nothing wrong with my grandma briefs. It wasn't like anyone was seeing them anymore!

"Shannon!" Dave put his hand across mine. "Eat your

salad. Smile at your colleagues. Isn't part of your job enter-taining the interns too?"

"Yes, it is." Dave was right. See, this was why I'd brought him. He and Emma, along with my other friend Phoebe, were my three best friends. I went to high school with Dave and we'd always kept in touch. He'd married his college girlfriend, but I'd never been all that close to her. Probably because she was threatened by my relationship with Dave and had banned him from ever seeing me again.

But since she was out of town and I needed a "spouse" for tonight's affair, why not borrow her husband? It seemed logical to both Dave and me. Luckily, his wife traveled quite a bit or we'd never get to see each other.

I turned to the intern on my right, a tiny little thing named Missy Stephens. Under five feet, she weighed about ten pounds, and was so timid that I don't think she'd ever looked anyone in the eye.

Except me. I could either take that as a statement that as support staff, I was not worthy of being intimidated by, or I could take it as a compliment that my social skills were so outstanding that I was able to make even the most timid intern feel confident. Dave would tell me to choose the lat-ter, and since he was my illicit date for tonight, it was his advice I would take.

"Having fun, Missy?"

She shrugged and said nothing.

"So what kind of assignments have you gotten so far?"

She flicked me a wan smile and mumbled something about research.

Okay, so she'd made eye contact with me. It didn't mean I could get her to talk. For the umpteenth time I wondered how she'd gotten the job. Maybe she'd had a twin sister do the interview or something.

"Shannon!" Jessamee leaned from around Missy's other side, and the two interns on her right were also staring at me. "Your husband is totally hot. We had no idea."

I glanced at Dave, who was chatting up one of the partners. I guess he was cute. I never thought of him that way. He was just Dave. "He's not my husband."

Jessamee looked thrilled by the news. "He's got a wedding ring on. Are you having an affair with him?"

"No." Unbelievable. If I were, would I be stupid enough to bring him to a firm outing and then tell a bunch of interns about it? But I just smiled demurely and said nothing. Imagined Jessamee at work at two in the morning for the third day in a row without a shower or a change of clothes, and I felt better.

"Oh." Jessamee and her little friends had the gall to look disappointed. "So who is?"

"What?"

"Well, who's dating who? Who's married to who? You must know the scoop."

Suddenly all the interns at my end of the table were staring at me with eager anticipation on their faces. "Shouldn't you guys be worrying about work?"

They all looked blank. Work? What was work? They were here for the summer to play and be wined and dined. "It's night. Not time for work," Jessamee said. There was an underlying threat to her voice, reminding me that I was supposed to pamper her.

As I said before, bitch.

No, I was going to be positive. Her comment was good news, because it meant the illusions were already working. Lawyers didn't work after five o'clock, right? Of course not. The interns were slowly getting sucked into the myth. If I had scruples of any sort, I would probably feel bad about creating a fantasy world with the goal of luring talented young attorneys into it, then bashing them over the head with reality after they were roped in by big salaries and the pressure of their reputations.

Actually, I did feel sort of bad about it, but that was my job, right? That's why I made the big bucks. Oh, did I say "big bucks"? I meant measly little salary that barely covered bread and water for my meals.

"So tell us the gossip."

I rattled off a couple of attorneys who were married, or commonly known to be dating, but kept the sordid stuff to myself. Not that I didn't suck up that kind of gossip as much as the next person, but I wasn't about to repeat it to interns who might go around identifying their source to the wrong person.

They seemed satisfied for the moment, but unfortunately it allowed them to turn the conversation back to me. "So if this is spouse night, why are you here with someone else's husband? You're not married?" Jessamee continued to grill me.

"Nope." I could hear my mom's voice, *tsk-tsk*ing me for being single at age twenty-four. Didn't I want to take Max back? Such a lovely young man with a promising career.

"Boyfriend?"

I gritted my teeth. "Nope."

"Girlfriend?"

I actually did a double take, but managed to regain my composure enough to be pleasant. "Just because I'm not dating a guy doesn't mean I must be a lesbian. There's nothing wrong with simply being single, you know."

Jessamee giggled. "Of course not. But it's a little weird to be single and bring someone else's husband to spouse events. It's not like you're going to be meeting many available men when the guy you're with has a ring on his finger."

I smiled. "I found you an office in corporate, Jessamee. Right next to Otto. You can't get more connected than being neighbors with the managing partner." Shame on me. Being under Otto's watchful eye was no picnic—neither was listening to him lose his temper over every inconvenience. The office next to his was vacant for a very good reason: no one wanted it. If I'd had any heart at all, I'd have warned Jessamee about being *too* connected. Instead I enjoyed a small moment of victory. How much pettier could I get?

Jessamee nearly puffed out with pride. "Excellent. Thanks, Shannon." How smug did she look? Like she'd bested me or something. She promptly turned away to gloat to the intern sitting next to her. Suddenly, I didn't feel quite so guilty, especially when I watched her ignore the response of the intern next to her and start a conversation with an attorney who was sitting several seats down. When she announced that she was going to be moving to the office next to Otto, the attorney shot me a curious look.

I decided to check on the dinner.

CHAPTER THREE

By some miracle of the Preserve Shannon's Job Fund, we made it to the theater fifteen minutes before the show started, exactly as I had planned. Was I good or what? "I was never worried," I said to Dave as we played sheepdog to the stragglers of the bunch.

He laughed. "I could tell." Then his smile faded. "I heard those interns grilling you about me. You doing okay?"

"No problem." I patted his arm. "I'm really fine with being single." In fact, it was a relief to be single. Sort of. "And you? How's married life?"

Dave's wife was always a dicey topic between us. Probably because she was saving up the money to put a hit out on me. Good thing I had an unlisted address.

"She's good. We've decided to start trying to have a kid."

Whoa. "Seriously?" *Stab me in my gut, why don't you?* Not that I wanted kids, but Dave? My partner in crime since ninth grade? A dad? No way would we be able to keep up our clandestine, absolutely-no-sex, totally platonic affair. "Got day care planned?"

"Actually, Yvonne's thinking of quitting her job and

opening a consulting business. Then she'd work from home and be a mom."

"No way."

"Yep." He held the door open for me as we walked into the theater. "She's pretty excited about it, actually."

"I never saw Yvonne as the domestic type."

Dave lifted a brow. "There's a lot of things you don't know about Yvonne. Do you really think I'd have married some horrible woman who wanted to torture little children and neglect her husband and kids for some glorious career that required her to travel three hundred days of the year?"

"Well, I wasn't *sure* about the torturing of little children, but now that you mention it . . ."

Dave stopped in the middle of the crowded hallway and gave me a look.

"Sorry." I felt like a jerk now. "Really, I'm just having a bad week and everything. I have no right to take it out on Yvonne."

"No, you don't."

"I said I was sorry!" *Dammit.* I really couldn't afford to have Dave mad at me. It would put me over the top—the "top" in question being the one that plummeted me straight down the precipice of total misery, isolation, and depression. "I'm sorry!"

Dave stared at me for a long minute, totally oblivious to being bumped by the crowds rushing in to see the show.

Crap. I'd totally pushed it too far.

"Shannon! Shannon! Look who I found!"

I turned around to see Hildy walking toward me, towing Max behind her. Max? Holy mother-of-pearl. What was he doing here? My stomach did a flip-flop. He looked so good.

I heard Dave suck in his breath and felt him move beside me. Well, sort of beside me. His shoulder was actually in front of mine, like he was blocking me.

And there was Max, in his Italian suit, with his gorgeous hair, completely sexy body, and those perfect teeth.

How dared he show up at this event before I was fully immunized against him? With any luck, I'd be able to muster up enough irritation with his presumptive appearance that I would drop-kick him across the room instead of throwing myself into his arms and begging him to take me back.

I screwed up my courage to deal with whatever emotional reaction he evoked in me. I had made a decision, and it was the right one. Now I just had to stand strong.

Hildy coasted to a stop, her arm tucked through Max's. "I couldn't believe it when he came up to me and asked where you were. I thought for sure he must have been out of town, which was why you brought Dave." She smiled at Dave. "You'll have to switch tickets with Max so he can sit with Shannon. Have a good show, you guys. 'Bye!"

And then she left.

Okay, when I said Hildy was the nicest woman ever, perhaps I shouldn't have framed it as a compliment.

See, this was the big debate. Everyone at the firm knew Max, because, as my significant other for the last two years, he'd been at all the firm events, especially since I was the social director and all. And since he fit oh so well into this kind of society, everyone loved him. Begging the question: Did I tell everyone I broke up with him and listen to them all tell me what a fool I was and try to convince me to take him back? Or did I keep my personal issues private and hope that no one ran into him and escorted him over to me?

Interesting debate to which I would have to give serious thought.

After, of course, I extricated myself from this situation without getting back together with him. I swallowed and forced a light tone to my voice. "What are you doing here, Max?" I could barely see him around Dave's broad shoulder, so I sort of pushed Dave to the side. He moved maybe an inch. Dave had never thought Max was good enough for me, and he was thrilled I'd finally seen the light.

"Going to the theater," Max said. "You look really sexy in that dress."

"Thanks." It really didn't hurt to have my ego stroked, you know what I mean? *Ack! No, Shannon! Be strong! You hate him, remember?* After all, he did have that wee little incident with the barmaid three weeks ago (hence the breakup). Granted, it was only a little hot dancing at the bar, and he was tipsy and thought I wasn't going to be there, but it still pissed me off. Enough was enough. I wanted more than a boyfriend who flirted with other women the moment my back was turned.

Max nodded at Dave. "Hey, Dave. Thanks for taking care of my woman for me. Don't want the single guys hitting on her."

"Max!" I shoved him in the chest. Hard. It was mildly satisfying to hear an "oomph" pop out of his mouth. Did his chest feel good or what? I missed having a chest to snuggle up to. I lifted my chin. I was not so desperate that I'd settle for the wrong guy rather than be alone for a while. "I'm not your woman. We broke up. It's over."

"Like we've broken up before? You never stopped being my woman then." Max looked a little smug and not at all battered by my shove. Too bad. Obviously I needed to take some boxing classes to get a little more power in my follow-through.

"Okay, fine. I'll admit that we've broken up six times before and always gotten back together. But that was different. It's really over. We've been broken up for two weeks! Has it ever lasted that long before?" By my count, twenty-four hours was our record. A phone call from my mother had always put enough guilt in me to take him back. Two weeks was different. It was for real.

Max wasn't going to get anywhere with me, no matter how many members of my family or my professional life he hit up for a reference.

Not that he was accepting it, which really wasn't making it easy for me.

Max didn't look remotely concerned. "You need me."

"I need you to leave me alone."

The lights overhead flickered, ordering us to our seats. "Let's go, Shannon." Dave took my arm, and I was suddenly so, so, *so* glad he was there with me. Dave was over six feet tall, and he worked out. He was strong enough to keep me from throwing myself into Max's arms and begging him to take me back. I'd done that before, and each time I'd realized almost immediately that nothing had changed. And then it would take me months to get up the strength to try again. My birthday was in less than two months. I didn't have time to go backward. No way was I hitting the quarter-of-a-century mark with nothing to be proud of. Max held out his ticket. "Switch seats with me, Dave. Let me get some quality time with Shannon. She won't even take my calls."

"That's because she doesn't want you around."

I love Dave. Love him. Maybe I should have married him instead of letting him go off to a different college and fall in love with his lovely and charming wife who adored him. See? I could be a decent friend and say only nice things about the woman he loved.

I didn't even let myself look at Max as Dave pushed me past him, keeping himself between Max and me.

"Shannon." Max's voice had risen a couple notes, and there was a hint of desperation in his voice. "Don't leave."

Dave tightened his grip on my arm and made me keep walking. Neither of us said anything until we'd sat down and I'd taken a moment to look around and make sure Max hadn't somehow managed to get a seat right behind me. No Max.

"Wow." I leaned back in my seat. "That was interesting."

"What was?" An attorney sitting next to me asked. "Where have you been? You almost missed the start."

"Intern crisis. Lost ticket. Had to save the day."

Dave put his arm over my shoulders and pulled me close to him. "How did Max find out you were going to be here tonight?" he whispered.

"I had originally invited him before we broke up. I never gave him a ticket, but he obviously charmed his way in— or mugged a theatergoer to get their ticket. I'm so thrilled Hildy was nice enough to escort him over to me."

"You need to tell people at the firm, so things like this don't happen."

"No way." *Gah.* That was all I needed—to have everyone at the firm discussing my personal life. Especially since everyone who had ever met Max thought he was the one slumming by hanging out with me. I'm sure they would all shake their heads and agree that I must have been truly deranged to dump him, because I'd never do as well as him again. Besides, look at Van's reaction. No one would believe it was for real anyway.

"Shannon, this is serious. He's following you around." Dave kept his voice low.

"He's harmless."

"How do you know?"

"Because I went out with him for two years. He's not going to come after me with a knife."

"Aren't ninety-five percent of murdered women killed by a husband, boyfriend, or ex?" Dave asked.

"Dave! He's not going to murder me!" Dave didn't look convinced, and I punched him lightly in the arm. "Cut it out. You're going to wig me out."

"I still think you should tell the people at M and S."

"Fine. I'll think about it. Now, can we watch the show?"

He shrugged and looked annoyed.

On the plus side, at least we weren't fighting over my immature comments about his wife.

On the minus side, the attorney next to me was looking rather interested in our conversation. "Broke up with Max, huh?"

Super. "Yes."

"Too bad. Great guy."

43

"Apparently." I leaned back in my seat and prayed for the lights to go off.

"You guys went out for a long time, huh?"

"Yes." I elbowed Dave for some assistance, but he was chatting with the attorney sitting next to him. The disadvantage of having friends who were actually good at attending these kinds of events was that they talked to other people.

"Why'd you guys break up?"

I could hear the unspoken question: *He dumped you, didn't he? Figured out he could do better. Poor little social director. That was your only chance for the big time, wasn't it? Such a shame you couldn't get the ring on your finger before he figured you out.* I glared at the attorney. "It's personal and I'd rather not discuss it, okay?" The lights went out before I could get a response. Damn. It would have been an apology. I just knew it. Figured. Just my luck to miss it.

"Ready?" Emma popped into my office, wearing a skirt that didn't leave much to the imagination, cut low and cut high in all the places that would have been way wrong for my body. But of course, she looked totally hot. "It's nine twenty-five on Thursday night. Time to hit the bars looking for single men."

Was it that late already? I glanced at the clock on my computer screen. Yep. That late. Maybe I should become a lawyer. I was already keeping lawyer hours. Why not get the degree and at least be making buckets of money to be at work until ten o'clock every night?

"I hope you brought something else to wear," Emma said, flopping down on my chair. "It really cramps my style when you go out wearing a suit."

Of course I had. I hadn't forgotten my goal to get Blaine drooling over my body so he would became my slave at work in hopes of seeing my bare breasts. But I was in the mood to be difficult. "When I wear my suit, I attract guys in suits. My kind of guy."

"Puhleez. Any chick can attract guys in suits. Guys in suits are guys. If you have breasts, they'll be attracted." She pulled her tank top tight across her chest. "The trick is to attract guys who actually think of you as a woman and not a colleague, which is why the suit is a no-go."

"Maybe I want to be seen as a professional. Maybe if I wear a suit, some guy will come up to me and offer me some fabulous job and then I can quit this job and go earn a seven-figure income doing something I love." *Ha. So there!*

Emma lifted a brow. "And what job would that be?"

"What do you mean?"

"What job would you love? Didn't realize you'd figured that out yet."

Ah, the stickler. "Well, I'm not going to wear a suit to-night, so I don't need to know."

"Good." Emma watched me pile up my papers into a neat stack. "Are you going to do the Bud Light thing with me next Thursday night? Do you have an event?"

"No event." I switched off my computer, and my stomach did a little hop. Why in the world did it do that? Because I was thinking about how hot Blaine was and wondering what he'd think of me in my barhopping clothes? Granted, they didn't show as much skin as Emma's, but that was a good thing due to my cellulite and little bit o' love handles. But I also had breasts, the advantage of being slightly . . .

ahem . . . let's just say that I wasn't anorexic. I hid my breasts at work under my suit and my carefully chosen silk blouses, but sometimes you just gotta bring out the arsenal. "I'm going to the bathroom to change."

"Excellent. I'll check on Blaine."

Blaine. In all of our arguments this week, he hadn't once mentioned Thursday night. I'd bet he wasn't coming. Like I cared. "I doubt he's coming."

"Oh, he's coming."

The beauty of being Emma: She never worried about being stood up or ditched. Because she didn't care. There were plenty of men. No need to dwell on any one in particular.

Emma stood up. "I'll just swing next door and give him a little peek at what's in store for this evening, and he'll be sprinting for the elevators."

"Or you could come with me and give me opinions on my outfit." *Oops.* My tone sounded a little testy.

Emma wrinkled her nose. "Right. Of course. The bathroom it is."

What was my problem? Since when did I care if Emma was nice to one of my coworkers? He was a miserable beast and I hated him, so I certainly didn't care if Emma was friends with him. In fact, it would probably help my cause, wouldn't it? Of course it would. So I didn't care. And to prove it, I'd tell Emma to go warm him up for the evening. "Emma."

"Yeah." She grabbed my suit bag off the back of my closet door.

"You should go make sure he's coming." Oh, wow. That really hurt coming out.

"Who?"

"Dave." I was going to be struck down right then and there for lying. "Are Dave and Phoebe meeting us there?" Phoebe was part three of my trio of friends, Emma, Dave, and Phoebe. My foundation. I met Emma in college, knew Dave from high school, and Phoebe had been a paralegal at M&S when I first started. She'd been my one friend at the firm, and after she left to go to law school—ironic, huh?— we'd stayed good friends, though I still doubted she had the staying power to be a lawyer. She wasn't ruthless enough.

"Yep." Emma glanced at her watch as she led the way to the bathroom, not even glancing in the direction of Blaine's office. "They should be there in about five minutes, so we need to hustle. Don't want them to have to fend off too many hostile patrons while they hold a table for us." She raised her voice as she pushed open the door to the bathroom. "Blaine! Be ready in five!"

I actually heard him shout something back in response. Unbelievable. Blaine shouting through the halls of M&S. Leave it to Emma to turn him into something human. "Emma, can you not yell? I'd prefer not to get fired." *Oh, geez.* Now I was getting petty. What was wrong with me?

"It's late. Anyone who is still here would welcome the break. I wouldn't do this at two in the afternoon."

Imagine if I shouted things to Blaine. I was *so* sure he'd respond. Yeah, right. He'd probably try to get me fired. That "unbecoming behavior" thing again. Once more the beauty of being Emma reared its head. One, she didn't work here. Two, if she did, she still wouldn't care about losing her job or impressing anyone.

Emma went through an average of six jobs a year. It didn't phase her, and as long as her parents kept footing her share of the rent and utilities, it didn't bother me either.

She opened my suit bag and pulled out the three shirts I'd been debating between when I packed this morning. She held up a black tank top with a diving V-neck. "Oh, totally this one. This gives you serious cleavage. What pants?"

"Black jeans."

She held up my four-inch black heels. "Excellent choice. A woman in black tonight. Like a viper. I love it. Makes your hair look awesome."

"Really?" I'd never been one for the all black look, but this morning it had struck me as an option. I pulled off my shirt and bra and put on the black push-up one I'd bought the day I dumped Max.

"Blond hair looks great with black."

My hair, which used to be more of a light brown or dirty blond, now had fashionable blond streaks in it, thanks to Emma and Phoebe dragging me off for a day of self-improvement two weeks ago. I think that was after the invitation to my sister's engagement party had arrived. I had to admit I liked the blond look. And it did go with the black. Maybe I should wear black more often.

I tugged on the tank top, which was a little snugger and more risqué than I remembered—it couldn't possibly have to do with all those candy bars I'd been chowing, could it? The push-up bra didn't help matters, but Emma wouldn't let me take it off. I updated my makeup for an evening look, unpinned my bun and put my head upside down to fluff my hair, yanked on my jeans, admired the pedicure that still looked good, put on my sandals, and I was ready to go.

"That bra does wonders for your chest." Emma studied my breasts until I felt self-conscious and sort of shifted away from her. "Oh, get used to it. Everyone's going to be staring at those tonight."

"So maybe I should change my shirt."

"Too late." Emma scooped up my suit bag, which contained my more conservative options, and took off out of the bathroom. I hadn't even made it ten feet when she emerged from my office, my purse under her arm and my clothes locked away.

"Emma," I warned.

She just flipped me a grin and bolted into Blaine's office, emerging to grab my arm before I could wiggle by her and into my office. "Don't even try it. You're never going to meet more guys if you refuse to get out there and live a little."

"Why does she need to meet more guys?" Blaine's voice drifted out of his office, and I wanted to shoot Emma.

Emma looked into the office, while I chose to lean against the wall next to his door, so he couldn't see me and I couldn't see him. "Shannon broke up with her boyfriend of two years a couple weeks ago, and he's been rather a nuisance ever since. Really pressuring her. She needs a new love interest so she doesn't go crawling back to him for the zillionth time."

Okay, it was time to end this conversation. I tapped her shoulder. "You wait for Blaine. I'll go catch up with Dave and Phoebe."

"I'm ready." Blaine walked out of his office, and I could

49

see his profile as he stared at Emma. Yep, he still looked good. *Bastard.* He turned and glanced at me, then looked back at Emma. Then he looked back at me again, and I saw his eyes flick over my outfit much the same way he'd checked out Emma that first night.

See? There was a woman underneath those suits.

Blaine dragged his eyes away from my chest and looked at my face. "Nice outfit."

Sarcasm or genuine compliment? Suddenly I felt sort of like a hooker. Lawyer wannabe by day, cheap call girl by night.

"I picked it out," Emma said. "She thinks it shows too much cleavage. I think she should show off what she has. What do you think, Blaine?"

Oh, my God. I was going to *kill* her. I shot a glance at Blaine. "You don't need to answer that." I glared at Emma and started walking down the hall.

"Too much cleavage for work." Blaine's voice drifted behind me.

"Well, duh. You haven't seen me like this all week, have you?" Yes, being a snippy bitch was probably *not* exactly what Emma was talking about when she said tonight would be a good opportunity to become friends with Blaine. Next time she invited one of my enemies out to play, I was getting the flu and staying home.

"It'll look fine for a bar," he said.

I glanced back over my shoulder to check out his expression. His gaze didn't waver from my face. "Well, thanks, then."

Fine. He thought I looked *fine.* Be still my beating heart. Good thing I wasn't trying to impress him.

Emma caught up and tucked her arm through mine. "Don't worry," she whispered. "He was totally checking out your butt, but since you are a colleague, he's probably afraid to really tell you how hot you are. You know, sexual-harassment stuff."

Not that I cared whether Blaine was checking out my butt or anything. But on a more general level, it was nice to know he was at least looking.

So maybe tonight would be interesting after all. Maybe, indeed.

CHAPTER FOUR

I was getting annoyed by Emma's cozy flirting with Blaine, so I glanced up at the mirrored ceiling in the elevator to distract myself. That was when I realized how much of my breasts was visible from that angle.

Good Lord! I was dressed like a total slut! Sure, Emma's shirt was about as low as mine, but her boobs were so small that she just looked cute and appealing. Me? Ho alert!

The elevator hit the lobby and opened. Emma tumbled out with Blaine. "I'm going back up. I forgot something," I said.

Emma spun around, grabbed my hand, and hauled me out. "You are *so* not going to change that shirt. It's about time you admitted you had a body under there. Tell her, Blaine."

He lifted his brow, and I stopped struggling long enough to listen to his response.

The bastard was spared by Van's timely intervention. "Shannon!" he hollered from his stand, and waved me over.

Blaine had escaped, but it wasn't over. I was going to wrangle a compliment out of him by the end of the night. He'd be in my office first thing in the morning, handing over Isabel in hopes of gaining my favor.

"Give me a sec." With great trepidation, I left Emma flashing her wares at Blaine and ran across the lobby.

Well, actually, I ran two steps, then concluded that I wasn't one of those ultratalented women who could do decathlons in spiked heels. I did, however, manage to reach Van's booth without wiping out. "What's up?"

"Good God, Shannon. What's with that outfit?"

"I already feel like a slut. Please don't make it worse. What do you want?"

" 'Slut' wasn't what I was thinking."

I narrowed my eyes at him. "Do I want to know what you were thinking?"

"How do I know?"

I rolled my eyes. "Okay, fine. What did you want?"

He didn't seem to mind that I didn't want to know what he was thinking. "Max stopped by about twenty minutes ago."

Whoa. Max? With my ho attire and Blaine's disdain, I was feeling a little vulnerable right now. "What happened?"

"I told him he couldn't go up."

"And?"

"He seemed surprised. Really surprised, actually. We commiserated for a bit about how you seemed to be taking this breakup more seriously than in the past, and then he left."

"He didn't argue?"

"Nope." Van lifted his brow. "Don't tell me you wanted him to argue? That this is some sort of test of his love?"

"Don't be ridiculous."

"Is that what the outfit is about? Postbreakup blues?"

I glared at Van. "Don't you have any personal boundaries?"

He looked surprised; then his face cooled off. "Fine."

Oh, so now I felt like queen bitch. "Van! Stop it!"

He shot me a look. I knew that look. It was the "typical psycho female" look. Time to reclaim my reputation as sane and stable. "Well, thanks for sending him away."

He shrugged. "It's my job."

"We're going to leave," Emma called from the other side of the lobby. "We don't want to keep Dave and Phoebe waiting."

Crap. No way was I going to let them go off on their own. "I'm coming." I looked at Van. "Sorry I snapped at you. Really."

"No problem." He glanced across the lobby. "Good-looking guy. Have fun."

I frowned. With the number of people who worked in our building, there was no way Van would know all of them by sight. "You want to meet him? He just arrived from New York a few days ago." I'd never quite figured out what kind of person Van was interested in socially. He never talked about his personal life. Ever.

Van lifted a brow, and a small smile played at the corner of his lips. "Not tonight."

Evasive again.

"Shannon! We're leaving!"

Van waved me off. "Go."

I had a feeling I still needed to do some groveling to Van,

but it would have to wait until another night. I had one or two serious professional issues to deal with first.

By the time we got to the bar, I was in a . . . um . . . how shall we say it? A less than stellar frame of mind?

Pretentious Bastard had spent the entire walk over chatting up Emma. I'd even done a little experiment in which I pretended to have a problem with my shoe and stopped in the middle of the sidewalk, and they didn't notice. They got a full block ahead, while I was sitting on the curb faking an ankle injury. They didn't even notice when I sprinted . . . er . . . wobbled after them and caught up a half a block later.

It was official.

I was invisible.

It was Pretentious Bastard's fault. Emma was my friend. She'd never fail to notice my plea for help if she hadn't been brainwashed by him. Maybe in his secret life he ran a cult. Got rich business people to join and worship holy Blaine, but instead of bilking them out of all their money, he made them give all their business to M&S. And probably sex was involved too—obviously Emma had no money, so he was brainwashing her for the sex.

Well, good luck to him. Emma was way too grounded to fall for a cult leader like him who was so obviously a fraud.

He flashed a grin at the bouncer as he walked into the bar. Did he see another victim to suck into his cult? *I'm on to you, Blaine.* He'd be sorry he pissed me off when I exposed his multimillion-dollar scheme and sent him to prison, so he lost his money, his reputation, his connections, and his law license.

"Shannon! Emma! Over here!" My friend Phoebe snapped me back to the present, and I waved at her.

She and Dave were sitting across from each other in a booth, and they'd spread out to take up as much space as possible. True friends. Let's see Blaine try to suck them into his little cult. Never.

Emma and Blaine veered in front of me toward the table. Emma slid in next to Dave, while Blaine claimed the spot across from her.

They were two-person benches. Which left me standing.

Have I mentioned that I hate Blaine? As the last one to be invited, he should be the one without a seat.

"Grab a chair," Emma said.

"Right. Sure." Not a lot of spare chairs in a bar.

I turned back to my friends, but Emma was busy introducing Blaine to Phoebe and Dave.

Um, hello? These were my friends. My night out. And I was being ignored in favor of a coworker I hated. *Fine.*

I stomped off, glancing over my shoulder at them, but they didn't even notice. Figured. No sense in making a scene if no one cared. I walked over to the bar, where there were tall stools. None were free, but maybe one would open soon.

I might as well stand here as stand at the table being ignored.

"Hi." A guy in black jeans, a black T-shirt, and shiny black shoes, with slicked-back black hair and a gold chain, leaned casually against the bar. "Here alone?"

I eyed him, and watched his gaze settle on my breasts. Well, that was what I'd asked for, right? Of course, it was supposed to be Blaine ogling my wares, not some stranger, but I couldn't exactly kick him in the nuts, could I?

Or maybe I should. Just because a woman wears a shirt with her breasts practically hanging out in full view doesn't mean a guy has a right to gawk at them.

"So?" He looked at my face. Impressive show of willpower. "Are you here alone?"

"Why do you care?"

He looked startled. "I don't know."

"If you don't know why you care, why'd you ask?" Gee, did I sound pleasant or what? Obviously I'd used up my allocation of good cheer during the work day, so in my personal life, where I actually wanted to be nice to people, I had nothing left.

Oily man glanced at my chest again, looked up, called me a bitch, and walked away.

Great. I felt so much better now.

The bartender gave me a beer, so I guess the breasts had done something good for me tonight. I peered across the room at my brainwashed friends, but Blaine and Emma weren't at the table. Maybe Blaine had been fingered by an ex-victim and the cops had taken him off to jail. Major bummer to have missed it.

I maneuvered my way back across the room and slid into the booth next to Phoebe. *Ha. Let Blaine find his own seat now.* "So, what's up?"

"You got a beer?" Phoebe pursed her lips in her trademark pout that men found so attractive. "We can't even get a waitress. Emma and Blaine went to buy drinks."

"No jail?" Too bad.

Phoebe and Dave looked confused, and I decided not to enlighten them. "It was my breasts. They blinded the bartender, so I grabbed the beer and ran."

Phoebe eyed my chest. "You are showing quite a bit more cleavage than usual."

"Emma's fault. She made me."

Dave did a quick drive-by of my chest, and his cheeks got red. "I think it's fine."

"Not too slutty?" Dave was pretty conservative. If he thought it was okay, then I'd feel better.

"No one could ever think you were slutty, no matter what you wore," he said. "You give off a conservative vibe."

A conservative vibe? That didn't sound too complimentary. "What do you mean?"

Dave shot a look at Phoebe, who said, "You come from a conservative family. You work for a law firm. It shows."

I stared at them. "That is so not true. I'm not like my family. I'm certainly *not* like one of the lawyers at my firm. That's ridiculous. I'm the antithesis of them. That's why my family wants to disown me."

"They want to disown you because you don't have an impressive job. It has nothing to do with your behavior or your attitude," Phoebe said.

"So my 'vibe' is exactly what my parents want?"

Dave shrugged. "I guess."

"Phoebe?"

"Shannon, relax. We aren't insulting you. We're simply saying that wearing that shirt isn't going to make anyone think you're a slut. You should be happy."

Yeah, happy that my parents had actually had some

influence on me, and that I exuded McCormickness everywhere I went?

"Hi." Emma dropped four beers on the table. "Blaine and I are going to go dance. Save our seats."

She giggled at Blaine, then grabbed his hand and dragged him through the crowd.

Un-friggin'-believable.

"So who is that guy anyway?" Phoebe asked. "He's hot."

"Phoebe! You're engaged!"

"So what? A girl can still look." She sighed. "Besides, it sucks being engaged to a guy who lives in Chicago."

Yeah, that could be a problem. Her fiancé had gotten the Chicago job a month ago and headed out. She'd applied to some law schools in Chicago to see if she could transfer, but it seemed to be too late to transfer for this year. So she was stuck. I actually felt bad for her, because Zach was a really cool guy and they were super happy together.

"I can relate," Dave said.

Phoebe raised an eyebrow. "How?"

"My wife travels a lot. Granted, she's not gone all the time like your fiancé is, but it's enough that I know how you feel."

"Really?" Phoebe leaned forward. "So do you sleep in the middle of the bed when she's gone, or do you keep to your side?"

"My side. What about you?"

"I sleep in the middle." She frowned. "Is that bad? Like some sign that I'm not keeping things waiting for him?"

I watched Dave and Phoebe bond over their loneliness,

and realized it was one of the first times I'd actually seen them talk. I mean, they knew each other because I dragged them both out on occasion, but now that I thought about it, it was usually me talking to each of them, and them not really talking to each other.

Which was too bad. They were both awesome people, and apparently they had some stuff in common. It would be good for them to be friends. Might help Yvonne relax if she knew Dave was out with two of us, instead of just me, homewrecker extraordinaire.

I decided to give Dave and Phoebe some bonding time. It would be great if they got to be good friends. They both knew Emma pretty well, so that would be the final key to a foursome that was inseparable.

"I'm going to the bathroom."

They both smiled at me, and Phoebe started to invite herself along, so I quickly changed my story. "I actually meant, I'm going to ask that guy over there to dance."

I waved my finger vaguely in the direction of the bar, and Dave craned his neck to peer past me. "Which one?"

"That one."

"Which?"

Fine. Dave was being overprotective. I turned around and scanned the bar. There was a guy in a suit holding a beer and sort of looking around, like he was hoping to see someone he knew. I started to point to him, and then stopped. He was the kind of guy my parents would like. Was that why I went after guys in suits? Because subconsciously I was still trying to do what my parents wanted me to?

Whoa. That would be a total sign of weakness. I wasn't

weak. I wasn't a McCormick—at least according to my parents. So forget it. No more men in suits. I scanned the crowd again. There was the slick breast starer who'd approached me before. Why not him? My parents would cringe. I pointed. "Him."

Dave and Phoebe stared. "The greaser?"

"Yep. I'll show you I'm not conservative. He'll think I'm a slut." As I started to march across the room, it did occur to me that perhaps there were some flaws in my thinking, but I decided not to worry about them for the moment.

I was about to discover the true Shannon. Couldn't let some sort of conscience or logic interfere with that kind of catharsis.

I marched straight up to the greaser, and in the recesses of my mind I realized that not only wasn't I the type to ask a guy to dance, I wasn't sure I'd *ever* asked a guy to dance.

Hmm . . .

I stopped, my hand hovering over the greaser's shoulder. I thought that perhaps—just perhaps—this wasn't the best idea.

Then he turned around.

And I panicked and froze.

Which meant my hand was still in the air, but now it was almost mashing his chin, since he'd turned around and all. He lifted a black eyebrow and inspected my hand.

This was way embarrassing.

I dropped my hand. "Um. Sorry."

He checked out my chest again, and then I could see that he recognized my breasts as belonging to the Bitch. He got this wary look on his face and sort of backed up. Great. I was so horrible I could scare off greasers. This was a sure sign from above that I should abandon this little venture right now before I got sucked in, but dammit! I didn't want to. So I pulled back my shoulders and gave him what I hoped was a challenging stare. Challenging in a good way, of course.

His eyes widened, then narrowed, then sort of crinkled, and I realized he was smiling. Well, leering. No problem. He was what I wanted, right? Right. So I'd just open my mouth and ask him to dance.

He waited.

My mouth wouldn't work.

He glanced over my shoulder, and I realized even my breasts were losing their appeal. Time to act. No worries if my mouth had ceased functioning. My hand still worked. Besides, if I was bent on shedding my conservative skin, then I would have to be the type to take charge. So I'd do exactly that.

I reached out and grabbed his wrist. Then I shot him a half smile that I hoped was mysterious and started pulling him toward the dance floor. It occurred to me that if he ripped his arm out of my grasp and ran away screaming, I might not be in the best frame of mind to cope with it, given my bout with invisibility earlier tonight.

But the greaser followed me nicely, right out onto the dance floor. I couldn't see Blaine or Emma out there, but it wasn't as if I cared about that or anything.

As soon as we started to dance, the greaser grabbed me around the waist and pulled me up against him.

Guess I should have noticed that it was a slow song. No problem. I flung my arms around his neck and started playing with the hair at the base of his neck. There were actually some curls back there. Interesting. I'd never dated a guy who had hair long enough to curl in the back. My parents would freak. "I'm Shannon."

"Dirk." He slipped his hands lower, so they were resting on the top of my butt.

Interesting. Dirk wasn't wasting any time. Either he was hopelessly smitten or he was a total letch. I'd prefer to consider him confident and assertive. A real man. And he did smell good. Some sort of aftershave or cologne? I closed my eyes and tried to pretend I was enjoying myself.

Nothing like having a man's hands on your body, right?

Hello. Lips nibbling on my neck. Hands now massaging my butt.

Wonder if he can feel my cellulite through my jeans? Not a good thought. Banned from my brain until further notice.

I tipped my head to the side to give him better access. Why not? That was what I was all about, right? Plus . . . I slid my hands over his shoulders . . . Dirk was seriously cut. Probably lifted for the sole purpose of picking up chicks.

Worked for me.

I opened my eyes and pulled back to look at his face. His eyes were totally black, and suddenly I realized that I found dark eyes a major turn-on. I was actually getting goose bumps.

Wow. Maybe I really was a slut.

Then his eyes closed and he was coming at me, lips puckered, tongue ready. *Hmm* . . . Maybe I wasn't all that into this after all. . . .

Too late. Attack of the monster tongue. For an instant I

considered biting down really hard, but then I figured I'd asked for it, right? I mean, this was the entire purpose: to show I could be a wanton woman if I wanted to.

Again, I had an inkling that there was a serious flaw in my thinking, but I shoved it aside. I was going to enjoy this makeout session if it killed me.

I flung my arms around Dirk and pressed my body up against him, returning the kiss with all I had. His hands started roaming my body, and there was skin-to-skin contact between his hands and my back. Was he actually going to undress me on the dance floor? A glimmer of excitement raced through me that totally startled me. Public sex excited me? Wasn't that interesting. *Huh.* Probably not something my parents would approve of. All the more reason, I supposed.

I flattened my hands on Dirk's chest, and I could feel his muscles flexing under my touch. Way cool. Max hadn't had muscles he could flex. Speaking of the ex, this was the first guy besides him that I'd kissed in two years.

See what I'd been missing?

Dirk slipped his hands under the waistband of my jeans and over the top of my butt while he chewed on my collarbone, moving progressively lower. *Good God!* He was practically at my nipple!

Okay, there was a limit. I couldn't go this far in a public bar. I grabbed Dirk's chin and manhandled him out of my chest. "Not here," I said. *Wow.* I was breathless. How about that? Kissing had made me breathless? Maybe I really did have a hot, sexual nature and I never knew it.

Dirk kept his hands on my butt. "Where do you want to go?"

"What?"

He started nibbling on my neck again, and I vaguely hoped he wasn't going to give me a hickey. I didn't have any silk blouses that had turtlenecks. "Your place or mine?" he asked.

Your place or mine? The words ground themselves into my brain with impressive force, and I stepped back. "Neither. I'm not going to go anywhere and have sex with you."

Dirk grabbed my hands and pulled me against him. "We don't have to have sex. We'll just have some fun and see what we feel like doing. My apartment is only a couple streets from here. Or yours, if you'd rather. Some women feel more comfortable at home. Whichever you prefer."

"Some women?" I twisted myself free again. "You do this often?"

He hesitated, as if unsure of the answer I wanted. "No? Never? You're my first?"

I actually started laughing. "Nice try, Dirk."

He grinned and went for me again. "So where to?"

I blocked his hands. "Actually, I can't. I have to get up early tomorrow, and I'm really not into the one-night-stand thing."

"It doesn't have to be one night," he said, trailing his finger down my arm. "We can go as many nights as you want."

Yeah, right. Like a one-night stand with a stranger would ever turn into anything. "Sorry, Dirk. I just got out of a serious relationship, and I'm not into taking a guy home tonight." I gave him a quick kiss. "It was fun, though."

And then I walked away, leaving him on the dance floor. I actually felt kind of bad about it. I hadn't been that pumped up about a kiss in a long time. But it probably wasn't the kiss. Maybe it was his body. Or that I knew my parents would impale themselves on their expensive champagne glasses if they could see me getting down with Dirk, with his black outfit, his gold chain, and his greased-back hair.

Either way, I showed Phoebe and Dave I could dump the McCormick vibe anytime I wanted to. The victory was mine.

Then I glanced up at the table. My friends and Blaine were all staring at me, varying degrees of shock on their faces. Except Emma, who gave me a thumbs-up.

Oh, hell. I'd forgotten about Blaine. This was completely embarrassing. I wondered if I could pass Dirk off as my brother. Or not. That might raise even more eyebrows.

I had about ten more yards to come up with an excuse that would make seeing Blaine in the hallway tomorrow morning bearable. Too bad my brain was mush and I couldn't think of a single thing.

CHAPTER FIVE

So I sat down at the table and ignored the entire fiasco. "What's up?"

"That guy, apparently," Dave said. "What the hell was that about?"

I eyed Dave. "What's wrong with you?"

He narrowed his eyes. "As your friend, I had every right to go rip that guy off you and toss him under a cab. I also have the right to throw you over my shoulder and cart you outta here if you ever do something like that again."

I stared at Dave. "Did you get possessed by my father or something? What's your problem?"

Phoebe patted my hand. "It was a little obscene."

"Oh, give me a break." Emma pushed Phoebe's hand off me. "Dave's just being a typical overprotective male."

"Emma!" Dave looked really annoyed. "How can you defend her? That guy could have been a rapist or something."

"In the middle of the dance floor?" Emma teased.

"Dave's right," Phoebe said. "That was quite a scene."

I was starting to feel a little embarrassed now. "People

make out in bars all the time. It's the first time I've ever done it, so why are you guys on my case?"

"Because it's not you," Dave said. "You're too good for that kind of thing."

I sat up. "No, I'm not. I'm not too good for it, so back off. Didn't I just prove it? I'm not good. I'm bad. I'm evil. I'm . . ." I stopped at the knowing look on Phoebe's face. "What?"

She looked at Dave. "Our fault."

"Ours?" He looked aghast.

"Yes. We convinced her that she was too much like her parents. So she rebelled."

Yeesh. This was getting way too personal. I looked at Blaine, and he unfortunately wasn't trying to cop a look down the front of Emma's shirt. He was listening intently to the conversation. Nothing like having your personal nightmares laid out on the table for Pretentious Bastard.

"Enough." I smacked my hands on the table. "I ditched him, didn't I? So you don't need to worry. It was an experiment and no harm was done. So back off."

When Dave opened his mouth to continue to harass me, I jerked my head toward Blaine. Dave glanced at Blaine, then shut his mouth, but he shot me a look that said the conversation wasn't over.

"I think it was great." Emma leaned forward. "So what's his name?"

"Dirk." Blaine still hadn't said anything. What was he thinking?

"Good kisser?"

Yeah, right. This is the exact conversation I want to have with Blaine sitting right here.

Emma tugged on my arm. "Was he a good kisser?"

"Yeah."

"Nice bod, huh?"

"Uh-huh." I picked up my beer and wiped some of the frost off the outside.

"Did you get his number?"

"No." I eyed Emma and lowered my voice. "He wanted to take me back to his apartment."

"Well, of course he did. You're totally hot." Emma sighed. "See? You're going to be a hit with the Bud Light girl thing."

"What Bud Light girl thing?" Dave sounded even more aggravated and overprotective. He shot a glance at Phoebe. "You doing it too?"

"Not yet, but it sounds like fun. Law school's sucking my bank account dry, so I'm all about some extra cash." Phoebe leaned forward. "So what's it all about?"

As Emma launched into a description of her new gig and Dave tried to talk them out of it, I leaned back and closed my eyes. What was wrong with me? Attacking strangers on the dance floor? For God's sake, I let him put his hands down my jeans and grab my butt. In public!

"You okay?"

I opened my eyes to find Blaine watching me. "I forgot you were here."

"No such luck." He was lounging against the bench, looking remarkably comfortable even though he couldn't have had more than six inches to sit on. "How'd your lunch go?"

"My lunch?" He looked so hot sitting there. So cool. And that suit. What could I say? I was a sucker for guys in suits. Or maybe just for Blaine. "What lunch?"

"The one that you had to round up those attorneys for Otto's big speech."

"Oh, right." *The one you almost ruined because you wouldn't release Isabel.* "Got it covered."

"Great. Glad Isabel was able to help."

"Isabel?"

"Sure. She took off the minute you hung up on me. When she came back, she said she'd gotten ten people, and Hildy had rounded up a few too."

"Oh." So he had released her. I felt like I should thank him, but why should I thank him for releasing my secretary to help me? On the other hand, this was what Emma had advised. Make nice. So I gave him a pained smile. "Thanks."

He nodded. "No problem."

We sat there for a moment while Emma and Phoebe squealed over something. I could rejoin my conversation with them, or I could take advantage of the moment. What had Emma asked him? Right. Where he was from. "So . . . um . . . this your first time living in Boston?"

He lifted a brow. "Yes."

"It's a great place."

"For what?"

"Um . . . museums. Bars. Theater. Restaurants. I don't know. Everything." Okay, this was stupid and boring. "I guess I could show you around if you wanted."

He cocked an eyebrow, no doubt bowled over by my apparent enthusiasm. "Maybe I'll take you up on that."

Yes, that was an evasive dismissal if I'd ever heard one. My parents would love him, with his cool manners and expensive suit. Hang on . . . brilliant idea alert. "You want to meet lots of influential people in the Boston area? Come to my sister's engagement party on Saturday. Everyone who is anyone will be there. Lots of potential clients." I'd help my reputation by showing up with him on my arm, and make him happy by introducing him to a number of potential business opportunities in the area. He'd owe me, he'd love me, and he'd be my slave after that.

"Saturday?"

"Yes. About six. Suit required."

"I was supposed to go with Emma to do her Bud Light thing."

If I wasn't so composed and collected, I would have tumbled off my seat in shock at that remark. First, what was Emma doing working at her stupid thing on the night of my sister's engagement party? Second, why had she invited Blaine? And third, what was up with Blaine actually wanting to do that? He was an uptight lawyer, for heaven's sake. I kept my voice calm. "Interesting that she'd invite you, because she's supposed to be at the engagement party too."

He looked surprised. "Really? She didn't mention that."

Wait a sec. Was I bordering on groveling? There would be none of that. So I shrugged. "Whatever."

"No, that sounds interesting. Hang on." Blaine touched Emma's arm. "Is it okay if I go with Shannon to her sister's engagement party on Saturday night instead of to that bar? Sounds like there will be some good business opportunities there."

Damn, I felt powerful right now.

Then Emma shot me an indecipherable look and I felt like a heel. Why should I feel bad? She was the one who'd been encroaching on my territory. "No, that's fine," she said, still looking at me.

What? She should be happy. Wasn't that her goal, to make me friends with him? "Aren't you coming, too?" I asked.

She shook her head. "I couldn't get out of work."

"Too bad." She lifted her brow and I scowled at her. "Don't look at me like that. You're the one bailing on me."

"I forgot about the party." Her words were a little tight, and I could feel Blaine watching both of us. For what? A screaming catfight? Hardly.

"Well, if you change your mind, I'd love to have you there."

She said nothing.

What was up with that? Emma never got moody about anything. Hormones, maybe?

Emma glanced past me, then nudged Blaine. "Can you let me out? I'm going to the bathroom." She bolted out of the seat as if she'd seen someone she knew.

Blaine slid back into the seat, and I caught him glancing at my chest. So I looked down. *Holy shit.* Was that nipple? I immediately yanked the front of my shirt up. It moved about a quarter of an inch. Apparently the problem with very low-cut, very tight tops was that there weren't a whole lot of options if you decided you didn't like them anymore. This thing was going down the trash chute the minute I got home.

I looked up to find Blaine watching me, the corner of his mouth curving up.

"What?" I snapped.

"Didn't help much."

"Thanks for noticing."

He didn't look remotely embarrassed that I'd just called

him on inspecting my breasts. "I was wondering if that was your normal weekend attire."

He sounded far from impressed. "It was an experiment." I tugged at it again. No success, though at least my nipples were definitely hidden now.

"That guy, too?"

Dirk. I'd forgotten about him already. Lovely of Blaine to remind me. "I'm on the rebound. Leave me alone."

"Self-destruction isn't admirable."

I scowled at him. "I've had enough of smug attorneys. I'm not being self-destructive. I'm fine, so back off."

He shrugged. "Fine."

"Fine."

"Just one question."

"What?"

"Are you going to dress like that on Saturday? No offense, but that's not the kind of image I want to project if I'm there on business."

Un-friggin'-believable. "Have a nice evening." I stood up and lightly whacked Phoebe on the shoulder. "I'm outta here. Tell Emma." Emma was welcome to Blaine. This night was officially over before it could get any worse.

Like there was anything left to salvage.

I shoved my way across the crowded bar, making a wide detour around Dirk, who was chatting up some buxom blonde. This was all Emma's fault. If she hadn't invited Blaine along on my personal night out, then at least my total humiliation would have been kept within friends. Now it would be all around work by the time I got there tomorrow.

Fabulous.

73

Unless someone mugged Blaine on his way out of the bar. It wasn't beyond possibility. He reeked of wealth and looked like he'd never gotten dirty in his life. An easy target, wouldn't you think? I stepped outside the bar and looked around for some deviants to alert to Blaine's presence, but all I saw were ordinary bargoers. No one who looked ready to risk jail just to please me.

Fine. I'd have to face him tomorrow. Or I could save myself the trouble and just shoot myself now.

Dog track morning dawned rainy and gray. Unfortunately lightning hadn't struck my building during the night, turning me into burned toast. Nope, I was alive and well, and had no choice but to go to work today and face my life.

I rolled out of bed and the infamous tank top was still on the floor. *First things first. Deal with that.*

I picked it up, walked into the kitchen, put it in the sink, lit a match, and set it on fire.

Stupid match went out.

So I tried again.

Same result.

I hoped the person who invented flame-retardant fabrics had been sent to Siberia for eternity with nothing but a box of matches and nonburnable tank tops. *Ha. A little cold, are you? Serves you right.*

"What are you doing?" Emma wandered into the kitchen, rubbing sleep out of her eyes.

"Trying to burn this thing."

"Why? It looks great on you." She fished it out of the sink. "What's wrong with you?"

"What's wrong?" I grabbed it out of her hand and shoved

it down the garbage disposal. "Oh, maybe the fact that Blaine actually saw my nipple last night because this thing was so low, and now I have to face him at work today. Oh, and perhaps the little incident on the dance floor with me nearly having sex in a public place?" I turned on the faucet, and then flicked the garbage-disposal switch.

Interesting noise. Not sure the tank-top-in-the-garbage-disposal concept was working all that well.

"Shannon!" Emma turned off the garbage disposal and glared at me. "If you break the disposal, we're going to be charged for it."

"It'll be worth it. Turn it back on." Wouldn't it be fun if it were Blaine's head in there too?

"No." Emma folded her arms across her chest and blocked the sink. "Why'd you take off last night?"

Last night. I forgot we were mad at each other. "Because I was tired of humiliating myself. Blaine made one too many derogatory comments, and I couldn't take any more. So I bailed. I told them to tell you I was leaving. Didn't they?"

"Blaine's not such a bad guy."

"I noticed you were snuggling up to him." I hadn't quite managed to keep my tone even on that one. Maybe I should take some acting classes. That might help me maintain my composure.

"Does that bug you?"

"So you admit the snuggling?" *Ow.* Chest pain.

"He's nice."

"Not."

Emma sighed. "Shannon, why don't you give him a break?"

"I did. I invited him to the party Saturday. You got pissed and he made a snide remark about my attire. It wasn't a raging success as invitations go."

Her cheeks colored ever so slightly. "I wasn't pissed."

"No?"

"Surprised."

"Why?"

Emma took a moment to fish the remains of my shirt out of the sink.

I waited.

She finally turned around. "I felt like you invited him to get back at me for the fact that I couldn't come. To punish me."

I blinked. "I hadn't thought of that, but now that you mention it, would it have worked?"

A smile tugged at the corner of her mouth. "I was a little annoyed," she admitted. "I felt like you asked him just because I already had plans with him."

"I didn't know you had plans with him until after I mentioned the engagement party. It certainly wasn't my first guess that you would have asked him to go hang out at a bar and watch you flirt with other guys. Sounds like a rather strange way to spend the evening, if you want my opinion." Or even if she didn't want my opinion—she was getting it anyway.

"I was being nice. He doesn't have friends."

Somehow I couldn't see a guy like Blaine desperate for something to do. Things probably just fell into his lap.

Emma cocked her head. "So then why'd you invite him to Lindsay's party?"

"To get my parents off my back. I figure if I show up with Blaine, then my parents can brag and I'll be acceptable.

It'll at least make the evening tolerable. Plus, it'll be good business for Blaine. If I can get him indebted to me, then I can leverage that to get him to back off Isabel's time. Unlike you, I'm being entirely selfish in the invitation." And I didn't feel one bit bad about it either. *So there*.

"You're right."

"About what?"

"That party is going to suck for you. You need all the help you can get. Take Blaine." She held up the shredded tank top. "I think you should wear this. With all the holes, it'll really show some skin."

"Oh, shut up." I grabbed it out of her hand and laughed.

We were good again.

One crisis down.

Now all I had to do was get the dog track party to fly, face Blaine, and hope that Jessamee's move to the office next to Otto was torturous and horrible. Ah, the small pleasures of life.

CHAPTER SIX

So which was worse?

a) Public humiliation on the dance floor of a bar, said humiliation involving nudity, sluttiness, nipples, and generally behaving in a totally embarrassing manner.

b) Getting back together with ex-boyfriend and having to deal *with the knowledge that I was never going to meet my soul mate as long as I was with him*. But he did know me better than anyone else and he did love me. *And my parents loved him.*

The advantage of (b) was that I wouldn't be tempted to be a slut again, I would be back in my parents' favor, and everyone at the firm would respect me again. The advantage of (a) was discovering I was a hotbed of raging desire with no morals whatsoever.

Short term, the latter was not a bad thing.

Long term, (b) was probably the better option.

I stared down at the Post-it I'd scrawled on. Had I lost my

mind? Was I actually considering getting back together with Max?

Obviously someone slipped a hallucinogenic in my beer last night. There was no other possible explanation for momentarily doubting my decision to dump Max.

I crumpled up the sticky and threw it in my trash can.

It was all Blaine's fault. The way he looked at me with disdain, as if he knew for a fact that I was a loser, whereas other people were just conjecturing.

That comment about my attire still pissed me off.

And unfortunately, there was nothing I could do about it.

He was a partner.

I was the social director.

I needed my job.

Marching next door and screaming at a partner for noticing my nipples just didn't seem to be the correct response, not if I wanted to keep my job.

And I was going to keep my job, dammit, if for no other reason than to spite my parents. And I liked it. Usually. Sometimes. Parts of it, at least.

My phone rang and I snatched it off the hook. "Shannon McCormick." Anything was better than thinking about Blaine and my nipples.

"Shannon. It's April."

My brother's gorgeous girlfriend. Another overachiever, plus she was gorgeous and made big bucks as a vice president of a bank. Loved her. "Hi, April. It's so nice to hear from you."

"Hi, Shannon. Listen, your brother and I were wondering if you wanted to go in on an engagement gift for your sister and Geoff."

"Sure. I'd love to." Maybe April would have some idea of what to buy a couple who could buy out the entire contents of a major department store with cash if they wanted to.

"Great. We were thinking maybe a five-hundred-dollar limit per person."

There went my rent for the month. Maybe I should start being a prostitute at night to make some extra bucks. Of course, that might get in the way of my evening duties as social director. Figured. Now that Dirk had shown me my dark side, I couldn't even make a profit off it. And since I couldn't admit to my family that I didn't have the money— it would be yet another sign of how I'd failed—I heard myself agreeing. This probably meant a shopping outing with April. Couldn't wait for that. With her perfect little figure and her stylish clothes, she always made me feel like a dirty laundry hamper. "Count me in. So you want to get it before the party?"

"I already picked out a nice crystal bowl. It'll be great for the dining room."

Yeah, it had better be nice. At five hundred bucks each, that was a thousand bucks for a bowl. Unless April and my brother were each throwing in five hundred, in which case we were talking a fifteen-hundred-dollar bowl.

I could upgrade my car if I had fifteen hundred dollars.

"So I'll just write your name on the card so the store can go ahead and wrap it up."

"Um, okay." So much for the excitement of shopping for my sister's engagement present. I'd been fantasizing about buying her some wonderful gift that showed our bond as sisters, but instead, my only contribution would be my name on the card and a check for five hundred dollars.

Great.

"So, see you tomorrow." April hung up, but not before I heard her ordering the salesperson to use different wrapping paper.

Had I mentioned how really excited I was about this party? Only about thirty-two hours away. How could I stand the anticipation? I wondered if my mom told April to call me about the present. A preemptive strike to stop me from showing up with an inappropriate gift that would embarrass the family.

A knock sounded at the door, and I nearly fell off my chair. Blaine. It was Blaine. I knew it. He'd ignored my subliminal signals to stay away (namely, the fact that my office door had been firmly closed since I'd arrived this morning and I'd asked Isabel not to let him anywhere near it). I needed some time to figure out how to deal with last night. I wasn't answering the door. "Come in." Why did my mouth insist on behaving in a socially appropriate manner when it would be so much more satisfying to just say what I meant? Like, "Get the hell away from my door and leave me alone, you miserable son of a—"

Jessamee Bouchillion pushed open the door and walked into the office. "Good morning, Shannon." She crossed her arms and gave me an evil look that made my toes curl. "What did you do to me?"

Besides kowtow to your every demand? Not much else. Haven't had a lot of spare time recently. "What's the problem, Jessamee?"

"Everyone's been giving me funny looks when I tell them I'm in the office next to the managing partner. What did you do? If you're trying to get back at me for threatening to get you fired, I'll report you. I know my rights. Retaliation is illegal."

Stifling the urge to tell Jessamee to stuff it, I gave her a demure smile. "You asked for an office next to a corporate partner. I gave it to you. He's the most influential person in the whole firm."

Jessamee narrowed her eyes and stared at me. Could there be more distrust oozing from her pores? The girl needed to lighten up. It wasn't as if the entire world were out to destroy her. Though she was entering the legal profession. Perhaps she was right on track. "Then why is everyone giving me those looks?"

Other than the fact that Otto is a psychopath and might very well come after you with a butcher knife if you fail to genuflect in his presence? "Because they're jealous."

"Oh." Jessamee considered that. "Well, that makes sense, then."

I nodded. Why didn't it surprise me that Jessamee would have no problem believing people were jealous of her? Hmm . . . wonder how that felt. April would probably know.

"Okay, see you later, then." Jessamee flounced out, leaving the door open.

I supposed I might as well get up and walk out of my office. It was past ten o'clock already, and I did need to get some work done that involved conversations with other people. If Blaine came by . . . well, I'd just deal with it, because I was cool and sophisticated.

I walked to my door, then leaned slowly out. Checked down the hall toward Blaine's office. Excellent. His door was shut. Wait a sec. What was he doing with the door shut? Was he avoiding me? Afraid I'd corner him and insist he come to the party?

Nope. I wasn't going to become paranoid about this. Not at all. I walked over to Isabel, still eyeing the door. "So is Blaine here today?"

"Yes." Isabel held up her finger and picked up my line, which was ringing. "Shannon McCormick's office, can I help you?" She waited a sec, then handed the phone to me. "It's for you."

I grabbed it. "Hello?"

"This is Dirk from last night."

Dirk? *Dirk?* How in the hell had he found me? "Dirk? You mean, you're the guy from the bar?"

"Yep. How are you?"

How am I? Shocked, horrified, terrified. "How did you get my number?"

"Your friend gave it to me. Emma, I think her name was."

Emma. I recalled with sudden clarity how she'd bolted from the table. I'd kill her for this. "Listen, now isn't a good time for me, Dirk. I have a meeting." When men were involved, normal standards of honesty didn't apply.

Isabel raised an eyebrow at me and I stuck my tongue out at her. Yes, I was mature. Not.

"Want to go out tonight?"

Um, the short answer would be "No." The long answer, "No." "Listen, Dirk, I'm sorry. I have plans. Thanks for calling, though. Bye."

I hung up. "Isabel, you won't believe what happened to me last night. I was at this bar and . . ."

Isabel's eyes flicked over my shoulder, and I turned around. There stood Blaine, with a stack of files in his arms.

And all I could think about was the fact that he'd seen my nipple.

"The guy from last night on the phone?" he asked.

"Um . . ."

He handed the files to Isabel, shot me a look, then walked back into his office and shut the door.

Crap. Encounter over. I hadn't come up with anything brilliant to explain last night, and hadn't managed to turn the phone call from Dirk into anything extraordinarily wonderful. Nope. Just stood there like a dope.

On the plus side, at least I'd faced him down and he hadn't brought up the nipple sighting. He hadn't even glanced at my chest. So that was it? He was Mr. Reserved again? A dignified attorney with no sense of humanity? Where was the passion in this place? Why didn't anyone actually say what was on their mind, show some emotion? *Come on, people! Let it all hang out! Or at least let some-*thing *hang out!* I felt like running down the hall, kicking open every door, and screaming at everyone to react, cry, laugh, do something!

"Shannon?"

I sighed and turned to Isabel. "Yes?"

She slipped a fax across her desk. "Confirmation for to-night. You're all good."

Tonight. Dog track night. I hadn't told anyone about the change in plans. The busses would be there at five thirty to pick everyone up. That was all they needed to know. That way no one could judge me or the event before they got there and saw how great it was.

Assuming, of course, that it was great.

Heaven help me if it wasn't.

* * *

I was a genius. No other conclusion was possible, not since I'd accepted at least a gazillion compliments on the dog track evening, and it was only eight o'clock.

The food was amazing, the service fabulous, the room we were in looked out on the dog track and had its own betting booth, so we didn't have to wait in any lines, or miss out on a race while we were eating. The attorneys were actually spending quite a bit of money, and the interns had all spent the twenty bucks I'd given each of them to entertain themselves.

Who would have thought the attorneys at M&S would enjoy the dog track? Maybe I'd have to arrange a trip down to the Connecticut casinos for later on in the summer.

I picked up my glass of wine and surveyed the room. Dessert was pending. Some people were sitting at the tables chatting, while others were out on the balcony cheering the dogs on. People had shed their jackets and ties, and I'd even seen a few sleeves rolled up.

I was a goddess. I'd salvaged the evening and managed to get the attorneys to actually quit being uptight.

I lifted my glass and toasted myself.

"Ms. McCormick."

Otto. I immediately stood up. "Mr. Nelson. So glad you could join us tonight." *Wow.* Otto was actually going to compliment me. Wonder if I could get a copy of the security footage from tonight so I could preserve the moment in immortality.

"Are you insane?"

I blinked. "What?"

"Gambling? Dog track? Handing out money to interns to

bet? What in the hell is wrong with you?" He was shouting at me, his cheeks were blotchy, and his face was about a quarter of an inch from mine. "What kind of firm do you think this is?"

Oh, God. I glanced next to me and saw several attorneys staring at us.

"Look at me when I'm talking to you!"

Did he actually spit on me? Was that saliva I could feel on my face?

"Do you have any idea of the number of generations that have put their guts into this firm to establish its reputation?"

"Um . . ."

"Answer me!"

He was friggin' yelling at me in public. Unbelievable. "Mr. Nelson—"

"Yes or no?"

"The firm has been around for one hundred and eleven years. Founded on September eighth, by two Harvard Law graduates who were from elite Boston families." The advantage of being the social director was that I'd learned the history of the firm so I could bore the interns with it at their first lunch.

"That's right. Harvard. Elite families. The foundation of this firm is reputation and prestige. Not something to be bandied about by you. If you can't respect this firm and all that it stands for, then I want you to resign right here and never walk in our halls again."

Oh, my God. I was being fired in front of everyone. Not just fired—yelled at. Humiliated. Destroyed. I bit my lower lip and ordered the tears to stay out of my damned eyes. I would *not* give him the satisfaction.

"Well? What's it going to be?" He was screaming at me. Screaming! Like he was completely insane! "Can you respect this institution or should I fire you right now?"

I had a choice? "I'm sorry, sir."

"That's not an answer!"

"Yes, I can respect it." I couldn't believe my mouth was actually functioning. My tongue felt like it had swollen up to about a zillion times its regular size, and my head felt like it was going to explode.

Otto glared at me, and I saw sweat dripping down his temple. He was insane. Crazy. A madman. At any second I was going to find a butter knife sticking out of my neck as I fell to the ground in the throes of death. And I'd lie there until the racing was over, until people had nothing better to do than deal with the body of their social director.

"From now on, every single event must be preapproved by me."

"Yes, sir." Preapproved? I had four events each week. I'd been at the firm for three years, and doing a kick-ass job as social director. The firm had been ranked number one in the polls for summer interns every single summer since I'd taken over. And suddenly I wasn't capable of making any decision on my own? It was like I was five years old. Incompetent, needing parental supervision.

"And I want a meeting with you every Monday to discuss your plans for the week."

Oh, God. A weekly meeting with Otto.

"Got it?"

Do you think I'm deaf or something? My ear is about one inch from your mouth and you're still screaming at me! "Yes, sir."

"And don't ever defame the firm like this again!"

Perhaps you could scream a little louder? Not sure the people in the parking lot could hear you clearly. "Yes, sir."

He glared at me for about another ten minutes, his mouth churning like he was spewing silent epithets at me; then finally he turned away and walked out.

All I wanted to do was cry. Then I looked around the room. Every single attorney and intern was staring at me. Even the people who'd been out on the balcony were inside now.

And everyone was silent. And staring. At me.

Even the serving staff from the track was staring at me, the dessert trays motionless in their hands.

So I had two choices. Burst into tears and make even more of a fool of myself. Or pretend nothing had happened and awe everyone with my emotional strength. I'd had enough humiliation this evening, thank you very much.

I didn't even have the privacy to close my eyes and count to ten to regroup. I simply smiled and clapped my hands together. "Glad I have everyone's attention. Dessert is ready to be served. We have decaf or regular coffee. After dessert, you may continue to bet and watch the races from up here, or you can go downstairs into the public areas. One bus will leave at nine thirty, and the other one will leave at ten o'clock. Enjoy the rest of your evening." I clenched my lips together and nodded at the waitstaff to start handing out the desserts. I needed to get out of there. Alone. I couldn't keep it together any longer.

But everyone was still gawking at me, and no one had moved.

So I turned to the server nearest to me. "Serve the damned dessert already."

"Oh, yes, ma'am." The man immediately ducked forward with his tray, and I instantly felt like queen bitch. Great, nothing like self-hatred to add to my emotional burden at the moment.

But his movement propelled others, and within five seconds the room was beginning to move again, person by person, like slow motion in a bad movie. Except the interns. They were all still gaping at me, but now they were whispering, no doubt wondering how a person as incompetent as I was could possibly be in charge. Would it ruin their careers to be associated with me? Should they petition for a new social director? Perhaps a mutiny would be in order. *Save yourselves! Protect yourselves from Shannon McCormick!*

Fresh tears battled for freedom, and I turned and walked out of the room. Not to the bathroom, because other attorneys would be in there. I shoved open the door to the back stairs and walked down to the public area.

Just get alone. That was all I needed to do. Then I could fall apart in privacy.

"Shannon! Shannon! Wait up!"

Dammit. Why did Hildy have to go and be herself *now?* Didn't she know that humiliation of this magnitude could be dealt with only in private?

I started running down the stairs, and I heard Hildy running after me. "Shannon! Stop!"

Cursing, I paused on the landing and waited for her. It was one thing to slink off in private and cry, but it was something else to actually be caught doing it. So I waited, and ground my fingernails into my palms to distract myself from the burning need to throw myself over the railing and see how many bones I could break in the fall. "Yes, Hildy?"

"Are you okay?" She finally caught up, breathing hard from the effort of chasing me.

"I'm fine."

She peered at me. "Are you sure? Because Otto really went off on you."

"Did he? I didn't notice." *Ow.* I wondered if I was drawing blood in my palms. Sure felt like it.

She actually laughed. "That's the right attitude. He's like that to everyone. Don't take it personally."

"Ha. As if I'd let that bother me. I know what he's like." Did I sound flippant enough? "I was just going to check on seating down here."

"Oh, good. I wanted to come down here, too." Before I could think of a valid reason why Hildy shouldn't accompany me, she tucked her arm through mine and started walking down the stairs with me.

What was up with that? I mean, I'd always known Hildy was nice, but chummy was a whole new level. Partners, even junior ones, didn't get chummy with social directors. Perhaps she was secretly working for Otto and was luring me to the edge of the track, where suddenly three huge guys would jump out and shove me in front of the dogs, who would trample me into a pulp. "Hildy—"

"Let's go down next to the track. I want to see the dogs up close."

See? I knew it. "Actually, I need to go back upstairs."

"Yes, you do."

I eyed her. "What do you mean?"

"You can't hide from everyone. The longer you wait to go back in there, the harder it will be."

"I have no idea what you're talking about." Why wouldn't she leave me alone?

"It's all part of the game, Shannon."

I stopped and removed my arm from hers. "What game?"

"The game. How you survive at a place like this. You take the grief, and then just keep quietly doing a great job and making it impossible for people not to respect you." She sighed. "You can't fight the system. Just go along with it and shrug it off."

Shrug it off? I'd just had my guts ripped out and shredded in front of everyone at the firm. Was she kidding?

"How do you think I made partner, Shannon? By fighting? No way. By blending in and playing the game."

"But that's—"

"Success." Her tone warned me not to insult her. "Look around you. See what it takes to get ahead and do it."

Get ahead? As if there were anywhere to go from social director.

"Come on." Hildy turned us in a half circle. "Go up there and show people that you've got what it takes."

She wasn't going to leave me alone. She was going to stalk me until I went upstairs and faced everyone. What was her problem? I'd just been humiliated. Destroyed. No job was worth this.

But I followed her up the stairs and walked back in. I saw a few people glance my way, but no one came up to me or said anything.

"Pretend it never happened," Hildy whispered. Then she walked off and left me alone.

So. Well. What was I supposed to do now?

"Shannon?"

I looked to my right to find Missy, the timid intern, standing by my side. I forced a smile to my face. "Yes, Missy?"

"Can I talk to you?"

"Sure. What can I do for you?" This was exactly what I needed. Some stupid intern crisis to distract me. Hell, I'd even like to have Jessamee come over and demand a new office. Anything to find an outlet.

"Alone." She turned away and walked over to a table in the corner.

I followed her. Or rather, I dragged my feet across the floor. If I was about to get a pep talk from an intern, I was going to go home and cry.

On the bright side, Blaine wasn't here tonight, so that was something positive, right?

I sat down across from Missy. "Yes?" How was I possibly going to make it through another two hours? I couldn't deal with this uptight world, with this type of corporate environment. A place where you were expected to accept that kind of treatment? Where it was okay?

It made no sense.

"I'm quitting," Missy said.

"Quitting what?" I tried to focus on her, tried to make myself care about her problems.

"My job." She looked surprised, like how could I not have figured out what she was talking about?

"Oh." Wait a sec. "Your job at M and S?"

"Yes. Can you pack my desk? I don't want to go back on Monday."

Oh, hell. This was all I needed. If Otto found out I had

interns quitting on dog track night, I'd be in even worse trouble than I currently was. "Why are you quitting?"

Her eyes widened. "Because of what just happened."

Great. "You mean with Mr. Nelson?"

She nodded. "I can't work somewhere like this. I'd never survive."

Not that I could conscientiously disagree with her on that one. As I'd mentioned before, she was about the meekest person I'd met in my entire life. She did, however, have the highest GPA in her class at Yale and was a third-generation attorney. A good perk for the firm, and Otto would have my head if I let her leave. "That was an aberration, Missy." Good Lord, I was going to be struck down for lying to an intern. "I screwed up."

"Taking us here? This was a great night. Everyone had fun."

Bless this woman. "It was more than that." Wait a minute. What was I doing? Trying to make it sound like I'd really deserved being yelled at in order to keep Missy there? I mean, it was one thing to work hard, but it was something else entirely to take the blame for something I didn't deserve.

Missy folded her skinny arms across her chest. "Do you know what I'd do if someone yelled at me like that? I'd die."

I'd die. That was what I felt like doing. But it wasn't my job to die. It was my job to make Missy think she wanted to work at M&S for the rest of her life.

But I looked across the table at her worried eyes and hunched shoulders, and I wondered how I could do anything but tell this woman to run away as fast as she possibly could.

CHAPTER SEVEN

"Missy."

"What?" She looked at me, and I saw trust in her eyes. *Oh, great.* That was all I needed, to have her trust me. Like this wasn't hard enough already.

"I think you should stay at M and S." I felt horrible, awful, terrible lying to her, when all I wanted to do was grab her hand and drag her from the building, telling her not to leave a trail that they could follow. *Run away! Run away!*

She pushed back from the table, shaking her head frantically. "No. No. No. I thought you'd understand. I mean, I saw your face. You can't possibly think I should stay."

I don't exactly have a good poker face. If she saw my misery when I was being yelled at, then so did everyone else.

Screw Otto. How dared he humiliate me like that! I'd worked my butt off for that firm, and I did a great job. He was lucky there was an event at all. If not for me, they'd be back to the pre-Shannon days, when the firm was ranked last on the list of firms for happiness quotient for summer interns. But no, he didn't care if anyone worked hard for him. He was a spineless bully who beat up on anyone who wasn't in a position to tell him that he was really an ornery bastard who deserved to have all his fingernails pulled off and his tongue chopped out and—

"Shannon?"

I looked at Missy. She deserved the truth. And I deserved to keep my job. "It's like this. If you can make it through the summer and get an offer from the firm, then you can use that as leverage when you interview at other firms in the fall."

Missy frowned. "What are you talking about?"

"Most people get offered permanent jobs at the end of the summer. They accept those jobs with a starting date twelve months out. If you intern here and then interview elsewhere, the first thing they're going to ask you is whether you got an offer. If you say no, then they figure there's something wrong with you, even if you explain that you quit on your own. If you say yes, then they'll believe that you chose not to go back."

Missy wrinkled her nose and looked very unhappy with the news.

"All you have to do is make it through the summer. That's ten weeks. Surely you can survive for ten weeks." It was all true. It was to her advantage to get an offer. And I wasn't acknowledging anything bad about the firm, and I wasn't lying to her that she really would be happy dumping her pride at the door and coming to work for M&S.

"I don't think so. . . ."

I patted her shoulder. "Give it until Monday to decide."

She frowned. "But he was such a jerk."

"It wasn't to you, was it?" A good thing, too. If Otto

chewed out Missy, I'd probably have to intervene. But he'd never yell at an intern. Not because he treated them differently, but because I was careful never to let an intern work with him on an assignment. As long as you weren't doing a project for him or in any way crossing his path, he could be fairly decent. Of course, Jessamee might end up tangling with him, but hey, I just couldn't drum up any regret about that one. "You can quit at any second, Missy. Why don't you just take it one day at time? You have the added benefit of getting paid very well."

Yes, she did, didn't she? Maybe if I were making Hildy's salary, I wouldn't feel bad about selling out and accepting being treated like scum. However, my minimum-wage salary would hardly cover the extensive therapy bills I was sure to accumulate. Which left me where? With my only option to leave the firm? To do what? Go to law school? Admit failure? Admit my parents were right, that I sucked so badly I couldn't even hold down a support position at a law firm?

No, thanks. I was going to stick it out and prove to everyone that I had what it took.

"I don't think I want to work here anymore," Missy said. "My grades are good enough that I can get another job even if I don't stay here."

Which was true. Ah, the luxury. Not like the rest of us, who actually had to fight for a job and suck it up even if it was miserable. I could just hear my mom laughing in the background. *See, Shannon? See what happens when you don't get a graduate degree? If you had one, then you too could pick and choose where you went.*

Shut up, Mom! I'm not going to be a lawyer!

"Tell you what, Missy. Do whatever you want. But come October when you can't get a job, you're going to look back at this summer and think that it couldn't possibly have been so bad that it was worth throwing away your future." I stood up. At least she was getting paid a lot of money to suffer. And she wasn't going to suffer anyway! Not this summer. Not with Auntie Shannon looking out for all the interns. I'd just spread my wings around them and protect them from real life and nasty lawyers.

Yep. I'd take a bullet for each of them. Already took one tonight. Still wasn't sure whether it had killed me or not. Perhaps I was suffering an agonizing death, the blood slowly leaking from my body and . . . I caught a glimpse of Missy's face. She looked rather shocked and upset by my words.

Oh, crap. What was I doing? My job wasn't to tell interns to suck it up. It was to protect them. But I really wasn't in the mood. I had my own problems to deal with. "Sorry, Missy. I didn't mean to come across so strongly. Let's have a meeting on Monday at nine and we'll discuss the situation some more. Don't do anything before then."

Maybe by that time I'd have my own emotions under control enough to talk to Missy.

"Don't you have to meet with Otto on Monday morning?"

Gee, thanks for that reminder. "We'll work around that. Call Isabel when you get in and she'll let you know when we can get together." Assuming, of course, that she had time to work on my schedule. It was unclear with Blaine still around. "Let's get back to the group. Might as well enjoy tonight. Nothing bad is going to happen to you here."

She eyed me suspiciously. "Something bad happened to you."

Excellent point. "Dessert, Missy."

I took her arm and guided her back to the main tables, depositing her next to Hildy and another young lawyer. Male, but young enough that he didn't have chauvinistic views toward women. Plus he was good-looking and he'd gone to Yale. If those two couldn't win Missy over, no one could. I eyed Hildy. "Missy's a little shaken up by Otto's . . . ahem . . . coaching of me. Might want to chitchat about it."

Hildy nodded and put her arm around Missy's shoulders and went to work. I walked away before I could listen to Hildy telling Missy how great M&S was and how she didn't need to worry about being miserable. In Hildy's mind, she probably wasn't lying. M&S wasn't miserable. But I couldn't stand there and listen to someone convince Missy to accept a job that would destroy her.

I know—I put her in Hildy's clutches, so I was as guilty as if I'd done it myself. On the other hand, Missy was an adult. Old enough to make her own decisions, right?

Yeah, right. I was a horrible person and I was going to burn in hell. And it wouldn't be after I died. It would be now; it would be Monday. And Tuesday and Wednesday and the rest of my career at this firm. All of it—hell.

By the time I got home, I was no longer embarrassed and humiliated. I was furious. How dared Otto berate me in front of everyone else? I slammed open the door to our apartment, kicked it shut, threw my keys on the floor, hurled my shoes into the living room, stomped into the kitchen, and yanked open the fridge door with a satisfying clank as three bottles of salad dressing fell out of the door onto the floor.

I grabbed an open bottle of wine and shoved the door shut, leaving the salad dressing on the floor. With any luck, I'd step on one, fall, and break my femur. I'd have to be in traction for six months, and I could spend my days watching soaps and living on disability. It would be great.

"What are you doing?" Emma appeared in the doorway, wearing her nondate sleeping outfit, namely sweats and a baggy T-shirt. When she had men over, she had a much more interesting assortment of nightwear to choose from.

I poured a glass of wine and sat down at the table. "The managing partner screamed at me in front of all the attorneys and interns. Told me I was incompetent and deserved to be fired. Also informed me that I wasn't capable of being trusted to make good decisions, so I have to run every decision by him for the rest of the summer." I was getting angry again just thinking about it. "Do you have any idea what I've done for that firm?"

"Yes, I do." Emma grabbed a glass and poured herself some wine, then curled up in another chair. "Why didn't you tell him to screw himself?"

"I did."

She lifted her eyebrows. "Really?"

"In my head."

She rolled her eyes. "Oh, come on, Shannon. That doesn't count."

"What am I supposed to do? Punch him in the face?"

"That would be a good start."

I snorted and leaned back in my chair. "Unlike you, I

actually need my job. I can't afford to lose it by pissing off some influential partner."

"Why do you need your job?"

I gestured at the kitchen. "To pay rent. To pay bills. To buy food." To buy my sister's engagement gift. "Unlike you, I don't have my parents supporting me."

She narrowed her eyes. "Don't make any snide remarks about that. My parents offer. What am I supposed to do, turn them down?"

"Yes! You've been out of college for three years! Try supporting yourself! Try taking a little responsibility for something. Anything!"

Emma set her glass down on the table, sloshing wine over the rim. "Hey! Don't get mad at me! I'm just trying to help."

"By telling me to yell at Otto and get fired? How is that helping?" My voice was getting louder, but I couldn't help it.

"Because you're miserable and you're in this stupid job just to prove your parents wrong or right or something. You think you're being independent from them, but you're working in a law firm. Oh, but you're not a lawyer. No, but you play the same game they do. Wear the same clothes, work the same hours, suck up to management. You're not the independent woman you think you are. You're everything you don't want to be, and you don't have the guts to realize it and actually take some risks. Instead you just let everyone else make you miserable, while you delude yourself that you're tough and independent. Well, forget it, Shannon! I'm sick and tired of hearing you complain and then doing nothing about it!"

I jumped to my feet and smashed my fist on the table.

"Don't ever accuse me of being like my family! You're wrong!"

"Fine. Be deluded. See if I care." And then she spun on her heel and marched out of the kitchen and into the bedroom. She slammed the door so hard that the glasses in the cabinet rattled and the calendar fell off the wall.

I shouted an epithet at her, and she screamed one back. Then she turned on her stereo and cranked it up.

Fine. I didn't want to talk to her anyway.

I grabbed my wine, stalked into the living room, and turned on the television. The tears creeping out of my eyes? An illusion. I was too mad to cry.

But dammit, this really sucked.

My one friend whom I could talk about it with wasn't speaking to me. No, I wasn't speaking to her, because she didn't deserve to be spoken to. How could she accuse me of not being independent? I would have thought she would understand how hard I was trying.

Trying to what? Succeed? Survive? Figure out what the hell I wanted from my life and my career?

I looked at the phone.

Maybe I should call Max. Maybe he would understand.

I picked up the phone and stared at the keypad. *Don't call him!* But I needed to. I needed to talk to someone who could understand. Someone who knew my family, who understood me, who knew I was good at what I did.

Max would understand. After listening to me for two years, he knew me.

I started to dial the phone.

"Don't call him."

I looked up to find Emma standing in the door. "Go away."

"You're calling Max, aren't you?"

"None of your business." I hit the last two numbers and lifted the phone to my ear.

"Shannon!" Emma ran across the room and grabbed the receiver out of my hand. She hit disconnect, then threw the phone across the room. "What are you doing?"

"I needed to talk to him!"

"No, you don't! You've lasted almost three weeks without him. If you call him now, you'll never break the cycle."

"Maybe I don't want to. Maybe I belong with him. He understands me, he makes my life with my family tolerable, everyone at the firm loves him. Maybe he's right not to let me walk away."

"And what are you going to do when you're on your honeymoon with him and you meet your true love, but you're wearing Max's ring on your finger?"

How dared she throw my confession that Max wasn't my true love back in my face? That was confidential information given during a moment of bonding. "At least he'd never accuse me of being like my family."

"Fine. Whatever. I give." She retrieved the phone and tossed it on the couch next to me. "Call him. I'm going to bed."

She walked into her room and slammed the door again as hard as she could.

I stared at the phone. God, I was so lonely. So miserable. Dave was with his wife. Phoebe was off in Chicago with her fiancé. I had no one to call except Max.

But I didn't pick up the phone.

After a long time, I retrieved the rest of the wine, put in a war movie, and imagined Otto's head on the body of every person who got killed.

And each time I went for the phone, I made myself wait another fifteen minutes. If I still had to call Max when those fifteen minutes were up, then I could do it.

But the wine took over before I succumbed. I fell asleep while "Otto" was getting blown up by a hand grenade between his legs.

If I caught my heel on a cobblestone on the way in, fell, and broke my collarbone, then maybe I'd have a legit excuse for skipping my sister's engagement party. Six weeks' worth of pain and my arm in a sling would be worth it, wouldn't you think?

I had a raging headache from the wine episode last night, and I still hated everyone in my life.

But I wasn't going to give any member of my family the satisfaction of knowing I was miserable. They'd gloat and wave law school applications in front of my face, and then I'd have to karate-chop them all into oblivion, and that would certainly be a damper on the party. Plus it would make me look bad, and after last night's humiliation, I was somewhat in favor of a low-key evening in which I lurked quietly in the background and didn't get noticed or ridiculed or anything like that. Engaging in various martial arts on my family members wouldn't be conducive to that goal.

Therefore, I was going to be chipper and positive and charming tonight. And try to avoid as many people as possible.

I forced a smile to my face and looked into the lobby of the Sleeping Pines Country Club, which was decorated with white roses. No, not decorated. *Saturated* with them, in an ostentatious display of money and connections. The paintings hanging on the walls were all originals that belonged in a museum of fine arts, and the expensive Italian-marble floors shouted, "Guess how much I cost!" The doorknobs were engraved gold leaf, as were the intricate designs on the ceilings. There was a man in tails at the front door, opening it for everyone, bowing obsequiously as each person glided past.

So not my style. No wonder my mom had been worried I would embarrass her. This place was seriously out of my comfort zone.

"Shannon? Shannon McCormick? Is that you?"

There stood one of my parents' friends. I wasn't sure of her name, but she looked familiar enough. Probably one of my parents' many "cocktail friends.""Hello," I said. "It's so lovely to see you." God, was I impressive or what? Charm oozed from every pore.

I did the requisite floating air-cheek kiss with the woman. "Shannon, your sister looks so beautiful. Soon to be married at age twenty-two. To a doctor! How wonderful!"

"Fabulous. We just love him." *Smile, Shannon. Get away before she asks* . . .

"So when are you going to follow in your parents' steps and go to law school?"

I gritted my teeth. "Oh, I don't know. We'll have to see."

"Shannon works at Miller and Shaw, you know." My mom magically appeared out of thin air, no doubt driven by her sixth sense to protect the McCormick family name from malignment.

"Oh!" The nameless woman looked startled and impressed. "I didn't realize you were a lawyer. At M and S? Impressive."

"I'm not a—"

"Shannon. Your sister is looking for you. Let's go find her." My mom interrupted before I could shatter the image by announcing I was the social director, not a lawyer. She grabbed my arm and dragged me away.

"Mom." I pulled free. "No matter how hard you try, some-one here tonight is going to figure out I'm not a lawyer."

My mom shot me a look; then she stopped and straight-ened my dress. "I'm glad to see you bought something decent. You look very nice."

Of course I looked nice. It was my sister's engagement party. Just because I wasn't living up to the McCormick family name didn't mean I had no social skills. "I even got it altered to fit me. How about that, huh?"

My mom eyed me. "Off the rack?"

"Of course. I'm a social director. I don't have the money to buy designer clothes." Like she didn't already know that. It was her way of gently reminding me what I'd given up by refusing to go to law school.

"I really wish you'd let me buy your dress for the rehearsal dinner. We could go to one of the boutiques on Newbury Street and get you something that's perfect for you."

Something up to her standards, she meant. My mom would have praised the heavens if I'd actually let her pick out and fund my wardrobe for the rehearsal dinner. Think of the control she'd have had over me then. It would have been a dream come true for her.

Well, too bad. There was a limit to what I'd do. I'd buy a decent dress and show up freshly showered, but I wasn't going to let my mom start funding my existence. The minute I did that, my independence would be gone. Not that I was independent, according to Emma. But what did Emma know about independence? She still got three grand a month for living expenses from her parents.

I took a deep breath. Hadn't I resolved to be positive tonight? No hating anyone, no bitter feelings about myself. Besides, what was the point in being confrontational with my mom, anyway? It wasn't like I'd change her, no matter how many psychic commands I sent in her direction.

Now, if Blaine was here, that might change her. At the very least, I might be spared disparaging looks for an hour or two. Not like there was any chance of him showing up tonight, though.

He'd been sequestered all day on Friday so I didn't have to see him, which spared me any post-nipple-sighting small talk, but I was astute enough to notice that by not seeing me all day, he hadn't had to get any final details about the engagement party. I'd finally left him a voice mail with the directions and said to meet me there, but I wasn't holding out any hope.

Not that I wanted to spend the evening with him after he'd insulted my clothes and gave me those smarmy looks when Dirk's name came up, but his presence would have made my family a lot more bearable, and for that I'd be willing to put up with him. Not that he was coming anyway.

Figured. I'd actually be dressing up to his standards

today, in my nifty black cocktail dress that was off the rack, but still mind-bogglingly expensive, at least for my budget. But my mom could smell bargain clothes like a dog could smell a cat under a bed. So what if I'd have to forgo groceries for three months? It wasn't worth the aggravation to push my mom that far.

My mom dumped me in a little discussion group of fifteen-year-olds, who all looked more sophisticated than I felt. Especially when I realized they were discussing the distribution of money from their trust funds. *Nice.*

I tuned out the conversation and glanced around the room. Typical McCormick family gathering. Lots of designer names on the clothes, not an off-the-rack suit in the place, and there was my little sister, Lindsay, looking radiant and happy while she hung on the arm of her oh-so-handsome doctor fiancé, Geoff Ziegler.

My dad had his arm around Geoff's shoulders and was laughing at one of his future son-in-law's jokes. And it wasn't his "work laugh." It was a real laugh. He actually liked Geoff. My sister had made my dad truly happy.

I studied my sister. Flushed cheeks, sparkly eyes, huge smile. She looked legitimately happy too. How could that be? How could living life to make my parents happy actually be emotionally satisfying?

So she had it all. My parents loved her. She loved herself. She loved her life. She loved her fiancé.

It would be so easy if I wanted the same things as my parents. Had the same goals. Would that make me as happy as Lindsay. What was wrong with me? Why couldn't I be happy with what my parents wanted for me?

"Shannon."

I turned to find my brother Travis standing behind me. His adorable little girlfriend was leaning on his arm, dripping with diamonds, as usual. Travis made very good money as a stockbroker, and he made sure everyone knew it. Did my parents proud. "Hi, Travis. Hello, April. So good to see you guys."

April gave me a smile, her eyes already drifting over my shoulder. "You look lovely, Shannon." She was holding a huge box beautifully wrapped in silver paper with gold wedding bells on it. A discreet card was tucked under the ribbon. I wondered if I should check to see if my name was actually on there.

"Where's Max?" April asked.

"I broke up with him." *Note the pronouns. I broke up with him.*

April looked startled. "Why?"

"Just because." Okay, a bit too much hostility there. How was I going to make it through the evening if I was already turning into queen bitch? But I was getting tired of trying to explain that I felt Max simply wasn't the one. People generally responded with blank or, worse, disdainful expressions. On the plus side, I had managed to refrain from calling him last night, and I was pretty proud of myself. And if I'd seen Emma at any point today, I would have apologized and thanked her for interfering. But she'd been gone by the time I woke up and she hadn't reappeared.

Which was fine.

It gave me a day of solitude to feel sorry for myself and to try to decide what image I was going to present at the engagement party to best hide my misery.

"I always thought Max was nice," April said. "I've run into

him at quite a few social functions and he's always been charming."

"Charming" didn't mean he was my soul mate. Travis looked at me sternly. "You dumped Max, and Mom says you're still at M and S as the social director. Is that true?"

I lifted my chin. "Yes."

He met my gaze. "Why?"

"Why what?"

"Why are you still there? You can't tell me you like playing mommy to all those lawyers."

He had me there.

Travis shook his head. "You could get into any graduate school. You're smart, you work hard, you could do anything. So why are you doing *that?*"

If only he hadn't added that last question, it could almost have been taken as a compliment. "Because I want to."

"Travis! April! When did you guys get here?" My dad slung an arm around each of them and started to walk off with them. "Come over and say hello to Lindsay and Geoff."

"Hi, Dad."

He glanced back over his shoulder. "Shannon! Didn't even see you standing there. Come with us." Then he kept walking without bothering to see if I followed.

Great. I wondered if I'd at least have gotten a perfunctory hello kiss if I were here with Blaine. Not that it mattered. I wasn't.

I stood there and watched the family reunion, and tried not to feel totally excluded.

Suddenly both my arms were grabbed and I was swept forward. I glanced up to find my attorney brother Ray and his lifelong best pal, Noah Quinlan, on either side of me. "Hi, guys."

"Can't be letting you feel sorry for yourself," Ray said. "You just have to get in there and mix it up."

It occurred to me that I must look pretty silly being propelled across the room by them. "Can you please let go?"

Noah released me, but Ray kept dragging me until I was in the middle of the McCormick clan. "We're here," Ray announced.

My family turned and Ray and Noah got their round of hugs. I wasn't going to humiliate myself by announcing *my* presence and then comparing the response I engendered. Lindsay accepted kisses and congratulations from everyone, and Geoff got his share of backslaps and handshakes. I gave Lindsay a hug. "I'm so happy for you." *Ow.* My face hurt.

She smiled. "Maybe someday you'll get married, Shannon. I'm keeping my fingers crossed for you."

"Gee, thanks." I gave Geoff a hug too, and wondered why he didn't smell like antiseptic. Shouldn't doctors smell like hospitals? Figured. Rich, loved her, and he smelled decent.

I stepped back as friends and business acquaintances swarmed the gathering, all of them wanting a moment with the treasured guests.

"So where's Max?"

I looked up to find Noah standing beside me, withdrawing from the crush around Lindsay and Geoff. As usual, Noah looked totally hot. I'd had a crush on him since I was about three days old. But being six years older than me, he hadn't even glanced in my direction until after I graduated from college. Max and I started dating soon after, so Noah and I'd only ever flirted harmlessly. "I broke up with Max."

Noah lifted an eyebrow. "Really? That's unexpected."

"Because he's so perfect?"

"Because your family loved him."

I sighed. "I'm trying to become my own woman. Make decisions for myself instead of because my family wants me to." Noah was an interesting part of my life. He was like family, so he knew all my ugly secrets, including the one my family tried to hide from the rest of the world—namely, that I existed. Yet he wasn't my family, so I could complain to him and he sort of got it. In fact, it was a sort of joke between us that my parents would trade me for him if they could. Well, I tried to make it a joke. I didn't always find it very funny, though.

"Good." Noah put his arm around my shoulders and squeezed. "Don't worry about everything so much."

"Easy for you to say." Noah was a lawyer at the same firm as Ray, obscenely successful, and a nice guy to boot. And did I mention totally gorgeous?

He pointed across the room. "Someone seems to be trying to get your attention."

I looked, and there stood Blaine, watching me.

CHAPTER EIGHT

Holy shit. Blaine had come. *Hallelujah.* For this, he could monopolize Isabel anytime he wanted. "Sweet." I glanced at Noah. "I'll see you in a minute."

"Sure."

I walked across the room as demurely as I could, nodding at people I didn't recognize as if I were in great demand. After a torturously long time, I ended up in front of Blaine. "You made it."

"Yep." He glanced around the room. "This is some kind of guest list."

Though I really appreciated the compliment about my parents' ability to attract the crème de la crème of society, a quick remark about my very expensive dress would have been okay with me. Not that I was dwelling on Blaine's utter lack of appreciation of me as a woman. "Come meet my family. They'll start introducing you around."

He nodded and followed me across the room, not touching me, but close enough that people could very well assume we were walking together. We reached the little clump, and my mom was in the middle of a very juicy conversation with someone who I think invented oxygen or something lucrative like that. "Mom."

She kept talking.

"Mom!" I touched her arm and she looked at me.

"Yes, Shannon?"

"I want you to meet someone."

My mom's eyes drifted from my face to Blaine, who was standing right next to me. She looked at me again, then at him, then turned her back on her little group and faced me. "Who is this?"

"Blaine Hampton. New partner at M and S. Just moved up from New York City."

Blaine shook my mom's hand. "So nice to meet you, Mrs. McCormick."

"Oh, call me Celeste."

I could see the wheels turning in my mom's head as she assessed his suit, his watch, his haircut.

"What firm were you with in New York?"

Blaine rattled off a name I didn't recognize, but my mom nearly passed out with glee. As a lawyer, she would know these things more than a peon like myself. "And you're here with Shannon?"

Blaine glanced at me. "Yes. She was kind enough to invite me."

"Oh, she was, indeed?" My mom must have sent some vibe to my dad, because he was suddenly standing next to her receiving the Blaine introduction. He sent me a few quizzical looks too, but Blaine reiterated to my dad that I'd invited him to the party.

I was thankful my parents were far too proper to do something as unseemly as ask whether he was messing around with their daughter, but it was apparent that the possibility had settled in both their minds, as my dad offered to take Blaine off to meet the rest of the family. I concurred, and watched my dad escort Blaine off into the McCormick family inner circle.

It was like Max all over again, only this time I wasn't actually dating Blaine, so I wasn't going to reap the benefit of my association with him for long.

My mom tucked her hands around my arm while we watched Blaine congratulate Lindsay. "He's quite handsome, Shannon."

"Yep."

"And dresses well."

"Yep."

"And a partner already?"

"Uh-huh."

"At such a young age. Impressive." My mom sighed. "I'm glad to see some good is finally coming out of that job of yours. It would be great to land one of the partners there, and then he could support you while you go back to school."

"I'm not going back to school. And I'm not going to use my job as a platform to prostitute myself into the arms of a lawyer." Two seconds with my mom, and all my goodwill was gone. Not that I'd really expected anything to change, but still. I'd hoped that the presence of Blaine might take some of the heat off me for at least the evening. My parents could tell all their friends I was with Blaine, and then everyone could conveniently forget that my job was a support position in which I earned less than the average family income for the country.

I heard my dad introduce Blaine to someone else, and

he definitely used my name as the connection. See? Daddy McCormick proud because loser daughter was able to bring Blaine to the party. Must use every opportunity to make black sheep look better.

Not that I was cynical or bitter or anything like that.

"This could be a little awkward," my mom said.

I didn't like the tone of that comment. I pulled my arm away and eyed her. "What could be awkward?"

"Oh, nothing. Must be off. I see an unattended guest." My mom vamoosed before I could corner her, and I had a very bad feeling in my stomach.

Max.

She'd invited him.

He was here somewhere. Lurking. Stalking.

I turned slowly, inspecting the room very carefully. Then I did a second circuit. No Max.

Why didn't I feel reassured? And how dared he be present when I was only eighteen hours away from relapsing into an I-can't-live-without-Max state? I was way too vulnerable to face him now. Max was safe and he knew me, and I wanted to go hide right now.

But I wouldn't. I was here with Blaine, and I was going to own him by the time the night was through.

Blaine was in a little group of gray-haired men who all looked very dignified, and they were shaking hands with Blaine and looking pleased to meet him. Great for him.

I looked around the room again. All these people talking to each other. Not to me. Which was why I'd wanted Emma to come.

Dave's wife was back in town, so he couldn't make it. Phoebe had gone off to visit her fiancé in Chicago. Emma was flirting with boys in a bar. Blaine was completely blowing me off. My family was ignoring me. And to think I'd been dreading this party. How ridiculous. Maybe I should look for Max. . . .

"Shannon!"

I whirled around to find Emma grinning at me. "Emma! You're here!"

"You bet." Emma was wearing a very short little skirt and a silk blouse that was a bit more daring than your standard business attire, but still perfectly respectable. Not a Bud Light girl outfit. "How's it going?"

"Terrible. I had my millisecond of fame when I introduced Blaine to my parents, but then I became obsolete." I was *so* glad to see her!

"They're just intimidated by the fact that you'll live a happy life instead of being trapped by money and power," Emma said.

"I'm really sorry about last night," I said. "You were right about Max, and thanks to your little intervention, I never did call him." I wasn't going to apologize for getting mad at her for all the other things she said. I still resented that, but I needed her. So I'd forget about the rest of the night.

Emma threw her arm around my shoulders. "No worries. I'm sorry, too."

She didn't specify, and I didn't push her. I had a feeling neither one of us wanted to revisit the specifics of that discussion right now.

"Let's go visit your sister. I want to congratulate her."

I followed Emma as she marched across the room, flashing smiles at anyone who looked her way. Big hugs for all of my family, and friendly chatter with them all. Interesting how my whole family seemed to love Emma, even though she was the antithesis of everything the McCormick name stood for. Guess that was the difference. She didn't actually have the McCormick name, so she was free.

She returned to my side. "Did you see Noah? He's looking really tasty."

"No kidding." My brother's best friend was in the group with Blaine now, and they were looking pretty chummy.

"Did you ever fool around with him?"

"Who?" Blaine or Noah?

"Noah. You guys always flirted."

"Nope."

"What a waste."

"Yep." Not that Noah mattered. I had my sights set on Blaine now. He'd seen me in my cocktail dress, been too awed by my beauty to risk comment, and was now aware of the family that I brought to the table. Oh, yes, he was all mine.

Blaine must have felt my psychic thoughts, because he looked over at me. Then he smiled.

I smiled back.

Then he excused himself from his little party and walked toward me. Oh, yes. Here it came. He was going to officially declare his lust for me.

He got closer, and his grin got bigger. *Wow. Nice dimples.*

Then he held out his hands. I started to lift mine in return when he grabbed Emma's hands and pulled her close, giving her cheek a kiss. "Emma! You made it! I'm so glad you were able to shift your work schedule so you could come for a bit."

Emma grinned at him. "It worked out perfectly. I was

able to make Lindsay's party, and you can still go with me to the bar."

Um, what?

"You look great, by the way," Blaine said.

"Thanks." She flashed him another smile.

What, do I have a rat on my head or something?

"Come over here. I want you to meet someone who might have an interesting job for you." He grabbed Emma's hand and pulled her across the room, back to his little clump.

Whoa.

What had just happened? Alternate reality or something? Please?

I watched Blaine introduce Emma to his gray-haired cronies. Saw Emma smile and toss her hair in that cute little way she had. Watched the exchange of business cards. Well, Emma took one and put it in her purse. It wasn't as if she had any business cards to offer.

It was dawning on me that perhaps it hadn't been my smartest move to leave the bar early on Thursday night. It had given Blaine and Emma plenty of alone time. What had happened after I left?

Was that why Emma had shown up at the party tonight? Not to support me, but to pursue Blaine? Was I just a tool for her angling?

As I felt a rising burn inside me, I caught myself. Emma would never go after Blaine. She wouldn't. She knew how I felt about him, and that would be enough. I took a deep breath and decided the best option was to get away for a moment and regroup, so I headed off to find the bathroom.

I enjoyed the porcelain bathroom for a good ten minutes, having a nice little pep talk with myself in the mirror. A pep talk that forayed into a generally supportive discussion with my reflection and an admonition to go back down there and socialize. If Emma could do it, so could I? Right? Surely not every overachieving person down there was a social snob. Some of those folks would be interested in good ol' Shannon McCormick, sans graduate degree and everything, right?

Of course, right.

Feeling much better, I fixed my hair, touched up my makeup, did a cleavage check, then opened the door.

There stood Max, leaning against the door frame as if he'd been waiting for twenty minutes. Blocking the door.

Crap.

"Hi, Shannon. You look lovely tonight." He smiled and took a step forward.

I shut the door in his face. Then I locked it.

He tapped lightly on the door. "Shannon, you can't keep avoiding me forever."

I looked around the room. No windows. Figured. In the movies there was always a window, and usually a rope ladder under the sink. I checked the ceiling. No ventilation shaft. Old country clubs like this apparently were not built for clandestine operatives to go racing around in their ceilings.

He knocked again. "We've worked through everything before. We can do it again, but you have to talk to me."

I sat down on the toilet. I could outwait him. Terribly unfortunate that I'd left my cell phone at home in the interest of carrying a very cute, teeny-tiny party purse.

"Shannon." He tapped again.

The toilet was too hard. I shifted to the carpeted floor and leaned against the cabinet.

"I'm really sorry about that night at the bar. I don't know what that was all about."

It was about your wandering eye. Damn, it had hurt that night when I'd walked in unexpectedly and seen him with another woman.

He knocked again, and I heard a soft thud, like he was leaning his forehead against the door. "Shannon. I love you."

Oh, God. I couldn't do this. I stood up and touched the doorknob, then stopped. *Be strong, Shannon.*

"You love me, too." *I do! I do!*

No, I don't! Well, I did, but not the truck-test kind of love. "Please leave, Max. I can't deal with this." How pathetic did my voice sound? I didn't have the strength to turn down his support tonight.

Suddenly I noticed Max wasn't talking anymore.

Silence.

I crawled to the door and peered underneath. Heels of men's dress shoes stared me in the face. He was still there, leaning against the door, apparently.

This was getting ridiculous. I was a grown woman. Surely I could walk out that door and shove him aside and make it downstairs without falling into his arms, right?

But I was afraid. I was afraid of going back out there and not being able to resist his apology. And then I'd be dating him again and questioning once again whether he was really the right one for me, or whether the right one had passed me by yesterday at Starbucks. Wondering whether Max had his hand on some other girl's butt.

"Are you waiting for the bathroom?"

Noah! I jumped to my feet and yanked open the door, jumping aside as Max staggered backward into the room. "Noah! Hi! Thanks for coming to find me!"

I sidestepped Max and grabbed Noah's arm. "Let's go."

Max was beside me in an instant. "Shannon! Would you just talk to me, for God's sake?"

I saw Noah hesitate and start to extricate his arm from mine. I immediately tightened my grip and shot Noah a look. He'd known me since I was born. Surely he'd understand my signals.

He glanced at Max, then back at me.

"Noah, let her go. I need to talk to her."

I started pushing Noah toward the stairs. "Max, I can't do this. I can't."

"You can't keep having your friends come between us," Max said, following us down the hall. "At some point you're going to have to deal with me."

I turned and stared at him. "We broke up. It's over." *Way to go, Shannon! Be strong!*

"No. It's not," he said.

Oh, God. Look at those eyes. Like puppy-dog eyes. He looked so sad. "Max . . ." *No! Be strong!* I cleared my throat. "Please leave me alone. *Please.*"

His eyebrows lifted, and I knew he heard the plea in my voice, the doubt. *Dammit!* Was I that weak? "Leave you alone so you can make a mistake that will ruin both of our lives? No way."

"Are you aware that following me around like you've been doing is called stalking? It's against the law."

He snorted. "It's not stalking. I'm trying to keep you from making a mistake."

121

That was it. Discussion was getting nowhere. I started walking again, and Noah stayed by my side.

This time Max didn't follow us, but I knew it wasn't over. Especially when he shouted out, "This isn't over!"

"Shannon?" Noah touched my arm as we reached the ballroom where the party was. "You okay?"

"Fine." I looked around. "Where's Emma?" God, I just needed my friends right now. Someone who would understand.

"She had to leave."

I felt my throat tighten. "What? Why?"

"She and Blaine went to her job. She tried to find you, but she couldn't wait."

"She and Blaine." I closed my eyes. It was absolutely amazing, but I'd actually managed to underestimate how bad this night would be.

"You and Emma in competition for him?"

I opened my eyes. "No," I snapped. "Don't be ridiculous. He's just a friend."

Noah studied me. "Is he?"

"He's a pretentious bastard who's usurping my secretary time and making my working life even more hellish than it is. The last thing I need is for Emma to be doing the nasty with him so I have to see him in the bathroom in the morning, you know?"

Noah lifted a brow. "Perhaps if he's dating your roommate, he'll have more incentive to be nice to you."

Ah. See? That would be a good thought, if I suspected Blaine had any kind of decency in his soul, but seeing as how he didn't, I failed to see how his shtupping my roommate would be of any benefit to me whatsoever.

Ray appeared at Noah's shoulder. "Family meeting in the cigar room. Now."

Apparently realizing I was seriously contemplating bailing, Ray grabbed my arm and directed both of us to the cigar room, named for the days when only men were allowed in there to smoke, because how could a man enjoy a cigar if there were women there to cramp his style? Impossible.

I stopped in the doorway. Mom, Dad, my two overachieving brothers, Noah, my sister and her fiancé, and Max? Wasn't he no longer family? He smiled at me from the other side of the room, and my gut answered with a thud.

Travis, my stockbroker brother with the $1.2 million house at age thirty-two, tapped his champagne glass with a spoon. "Can I have everyone's attention?"

Great. A private toast to the happy couple. So unfortunate I didn't have my own glass to raise in their honor. No problem. A quick trip to the country club bar would take care of that.

Travis tucked his arm around April and pulled her up against him. "April and I wanted to make the announcement in private so we didn't take away from Lindsay and Geoff's spotlight, but we had to tell you now, because you'll be figuring it out soon enough."

What? Had April been arrested for insider trading? That would be interesting.

Travis grinned at his girlfriend, then looked at the family. "We're going to have a baby!"

The place erupted into shrieks and cheers as my family swarmed them, bombarding the happy couple with questions about due dates, sonograms, and even diapers. My mom was mooning about her first grandchild, and my dad was clapping Travis on the shoulder, claiming some BS about how he was a real man.

Uh, hello? Was I the only one who noticed that the announcement was missing something important? Like a wedding date?

I stared at the ebullient room. What if I had showed up tonight and announced I was knocked up but I had no intention of marrying the father? That would be the final blow. I'd be excommunicated once and for all. Probably find myself becoming fast friends with a major Rhode Island crime family as they loaded cement around my feet prior to offering me a nice little swim in Boston Harbor, per orders of my family. But Travis and April? Golden children who could do no wrong. My parents saw only the good in what they did. Unlike me. The perpetual bad child.

I watched April whisper apologies to Lindsay for horning in on her and Geoff's celebration, but she explained that they felt it best to make the announcement now, so their news would fade as Lindsay's wedding approached. Give me a break. Yes, there wasn't that long between the engagement party and the wedding, but that's what happens when the bride has just graduated from college and is getting married right away. My parents couldn't miss out on the opportunity to show off their new son-in-law repeatedly, and since Lindsay had been tied up in senior year festivities, there'd been no opportunity until after her graduation. But with the wedding so soon, April could have waited for her announcement until after the wedding. Or she could have told everyone one by one over the phone, or even at a family dinner in two weeks. But she'd chosen Lindsay's engagement party. I might be a bitter, rejected woman, but even I wouldn't do that to my sister.

And I watched Lindsay hug April. What was up with that? If I did that to Lindsay, there'd be no hugging, that was for sure.

Why couldn't I find a secret stash of papers in my parents' safe listing the details of my adoption and the identities of my real parents?

"You know they love you."

I looked up to find Max standing next to me, and something cracked inside me. How could I turn this man away? He knew me. Knew what made me tick. "Max . . ."

He gave me a soft smile, then walked away.

I almost laughed at his retreating back. So that was his plan now? Break me down piece by piece until I was a crumbling pile of gook, begging for him to come back to me? Touch my heart, and then run before I could get annoyed?

Unfortunately, it felt like it was working. I so needed to go home and look at my Max pro/con list, of which the con list was way longer.

"Want to get a drink?"

This time when I looked up it was Noah standing next to me. Noah. I'd forgotten about him. He would understand what I was feeling. Not as much as Max, but enough. "Sure."

He nodded and tucked his hand under my elbow. "To the bar in the ballroom or the club?"

"The club." No more festive atmosphere for me, thanks. Off to a secluded place to drink with Noah sounded much better.

Wait a sec. Off to a secluded place with Noah? When I was single for the first time in my life? I was suddenly feeling better.

Much, much better.

CHAPTER NINE

"So tell me, Mr. Almost Family." I paused for a long drink of the chardonnay the bartender had brought. "How is it you stand being around them?"

Noah wiped some of the frost off his beer. "You have a great family. Give them a chance."

"Me give them a chance? What about the other way around? Until I get a graduate degree or invent electricity, I'm never going to be good enough for them."

"Maybe that's your own fault."

"According to them it is." I scowled at Noah. "I didn't realize you shared the same opinion." Part of my crush on Noah had been that I always thought he saw me as something more than a failed McCormick.

He scowled back. "You are way too sensitive."

Oh, so that was great. I was too sensitive now? The way I saw it, I actually put up with quite a bit.

"Did it ever occur to you to stop worrying about what they think? Enjoy them and live your own life. Easy enough."

"That's what I've been trying to do. It's not that easy." I

frowned. "The standards are different for me. Travis and April aren't even getting married, and no one cares. Can you imagine if that were me?" I shook my head. "It's all about the money."

"So make some."

I eyed Noah. "There's more to life than making money."

"Then don't."

"Well, aren't you Mr. Helpful?"

He lifted a brow. "What do you want me to say?"

"How about, 'Gee, Shannon, I think you're great the way you are, and I think you're getting a raw deal, and I still think you rock, even though you're just a social director.'"

"I'm here with you, aren't I?"

I blinked. "Yes."

He shrugged and took a sip of his beer. "There you go."

I had to lean back in my chair for that one. Noah knew all my ugly secrets, and he was here in the bar with me while legions of well-connected people were mingling in the ballroom?

I offered nothing. Yet he was here with me. Interesting.

Hey! Don't let your wine-fogged brain read too much into that, Shannon. He's like your big brother, not some guy who has been lusting after you for years, just waiting for you to become a free woman.

The bartender slid another glass of wine across the bar. Was it my third? Not my fourth. I'd never drink four glasses. Except when I was home alone on a Friday night feeling lonely and watching old war movies. "Thanks."

He nodded and glanced at Noah. "You driving her home?"

"No." I sat up. "I'm taking a cab."

Stephanie Rowe

Noah smiled and trailed his fingers over the back of my hand. "I'll drive you."

Check it out. He was touching me, and it didn't feel very sisterly. I picked up my drink and swirled the wine, eyeing him over the rim. "I've always had a crush on you."

He lifted his brow. "I know."

Oh. So much for that revelation to bring us together. "I hid it well, huh?"

He laughed and tucked my hair behind my ear. "No, not really."

My heart hit a speed bump and I set the glass down. "Why are you touching me like that?"

His hand froze. "Like what?"

"You know what." I grabbed his hand and pushed it away. "Like you actually noticed I'm a woman."

Noah frowned. "Maybe we should go back to the party."

"Yeah, sure." Good idea. Things were getting too weird. I left my wine untouched and headed back to the party. I stopped at the door to the ballroom. "Um, Noah?"

He stopped next to me. "Party seems to be over."

"You think?" All that remained were a few of the facility's people disassembling the tables and chairs.

One part of me was glad I'd been spared the ordeal of the party. The other part? Well, I felt like a heel for bailing on my sister's event, even if she wouldn't care. And what about Blaine? *Oh, wait. That's right. He left with Emma.* And Max? No, that was good too. If I'd seen him again, I was quite sure I would have been too weak to resist a friendly face.

"Come on. I'll drive you home." Noah put his hand on my back and guided me out of the country club. Even the

128

white roses in the lobby were still perky and happy. So I picked up two vases and carried them out. I might as well get a little something out of the evening. Noah lifted his eyebrow, but wisely kept his mouth shut.

By the time we arrived at my apartment building, I was asleep. I woke up to discover I'd drooled all over his jacket, which I'd balled up into a pillow. I also woke to find Noah gently stroking my cheek while saying my name.

Dammit! There was that "this does not feel like a brotherly action" siren again. I sat up and looked at him. And then I saw his eyes flick to my chest. No way there was nipple action again!

I glanced down. No nipples, but barely. With my shoulders forward, there was a nice gap in the front of my dress. And Noah had noticed. I looked at his face again, and there was no mistaking the interest there. Noah was obviously enjoying my womanly attributes.

And I'd noticed long ago that he was a man.

I was single.

He was here.

"Noah."

He grunted.

"Want to come up for a few minutes? For a drink?"

For a long moment he said nothing.

Neither did I. I wasn't sure what to say. A part of me was nearly orgasmic at the thought of taking Noah upstairs, but a much less welcome part of me was shaking its head and ordering me not to do something so foolish. This was Noah! He was practically one of the family!

And he was hot.

So what was the problem? Wasn't that what I wanted? A man whom I adored, who knew what I was really like and liked me anyway, who knew what my family was like and didn't want me just to take advantage of the McCormick family name? Noah was already connected with them. He didn't need me for an in.

Tonight would be only about us.

"One drink," he said.

Good God! He was coming upstairs! I managed a smile. "Great."

He followed me into the lobby, up the elevator, and down the hall, saying nothing. The casual camaraderie that had been our relationship for the last twenty years had vamoosed, replaced with a silent sexual tension.

Sexual tension with Noah. What a concept.

I opened the door and let him in. "My palace."

He stepped inside and took a glance. "Haven't lived like this since I was in law school."

"Yes, well, that's because you make lots of money and I don't." I pulled open the fridge. "Anything look good?"

"No." He shut the fridge and turned me so my back was against it, his hands pressed against the freezer on either side of my head. "You realize this is the first time we've been single at the same time since before you went to college?"

"So you're single too? Wasn't sure." I swallowed hard. Did he smell good or what? Like some very refined and perfect cologne. Subtle, but rich and pure. Probably cost a hundred bucks an ounce.

He trailed one finger over my collarbone. "I like this dress."

"Thanks. My mom was disappointed it was off the rack."

His finger came to rest over my lips, and he shook his head. "Stop it."

"Stop what?" Hard to talk with his finger still on my lips. Hard in a good way, I mean.

"Stop putting yourself down."

I frowned. "Do I put myself down?"

He made this noise that was sort of like a disbelieving grunt.

So communicative. Typical guy. "Um, Noah?"

"Yeah?" His finger had trailed off my collarbone and was now drawing circles on my chest. Which was bare, due to my cocktail dress. Which meant we had some skin-to-skin contact going on right now.

I hesitated. What to say? A part of me wanted to ask him what was up: one-night stand or the first step of our new relationship, from friends to lovers? But then I might scare him away. But if I did, then that would be good, right? Because if having a discussion about the repercussions of tonight scared him, then he didn't want repercussions, which meant I didn't want him.

That's right. I was a relationship girl. Not a one-night-stand girl. I'd never slept with a guy before I had some serious commitment, and I wasn't about to start now. Sure, I was lonely. Sure, my job sucked. Sure, I was vulnerable. Sure, I was afraid I'd tumble back into Max's arms at any second. Didn't mean I was going to be handing off my body to the highest bidder.

Then Noah kissed me. Not on the forehead or the nose. On the lips. Yessiree. His lips. On mine.

This was no "you're like a sister" kiss. No way. *Hello, Noah's tongue. Let me welcome you.*

I was kissing Noah. Noah! His hands were still on either side of my head, pressed up against the freezer. His body was still a good six inches away. All that was touching were our lips.

I'd never realized exactly how much talent a man could have in his lips. Or maybe it was because I'd been dreaming about those lips for the last two decades of my life. Whatever it was, I felt like my body was going to explode right there. My stomach was all loopy, nerve endings in my nether regions were squirming for attention, and I felt the most incredible sensation of *wanting*.

He broke the kiss, but kept his lips against mine. His breath was hot in my mouth, and it was sweet, delicious. Loved it. "Emma."

"My name is Shannon." Whoosh. The flame went right out. I'd never had a man whisper someone else's name when kissing me. Definitely not the best feeling in the world.

Noah smiled and kissed me. "I meant, is Emma coming home tonight? It might be awkward if she walked in right now."

"Oh . . ." Pilot light was lit again. "So you think we should stop?"

"Or move."

"Move." *Like, to where?*

"Do you have a room where we could close the door? You know, so we don't cramp Emma's style." He nibbled for a moment on the right side of my neck. "Like a den or something?"

I was going to burst into flame right there. "Um . . . no den. Only three rooms have doors. Emma's room. The bathroom." I swallowed. "And my bedroom."

"If we went in Emma's room, it wouldn't solve the problem." He removed one hand from the freezer and let his fingers drift down my arm. Then he brought my hand to his lips and gently sucked on each finger, his blue eyes locked on mine.

Oh, wow.

He set my hand on his chest. His muscles twitched under my touch. "And the bathroom seems rather cold. And tile is hard. And what if she needs to brush her teeth?"

"Wouldn't want that." I watched my fingers stroke his chest. Did I tell them to do that?

Now that my arm was no longer by my side, Noah took advantage. His hand started on my shoulder; then his fingertip trailed down my side, over my ribs, and the back of his hand brushed the underside of my breasts.

"So I guess that leaves your room." He suddenly thrust his arms behind me and hauled me up against him, his lips fierce on mine. Demanding, like he owned me. Like he was the man and he wasn't going to stop until I was chanting his name and writhing beneath him in the throes of multiple, overwhelming orgasms.

I was down with that, and as a polite hostess, it would probably be best if I showed him exactly how supportive I was of his plans.

So I wrapped my arms around his neck and tried my best to inspect his tonsils, by Braille, of course.

"Which way?"

"Second door on the right." Interesting how difficult it was to articulate when my tongue was exploring his molars.

He seemed to conclude he'd gotten the gist of it as he

lifted me up against him. *Hmm . . .* I was kind of heavy. To be helpful, I wrapped my legs around his waist. Purely for altruistic purposes, so he wouldn't pull out his back or anything like that. Because we had that kind of considerate relationship.

When I felt his hands on my bare fanny, it occured to me that I hadn't given serious consideration to what would happen to my short, tight dress when I anchored my legs around him. Nowhere to go but up. Like around my waist.

Guess he knew I was wearing a thong by now.

Interesting. My precarious position gave me an insider's view to the fact that he seemed to be liking what he was finding. Liking it quite a bit. I hoped his suit pants were loose in front.

I felt him shift, and then heard my door slam. What a rugged hunk of meat, kicking my door shut. This was like Dirk, only a thousand times better because I totally wanted Noah as a person and as a lover and because . . . well . . . it was *Noah.* Need I say more?

He set me down on my feet next to the bed, but he didn't move his hands from my butt. *Nice move, Noah.*

"Hey." I broke the kiss.

"What?" His hands paused in their commendable effort. "You think we should stop?"

And force me to live the rest of my life in sexual frustration because I'd never find another man who made me this hot? *Not on your life.* "I want to see you."

He lifted a brow. Well, I think he did. It was really dark in my room with the shades down, blocking out all the city lights.

I pulled away from him and yanked open the shades,

bringing a faint light into the room. Enough that I could see him. Noah. In my bedroom.

Hey, if I was going to have fantasy sex with Noah, I was going to do it right. My way. After all, Dirk had shown me my passionate sexual side, right? So it was time to find out how far it went.

I walked back over to Noah and tugged off his tie, slapping his hands when he reached for me. "I've been fantasizing about your body for the last twenty years. Don't rush me."

He grinned and let his hands drop to his sides. "You'd better hurry up."

Ah, the man could barely wait to get his hands on me. Must be those breasts. Yes, he'd be getting to see my nipples tonight. If only Blaine could see what he was missing . . . *Hey. Don't think about Blaine.*

Blaine. Blaine. Blaine. Suddenly his pretentious face was everywhere in my brain, that snarky look of disdain on his face. *Shannon, I didn't realize you were a slut. Two guys in the same week?*

Shut up!

I quickly unbuttoned Noah's shirt and pulled it off his shoulders. While he was shrugging it over his wrists, I flattened my hand across his chest and stared. Well muscled, not an ounce of fat, and the perfect amount of hair.

"So?" His eyes were dark and he was watching me.

"Jury is still out." Look at me, with my witty lawyer joke. Obviously being on the verge of a major sexual encounter with a really hot lawyer seriously reduced my antipathy toward attorneys. "Need more evidence." I set my hands on his belt. "May I?"

He nodded once.

Good enough for me! I unfastened his belt and his fly and let his pants drop to the floor. Black silk boxers. As if that should be a surprise. If I checked the label, I had no doubt it wouldn't be Fruit Of The Loom.

"I think your boxers cost more than my car."

"If they offend you, perhaps we should get rid of them."

What a wise man. I hooked my thumbs over the waistband. "They offend me greatly. It's them or me, bucko. Make your choice."

He tilted his head. "I'm not sure. They were very expensive. I'll have to weigh my options."

I felt my insides begin to simmer and bubble at the heated look in his eyes. "How can I help you decide?"

"Being a lawyer, I like to gather all my facts before committing."

Oh . . . committing. An unconscious use of the word? He was falling for me bad. "Gather away."

His eyes darkened and he reached for me. My breasts perked up. *Come and get us.* But his hands went to my shoulders. He turned me away from him, so my back was toward him. His lips and tongue went to work on the nape of my neck while his hands tackled the back of my dress.

A tug, and then a *zzzip,* and then my zipper was down and my dress was around my ankles.

He slipped his hands under my arms and cupped my breasts, even as he continued to nibble on my shoulder. Suddenly I was very fond of the fact that my dress had had a built-in bra. No extra layers needed.

"Mmm . . ." His fingers played with my nipples, which

were more than happy to sit up and pay attention. "So I'm thinking it might be a good trade."

Trade? What was he talking about?

"My boxers for your panties."

Ah. Seemed like a fair deal. "I don't think my thong will fit you."

He rested his chin on my shoulder and let gravity pull his hands downward to the apparel item in question. "I don't want to wear it." And then he made it very clear what he wanted my panties for. "I just want it out of the way."

Yeah, I was getting that picture. Sort of. My brain was getting really foggy and I wasn't sure I still had full cognitive function. I did manage to pull myself together enough to turn around and rid him of his very confining boxers while he was returning the favor.

And then we were on my bed. Both of us naked. And I started to giggle right when Noah moved downward and parted my legs.

He stopped and looked up at me. "That's a first."

"What?" I giggled again.

"I was expecting you to maybe moan a little. Not laugh." He frowned. "I think I'm offended."

I squeezed my eyes shut and ordered myself to stop laughing. All that did was make me snort when the laugh finally burst out. I opened my eyes and looked at Noah, who was actually looking offended. "I'm sorry, Noah. It's just . . . well, it's you. And me. And we're naked." I mean, I'd known him my whole life. He was like my brother. And now we were naked together?

His eyes darkened and he scooted up. "Yes, you're right. We're naked. And you're gorgeous with an incredible body.

137

And I want to make love to you until you can't think anymore."

The giggles disappeared immediately. "Oh. When you put it that way . . ."

This time, when he began his ministrations I wasn't laughing. When I moaned, I felt Noah grin. Yeah, yeah. Gotta love the male ego. With the last of my willpower I managed to fumble for my nightstand drawer and pull out a condom for him.

What? I'm not a slut. It was my stash from Max.

Being the accommodating guy he was, he accepted my offering and made short work of it. One-handed, by the way, with the other one taking up where his mouth had left off. The man was all talent, and I decided I would forever be his love slave.

Or sex slave, rather. We so weren't at the love stage yet. *Yet* being the operative word. I had no doubt we were meant to be together. How could we not? Friends and lovers. The perfect combination.

He slipped his knee between my thighs and I moved to welcome him. When I felt him slip inside, I was absolutely certain I would die. Explode. Shoot to the heavens and never return. *This* was what sex was all about.

He groaned and closed his eyes, and I wrapped my legs around his waist and let him take me along. It started in my toes, a tingling that moved up my feet, grabbed my legs, then shot upward, taking over my whole body until I was unable to move or think or feel anything except the most incredible electricity igniting every single molecule in my body.

I was *so* writing in to *Cosmo* about this orgasm.

CHAPTER TEN

I woke up in the middle of the night to find Noah sprawled across me, still naked, still gorgeous, and still there. He hadn't bailed and left me with a note on the pillow. Remember how he uttered that magical word *committing* during our lovemaking? He was whipped.

And I had to go to the bathroom.

I climbed over him, pausing a moment to kiss him thoroughly just because I could; then I grabbed the doorknob. For a night that had begun as one of the worst of my life, it had certainly ended as the best one. Ever.

See? That was why I'd broken up with Max. Because I'd believed in my soul that he wasn't the right one for me. How about that?

Less than three weeks later, I'd proven it.

My heart all warm and snuggly, I flung open my door and found Blaine standing in the hallway in his underwear. Tighty-whities that left nothing to the imagination. Interesting body. Good, but nothing like Noah's. "What are you doing?"

He looked horrified. "Going to the kitchen."

Now, if that wasn't the most inane answer. How about, *Having sex with your roommate, hope you don't mind?*

"Shannon?" I noted the shocked look on his face, then remembered I had been naked when I'd gotten up and I hadn't remedied that situation. Full-frontal for Blaine.

I slammed the door shut and cursed. Monday was *really* going to be awkward now. Emma was damned lucky I'd ended up with Noah tonight or I'd be unbelievably pissed at her. As it was, she was going to have to do some serious groveling to get me to forgive her. And regardless of that, I still had to work with Blaine, and he had now seen me entirely naked. No more, *Oops, he saw my nipple.* We were talking full monty now.

"Shannon?" Noah was propped up on his elbows, his eyes squinty with sleep. "Anything wrong?"

"I was just going to the bathroom."

He frowned. "I need some water."

I started to offer to get him some, and then I smiled. "Go ahead and help yourself. There's bottled water in the fridge. I'll meet you back here."

He grunted, rolled out of bed, and grabbed his boxers. Smart guy. He remembered I had a roommate.

I let him go out ahead of me, then sneaked to the bathroom clad in an oversize T-shirt. I heard the rumble of male voices from the kitchen, and I smiled. Yes, indeed. This was turning out to be quite a good night.

I smiled at Otto, watching his mouth rattle on and the sweat trickle down his face. I could see him spewing at me, but it was all drifting happily past me. My great-sex-with-Noah force field was still protecting me. Nothing, not even

Otto, could get through my bubble of happiness. What would Noah do for my birthday? My twenty-fifth birthday with the man of my dreams on my arm. I might not have my career figured out, but things were definitely heading in the right direction.

Otto's mouth stopped moving.

So I nodded. I wondered what Noah was doing now. Was he thinking about me? He'd stayed for pancakes on Sunday morning. Since Blaine had stayed too, it had made for a rather interesting Sunday morning.

As I said, if I hadn't hooked up with Noah, Emma would have been dead meat. As it was, I had still felt viciously embarrassed when I saw Blaine that morning. I mean, he'd seen me totally naked! So she was still in trouble for that. I didn't need my office hell following me home.

I realized Otto was staring at me expectantly. *Shit*. "I'm sorry. Can you repeat your question?"

His beady little eyes narrowed. "Ms. McCormick, I asked you for your list of activities this week. I assume you brought it?"

Double shit. Noah's protective bubble popped. Where was my brain? A mind rocking orgasm wasn't going to impress Otto. Only preparation and genuflection would impress him. And I'd done neither. "I'm sorry. I thought we were going to talk about them. I didn't realize you needed the actual list." Did that sound lame or what? I hadn't let myself get caught unprepared by Otto since my first month at the firm. A little sex and my brain shut down?

Otto's forehead started twitching and he leaned forward. He resembled a cobra, and I considered lifting my arm to cover my face in case he started spitting venom at me. "Ms. McCormick, you do realize you're on probation, don't you?"

It was all I could do to keep my mouth from dropping open and tears from flaring in the corners of my eyes. "Probation?" *Nice squeaky voice.*

"You can't afford to come to meetings unprepared."

Really? Hadn't figured that one out for myself.

"I want that list on my desk in twenty minutes. And I want an updated list waiting for me when I arrive every morning."

Oh, sure, I have plenty of time to start tracking my activities minute by minute. That's such an efficient use of my time. But I nodded—no point in trying to fake a smile. He didn't care, and I hated him so much that a smile would have morphed into some screaming-epithet monologue. I'd put people with Tourette's to shame. So I clamped my lips together and stuck with one simple nod.

"Fine. You're excused."

You are a bastard in the truest sense of the word. I stood up and walked out. The instant I got into the hallway, tears sprang free. And I mean, they *sprang.* There was no holding them back.

And my office was on the other side of the floor. I looked down the hall, and even through my blurred vision I could see people milling around. No escape. I couldn't even make it to the ladies' room without being caught.

Then I saw Jessamee walking down the hall toward me. *Crap.*

I did what any sensible woman would: I bolted for the emergency stairwell. The door slammed shut behind me, but I ran down a flight in case someone like Hildy was hot on my trail.

But no caring soul yelled my name, which made me feel even worse. Shouldn't someone have noticed that I needed help? That my rushing off to be alone was a sign of my desperate need for comfort?

Apparently not.

So I sat there and let myself cry. I mean really cry. I cried for myself, for all the miserable things that I let bother me, and for the fact that I was immature enough to let them bother me. I cried because Blaine hated me. Because he'd seen me naked. Because I had to pay five hundred dollars for my sister's engagement present. Because I was unbearably tired of fighting my parents' expectations. And I cried because Emma had betrayed me by sleeping with Blaine.

It took me almost forty-five minutes to run out of things to cry about.

And then I gave it another five minutes of crying to cover new things that I didn't know about yet.

Then I had a mother of a headache and my silk blouse was all wet from my tears. I had no doubt my eyes were puffy and I'd wiped all my makeup off.

Then I realized I'd missed Otto's twenty-minute deadline for my list to show up on his desk, which reopened the floodgates.

Eventually, there were simply no more tears.

Interesting. I'd never actually had a tear drought before. That was probably good. Running into tear droughts frequently was an indication that things really sucked.

I sat there for a few more minutes, my body completely exhausted, my brain nothing but goo. But the awful knot of tension in my stomach was gone for the moment. I tested a smile, and my face didn't crack.

So I could go back in there and manage a brilliant smile to blind everyone long enough for me to get back to my office, where my makeup repair kit was. Right. I could handle this.

I stood up, feeling much stronger than I had since I'd broken up with Max. No wonder nervous breakdowns—or whatever they were called nowadays—were so popular. They were very cleansing. Perhaps I should do it every day. Or maybe every other day. They were also very time-consuming.

I stood up, figured out how to fold my arms across my chest to hide the wet spots, and took my hair out of its bun. I fluffed it around my face so it sort of fell forward over my tearstained face. It felt sort of vampy, which was fun. I lifted my chin, practiced another smile, then marched back up the stairs to return to hell.

Turns out, emergency stairways were locked on this side.

Argh! I yanked on the stairwell door, then kicked it, then yanked again. Locked!

Crap. I was on the thirty-first floor.

I considered banging on the door until someone opened it, but that wouldn't exactly be conducive to sliding unobtrusively back to my office, would it? It was one thing to breeze by people and have them wonder if your eyes were puffy, but if I emerged from the stairwell with puffy eyes, there wouldn't be a whole lot of guesswork.

Dammit.

I stared down the stairwell. Thirty-one flights was an awful lot to walk down in heels and a snug skirt.

Then I considered the fact that Jessamee's office was

directly across from the stairwell, and she'd be the one to open it in response to my frantic banging.

I decided to bond with the stairs.

Forty-five minutes later, Isabel gasped when I walked by her cube. "Shannon? What happened to you?"

I looked down at my torn nylons, courtesy of taking off my heels on floor twenty-one. Sweat was dripping down my temples, and I was covered with a thin coat of dust— apparently I was the only one who'd ever chosen to traverse that particular path in the last one hundred years. My makeup was long gone, my blazer swung over my shoulder, and I had no doubt there were sweat stains on my silk blouse, but I hadn't even bothered to stop in the ladies' room to check. Some things were too depressing to face. So I gave Isabel the brilliant Shannon smile. "Had a little mishap with the vending machine."

She stared.

"I have to write a memo for Otto, and then I need to take a couple hours off. Can you clear my schedule until, say, two o'clock?"

"Otto called. He said you were late with the memo."

I braced my body and ordered myself to be strong, but I still flinched. *Dammit.* "I know I'm late. That's why I'm doing it now. Tell him I got hit by a truck but that I am writing it while in traction because I'm so dedicated."

I saw Blaine's office door start to open, so I bailed into my office and shut the door.

I hadn't even opened my desk drawer to retrieve my makeup when my phone rang. I hit the speakerphone. "Shannon McCormick."

"Hi, darling."

"Mom." Tears sprang into my eyes again. "I'm having the worst day."

She was quiet for a moment, and suddenly I felt stupid. We didn't have that kind of relationship.

"I'm sorry." She sounded sincere, and the tears came harder. "Is there anything I can do?"

"Get me a new job."

Her tone changed immediately. "Well, Shannon, if it's your job that's the problem, then that's your own fault, isn't it? I have no sympathies for your staying in a miserable job because you're too stubborn to listen to us. It's time you grew up and took responsibility for your decisions. Dump the job and go back to school."

I stared glumly at my desk. "That's your answer for everything, isn't it? Go back to school and get a new career?"

"It's a good answer when you hate your job."

I hate it when my mom is right. "So what do you want?"

She transitioned smoothly to the new topic. Not that she was the doting type who'd want to spend hours commiserating with her daughter. "I thought it would be nice if you threw April a baby shower."

I could think of no socially acceptable comment.

"Lindsay has her hands full with her own wedding, and as mother of the bride, I'm very busy as well. Besides, you and April are almost the same age. It will be a good bonding experience."

"Do you care that they're not getting married?"

My mom hesitated, and then she said, "April is a wonderful woman and she'll make a fabulous mother."

So she did care. I couldn't believe it. That was as close as my mom would ever come to admitting anything negative about any of her golden children, but it was something. Sure, it was totally immature of me to be glad that Travis was a little bit in the doghouse, but hey, did I ever claim to be mature? "Sure, I'll do the baby shower." Just the thought of my mom sitting there being unhappy that her first grand-child was going to be born out of wedlock was a good enough reason for me.

"Great. I'll pay for everything, as long as you set it up."

I decided to forgo my "never take money from my parents" mantra for this one occasion. "Okay."

"Thanks, Shannon."

"Sure." Who knew? Maybe this was an olive branch from my mom. Her first step toward acknowledging publicly that I was actually her daughter. Well, maybe not that far. She'd probably tell everyone at the party that I was the caterer.

I bade farewell to Mommy Dearest and hung up the phone. I smiled. I just might be able to have some fun with the baby shower after all.

The phone rang again. "Shannon McCormick."

"It's Noah."

The warm bubble swelled up again, and I leaned back in my chair. "Hi."

"Are you free for dinner tonight?"

Some of my glow faded. "I'll be at work until ten." By the time I got back from cleaning myself up, I would be way behind.

"Tomorrow?"

"Red Sox game with the firm."

He was quiet for a moment. "How about I stop by while you're at work? I'd really like to see you."

Okay, I was in heaven. My life was perfect. I still couldn't believe it. Noah and Shannon. A couple. I wondered how we'd tell my family? Would Noah want to announce it? We could invite everyone to his condo for a dinner party and tell them then. Or maybe he'd want to tell Ray first and then quietly make the rounds? "That would be great."

"Okay. I'll be by around eight or so?"

"Great. I'll tell security to let you up. Thirty-first floor."

"Right."

"And Noah?"

"Yes?"

"I don't recommend the stairs. Use the elevator."

I was still laughing when I hung up the phone.

My good humor lasted until I checked my voice mail and got a message from Missy that she was home sick. Yeah, right, allergic to Otto. As wonderful as it was to have Noah sniffing around my skirts, I did still need to make a living and keep my job. Which meant not allowing a third generation attorney and Yale superstar to quit on week two. Somehow I doubted that would go over too well with my probation. I buzzed Isabel. "Can you get me Missy's home number and address, please?"

"Sure."

Excellent. Blaine had actually allowed Isabel the thirty seconds it would take her to retrieve the information for me. Probably a direct result of the peep show I gave him. I was not ready to admit it was worth it, however.

A light tap sounded on my door. *Crap.* I still looked like hell. "I'm on a call."

The door opened and Hildy slipped inside. "Isabel said you were free."

Seeing as how my phone was hung up and my hands were full of makeup, I couldn't exactly call Isabel a liar. "Hi."

"You look like hell."

I was startled by that response. Hildy was always the tender, supportive type. "Thanks."

"Well, you do." She sat down in my visitor's chair. "I was stopping by to see how you were doing after Friday night, but I guess I have my answer."

"Actually, I got locked in the emergency stairwell and had to walk down to the lobby. Thought it was the bathroom."

She pursed her lips. "I talked to Missy on Friday night. She's pretty shaken up. I think we might have lost her."

I decided to swallow my pride and apply my makeup in front of her. "I'll take care of that."

Hildy continued to sit there, but said nothing.

Finally I set down my makeup and looked at her. "What?"

"Have we lost you?"

I frowned. "What do you mean?"

"Are you going to leave?"

I blinked at the genuineness in her voice. She cared? Really cared? "Not at the moment."

Hildy nodded and scooted forward. "Shannon, this isn't an easy place for women. We both know that. It takes a special woman to make it here. Someone who is strong and talented and smart, who can blend in and make people happy while still carving out a place for herself.

Women like that owe it to other women to fight, so as to clear the path for other women."

I frowned. No wonder Missy had run away screaming. This wasn't exactly warm and fuzzy stuff.

"Don't you know what I'm saying, Shannon? You're one of those women, and we need you."

I stared. "What?"

"You have the right personality, and with your family's connections, you have all the credentials to make it to the inner circle. You need to stay here."

I frowned. "I've never heard of a social director making it to the inner circle." The reference to my family's connections made me distinctly uncomfortable. Perhaps I should tell Hildy I was a black sheep and publicly disowned.

Hildy laughed softly. "No, not as a social director. As an attorney."

My gut tightened. "I'm not an attorney."

"Easily remedied. Go to law school at night and continue to work here during the day."

"I work at night too." Stupid thing to say, but I was too floored to actually address what she was suggesting.

"Only during the summer. You could work around it the rest of the year." Hildy leaned forward. "This is what I do, Shannon. I look out for women who can make a difference. You're one of those women."

I had no idea what to say. My first response was the same as usual to anyone who suggested my being a lawyer: No, no, and no.

But this was the first time anyone had suggested it in a way that actually made me feel good. *Be a lawyer because you're the best,* as opposed to, *Be a lawyer because you suck and are an embarrassment in your current job.*

I realized suddenly that Hildy was studying me. When I looked at her, she smiled. "Let's go to lunch this week and talk about it. I have connections and could still get you into school for this fall."

This fall? But I didn't want to be a lawyer. "I haven't even taken the LSAT."

She smiled. "My husband is the head of admissions for one of the law schools in town. I have ways of persuasion." She winked then, and I almost fell off my chair. Hildy making a sex joke?

She rapped her knuckles sharply on the desk, then stood up. "I'll have my secretary talk to Isabel and set up a lunch."

"Um . . ."

"First step, go home and change your clothes." She smiled and left before I had a chance to tell her there wasn't a chance in hell I was going to follow in her footsteps.

I leaned back against my chair. *Wow.* Hildy thought I was something special. It was the most bizarre feeling. I mean, Max had always claimed to think I was special, but he was my boyfriend, so he had to if he wanted any action. But there was no ulterior motive for Hildy.

Which meant she really believed what she'd said. That I had something to offer.

How about them apples?

I couldn't wait to tell Emma. And Dave. And Phoebe. I smiled. And Noah.

But first I had other things to take care of. Not that I was going to jump on the Hildy locomotive, but now that she'd brought it up, I certainly didn't want Otto to take the choice away from me.

Which meant I needed to kick some serious butt on this memo.

And then change my clothes.

And then find Missy and reel her back in.

And be back in my office by eight so I could be here when Noah came by.

Yes, indeed, I had quite a full day planned. And for the first time in my life, *attorney* wasn't a dirty word. Well, maybe a little, but it was looking a bit brighter.

CHAPTER ELEVEN

I tried calling Missy from my cell phone for the seventeenth time as I stood outside her apartment door. Still no answer.

So I knocked on the door. "Flower delivery for Missy Stephens."

I heard the television volume lower. "Hello?"

I repeated my intro, and felt guilty for lying.

The lock clicked and Missy opened the door. Her mouth dropped in astonishment to see me on her doorstep. I smiled. "I lied. I have no flowers." Come to think of it, flowers would have been a good idea.

Note to self: The next time I have to track down an MIA intern at her apartment, bring bribery. "Can I come in?"

She wrinkled her nose. "I'm sick."

"Really? You look like you just got back from a run." When she frowned, I added, "The sweaty clothes and running shoes give it away. Let me in. You stood me up for our meeting today, and my feelings are hurt." I wondered if Missy had an eating disorder. She already weighed about six pounds and could hardly afford to be burning calories on a run.

The corner of her mouth curved up. "No, they're not."

Actually, my feelings had been hurt more than once today, but it had nothing to do with Missy. "Of course they are." I gestured inside the apartment. "May I?"

She sighed and opened the door. "Fine."

It was great to feel welcome.

I stepped inside and decided I wanted an apartment like this when I won the lottery. Apparently Emma wasn't the only one who had parents willing to support their children in high style. Then again, if I were in law school, my parents would be begging to spend lots of money to support me.

The difference was that I wouldn't have accepted it.

"So you're here to convince me to stay. It's too late. I've already decided."

I ignored her, walked into the living room, and sat down on the couch. "Got a boyfriend?"

She frowned and stood in the doorway. "I'm not changing my mind, Shannon."

"So that's a no, huh? Me neither, but I'm hoping." Oh, yes, I was hoping. I'd even tucked a couple condoms into my purse this morning. I'd never considered having sex in my office, but now that my true sexual nature had emerged, who knew what I'd be tempted to do? If Noah started something . . . well . . . who would I be to discourage innovation?

But back to the present. A present I had to remedy if I wanted to seriously consider Hildy's suggestion. Or at the very least, keep my job. "Why don't you want to come back?"

Her mouth dropped open. "Because of what Mr. Nelson did to you. It was horrible, and no one seemed to think there was anything wrong with it. I can't work in that kind of environment."

I narrowed my eyes and studied her. Did she need Supportive and Loving Shannon, or did she need Cold, Hard Truth Shannon? She was very wimpy, but I'd been giving her the love since she started, and it was clear how well that wasn't working.

So I took a risk. Besides, after being battered to hell by Otto, I wasn't really in a touchy-feely mood. "Do you want to be an attorney?"

Missy rolled her eyes. "Of course."

"Where? At a big firm, or doing public-interest work for a government agency, making eighteen thousand dollars a year and waitressing at night so you can pay rent?"

She lifted her chin, and for the first time I saw the generations of Yale-trained attorneys in her eyes. "I'm going to work at a big firm and be partner."

Exactly the answer I was looking for. "Then you need to realize there's an Otto wherever you go, whether it's Boston or New York or anywhere. A big firm has old-school attorneys who bring big bucks and connections to the firm, and they can get away with anything. If you leave M and S, you'll have to find another job. And when you run into an Otto there, are you going to leave again? You'll run out of firms pretty soon, and you won't be partner." Okay, so I'd given her the combo: cold, hard truth delivered in a loving and supportive way. I didn't quite have the cold, hard nature, you know?

Missy studied me very closely, as though searching for the truth.

I leaned back on the couch. "Ask anyone in your family. That's the way of the profession, Missy. Learn to deal with it, or find another career." I crossed my fingers behind my back and hoped that her thoughtful, slightly stunned look was a good sign. I was totally screwed if she didn't come back, and I knew it. I sat up. "You met Hildy. She's nice, right?"

Missy nodded mutely.

"See? You can be nice and still succeed. The trick is to stay out of the way of the Ottos, and if you have to work with them, don't screw up."

She lifted a brow. "How did you screw up with the dog track?"

The truth? "I knew he'd be pissed and I did it anyway. Pushed my luck."

"But it was the right thing to do. It was fun."

"I'm not my own boss. I have to play the game." Like Hildy said. *Hmm* . . . Had she lodged herself in my head? It seemed much easier to talk about the Otto fiasco now that I had Hildy humming along that I was talented and valuable. Amazing what a little positive feedback could do for one's emotional stability. "So do you. No matter where you go."

Her lower lip stuck out in a pout. "I don't like it."

"Then don't be an attorney in a big firm." I sat up for the zinger. "But if there's any chance at all you want to work for a big firm, then you need to suck it up and learn how to succeed. Nothing bad is going to happen to you this summer. It's my job to make sure of that. But you can use this summer to keep your eyes and ears open. If you're observant, you should be able to figure out what it's really like to work here. Then you can make your choice as to whether you can handle it." I met her gaze. "Trust me, you are safe this summer. It's a no-risk opportunity for you." I would have mentioned the paycheck as added incentive, but from the look of her palace, I doubted she was worrying about footing her own bills. "So what do you think? Suddenly recovered from the flu?"

She still looked annoyed. "I don't know. I have to think about it."

I cursed under my breath, but kept my face serene. "Well, give me a call when you decide, or if you want to talk more." I tried to send her brain vibes not to quit, and then I let myself out.

I had no idea what she was going to do. But I knew that if she chose not to come back, I was going to lose my job.

I bit my lip as I waited for the elevator. Regardless of my long-term goals, I had worked damned hard for the last three years, and I was good, and I didn't deserve to be fired. I closed my eyes and tried not to think of what my family would say if I got fired from a job that wasn't even worthy of me.

Come on, Missy. Don't let me down.

I dropped down to the lobby at seven thirty. Van usually came on at seven. He was there as usual, and I felt a rush of relief at his welcoming smile.

"Hey, Van." I leaned on the counter and grinned.

He took in my corporate attire. "Back to the old Shannon, huh?"

Nice. I'd forgotten that he'd seen me in the slut outfit. "Yeah, that was a mistake."

He tilted his head. "What happened?"

As if I wanted to go there. "So there's a guy coming in about a half hour named Noah Quinlan. Go ahead and let him up." I couldn't keep the smile off my face when I said it, and Van lifted his eyebrows.

"New guy?"

I shrugged, but I couldn't stop smiling. "Hopefully."

Van leaned back in his chair and studied me. "This is the first time you've ever been interested in anyone other than Max. Maybe it really is over with him."

I grinned, my heart racing at the thought of Noah. "Believe me, I have eyes for no one but Noah now. I've known him since I was born, practically, and now . . ." I felt my face turn red.

Van met my gaze. "Slept with him already?"

"Shut up!" My cheeks felt like they were smoking, and I threw a pen at Van.

He looked startled. "I was kidding. You really did?"

How in the world had we gotten on this topic? This was way more personal than Van and I ever got. But now I had to explain, or he'd think I was a slut. "He's my brother's best friend. I've known him for twenty years. But now that we're both single . . . well, it makes sense, you know? We already know everything about each other." Well, not everything, but Noah knew me very well.

Van looked amused. "You don't need to explain yourself to me. I don't care what you do with who."

I frowned. What was that about? We were friends, weren't we? Shouldn't he care a little about what I was up to? I tried to ignore the fact that my feelings were somewhat bruised.

He shoved a clipboard across the desk. "Fill in his vitals here, and I'll send him up. Does he have a key?"

"No. So can you call once he's in the elevator?" I jotted down Noah's info, still undecided on what I thought about the fact that Van didn't care what I did. But why should he care? And why did I care whether he cared?

"Yep."

I handed him the clipboard. "Okay. Thanks, then." I hesitated, feeling like I needed to conclude the conversation in some way, but then someone else stopped to ask for directions, so I left.

Noah didn't show up at eight o'clock. Or eight thirty. Or even nine thirty. On the plus side, that let me get through all my major work, which meant that when he finally got there, I could leave with him. *Heh, heh, heh (suggestive laughter).*

On the negative side, I became a little obsessive. Called Van four times just to make sure the phone lines hadn't broken and I'd left Noah standing in the lobby waiting for me to unlock the door. Called Van once more and then hung up when he answered, feeling stupid. When it occurred to me that Van probably had caller ID for all the lines in the building, I decided that the hangup route wasn't the optimal step.

I finally called Dave at nine thirty and filled him on the

Noah thing. He was shocked and ordered me to go out with him on Wednesday night to give him the scoop. I told him to invite Phoebe too so I could do the double duty. And when he asked about Emma, I have to admit, I got a little immature and told him that only my true friends were invited on Wednesday.

I'd have to do a little explaining on that one come Wednesday, because before Dave could probe further Yvonne arrived home, and he had to go. Which left me alone in my office with no Noah, and no one to call.

Should I wait? Or would that be giving Noah too much power? Lead him to believe it would be okay for him to be two hours late for our dates and I'd still be there for him? *Yuck*. Hated that.

So I should leave? But what if he had a legit excuse and was so bummed that I wasn't there when he arrived that he decided I was cold, heartless, and unforgiving and ended the relationship before it began?

I frowned, then called Van.

He was laughing when he answered the phone. "I think you have it bad for this guy."

See? I knew he had caller ID. "Dating etiquette question for you."

"Go ahead."

"He's almost two hours late, and I'm finished with my work. Should I stay and give him a little more time in case he had some crisis? Or should I leave and risk disappointing him when he appears?"

"Leave."

I frowned. "Why?" It was so aggravating that men didn't like to go into all the touchy-feely conversations. I needed to flesh out the pros and cons. This was a very big decision.

"Because he's late."

"But what if he has an excuse?"

Van made some noise of exasperation. "Does he own a cell phone?"

"Yeah."

"There you go."

I scowled and blacked out Noah's name with a marker. No more doodling of his name on my desk blotter. "So I should leave?"

"No matter how many times you ask me, I'm not going to tell you to wait for him."

"But don't you think leaving is a little harsh this early in the relationship?"

"Don't you think being two hours late for a date is a little harsh this early in the relationship?"

I rolled my eyes. "Maybe."

Van sighed. "Tell you what. I worked an earlier shift today, so I get off at ten. Let's go out for a drink."

I blinked. "Are you asking me on a date?"

He laughed. "No way. You have too much going on in your personal life for me to keep up. Besides, I still like Max. Nice guy. Brought me a six-pack tonight. Granted, he was trying to bribe me, but still."

My heart caught. "Max was there tonight?" So Noah was standing me up and Max had come by? Max, whom I'd treated so badly, was still there for me?

"Yeah." He paused. "I didn't tell him about Noah."

Oh, God. I could only imagine if he found out about Noah? That would totally hurt him.

"Shannon."

"What?" My life was a mess. A disaster.

"Be in the lobby in ten minutes. I'll buy you a drink."

"Fine." I slammed down the phone and folded my arms across my chest. Should I be hanging Noah out the window too? No, that couldn't be right. Noah would never jerk me over. There had to be an explanation.

Maybe he didn't have my work number or my cell number. Maybe he'd been trying to reach me. I grabbed my cell phone and scrolled through to Noah's cell, put in there long ago as a family friend. I hesitated with my finger hovering over the send button, then finally hit it and waited.

It rang six times and then went into voice mail. Which meant he could have looked at his phone, seen I was calling, and chosen not to answer.

I scowled and tossed my phone on the desk. *Bastard.*

My phone rang and it was Van. I glanced at the clock as I picked up. "I still have seven minutes. I'm coming."

"This is front-desk security calling for Ms. McCormick. I have a visitor for her. Could you please check and see if she's still in?" Van's voice was all formal and proper, and he was clearly trying to give me an out.

"Is it Max?"

"No."

My heart skipped. "Noah?"

"So Ms. McCormick has already left?"

I closed my eyes. If it was anyone but Noah, I'd follow Van's lead and play the game. But this was Noah. The one guy whom I could date where no games would be involved. "No, Van. I'm still here. Send him up."

He was quiet for a long moment, and I wondered if he'd

even do as I asked. Finally he muttered his acquiescence and hung up the phone.

I slammed my chair back and smashed it into the wall as I leaped to my feet and raced to the bathroom. I checked my makeup, teeth, breath, hair; then I sauntered coolly into the reception area just as Noah was stepping off the elevator.

He was wearing athletic shorts, a T-shirt, and a baseball cap. He looked like a total jock, and his quads were flexing with each step. My stomach did a triple flip as I recalled my intimate knowledge of his legs, and I was very glad I hadn't listened to Van. I opened the door and smiled. "Hi."

He stepped inside and didn't touch me. "Sorry I'm late."

I frowned. Granted, there was no need for major public displays of affection, but a quick kiss? A touch of my arm? There was barely anyone around, and a little PDA would have been fine. "Let's go to my office."

He nodded and followed me down the hall. I caught a whiff of yummy cologne, but it was only a whiff. The predominating odor was that of a sweaty guy. Couldn't he at least have showered?

Then I frowned. That was why he was late? Because he was working out? I slanted a look at him, and he gave me a half smile.

My stomach tightened. There was a weird vibe going on here. I led the way into my office and retreated behind my desk. I wasn't sure why, but something in the air was telling me I needed protection.

Noah shut the door and leaned against it. "I'm really sorry I'm late."

"Were you late?" I made a big show of looking at my

clock. "I didn't even notice." I blinked. "Wow, it's ten o'clock already?"

I wasn't sure whether he bought it, but it made me feel better. I mean, it might be Noah, the love of my life, but a girl still needed to have a little pride, you know?

"I was playing squash with Ray."

"My brother?"

He nodded.

Huh. "Did you tell him about us?"

Noah sort of did this evasive thing with his eyes. "I tested the waters."

Tested the waters? What kind of declaration of love was that? "And?"

He shook his head. "No-go."

I blinked. "No-go? What does that mean?"

"Ray was really against it."

"So what? Since when does he have any say in who you or I date?" I felt a roiling anger inside of me. No-go? That was how he dumped me? *It's a no-go?*

"He's my best friend, and your family means more to me than my own family does. He said everyone in your family would consider it a betrayal if I took advantage of you."

"I'm twenty-four!"

He shrugged. "He made sense. Shannon, I had a great time on Saturday night, I really did. And I'd be willing to give this a shot, but I can't risk losing your entire family if it doesn't work out."

I was too shocked to respond. Totally dismissed.

"So, um, I guess that's it. Sorry again." He gave me a smile. "Maybe sometime it'll work out, you know? I just think we need to back way off for now. There's too much at stake."

I found my voice. "We've already crossed the line, Noah. You can't pretend it didn't happen. As long as we've already gone this far, why don't we see it through?"

"Because we haven't hurt anyone in your family yet. If we keep going, that's going to happen."

So as long as it's only me you hurt, that's fine?

"So are you okay?"

Oh, yeah, fine. The guy I'd adored my whole life used me and then dumped me? I couldn't even fathom it. Of anyone in the world, I never thought I'd have to worry about being used by Noah. As he said, too much at risk. "Decision made?"

He nodded. "I'm really sorry. I wasn't thinking on Saturday. It should never have happened."

He smiled again and then walked out.

I'm such a loser.

Slut.

Idiot.

Pathetic useless creature.

Slut.

Fool.

Slut.

I can't believe this!

I couldn't even cry. I felt as if there were a two-thousand-pound weight crushing my body. I couldn't move. Couldn't respond. Couldn't think.

My phone rang. I looked down. It was Van. No doubt he saw Noah leave without me.

I was completely incapable of facing Van. He knew everything. He alone would know how stupid I was, that I was a slut, that I was a fool.

My forehead dropped to the desk and I closed my eyes, squeezing back the tears that had decided to make an appearance. *Oh, God.* I felt so empty. So betrayed. So nothing.

A light tap sounded on my door, and I dove under my desk. No way was I here.

The door opened and shut.

Just when I was about to climb back out from under the desk, I heard footsteps. *Crap!* Someone was in my office! I crunched into a little ball under my desk and prayed that whoever it was wouldn't find me back here. There would be absolutely no explanation that would save my pride.

Feet came into view behind my desk: polished black shoes and black trousers. A man. Noah? Had he come back?

No, he'd been wearing sneakers.

Blaine. *The bastard.* It was as if he could sniff out my vulnerabilities.

He sat down in my chair.

Or maybe it was a spy that Otto had sent to search my files for evidence that would justify firing me.

Then he pushed the chair back and Van's face appeared. "Hi."

CHAPTER TWELVE

I stared at him.

He didn't smile. "Are you stuck?"

I swallowed. "I dropped something. Something important."

He nodded, as if he completely believed me. "How about that drink?"

What? Wasn't he going to ask me about the fiasco with Noah? About why I was hiding under my desk with tears still streaming down my face? Miss Puffy Eyes herself. "I'm not really in the mood for a drink."

He lifted a brow. "Seems to me you might be in the perfect mood for a drink." He was still leaning down, chatting with me as if it were absolutely normal for him to be sitting at my desk talking to me while I was huddled under it.

"Chocolate."

He nodded. "I think we can work that out." He held out his hand. "Come on."

I declined his hand, not really in the mood for being dependent on guys. He shrugged and slid my chair back so I could climb out. Let's just say the effort of extricating myself from under the desk without exposing my thong to Van wouldn't exactly have qualified me for the Lady Grace award of the year.

Obviously the short, tight skirt I'd worn to impress Noah had failed miserably. I stood up and realized I was between Van's knees. He lifted his hand and touched my hip, then dropped his hand and sort of looked over my shoulder. I glanced down to find my skirt had hiked up over my left hip, giving Van a very clear view of certain private things. And he hadn't even looked. True gent.

I fixed my skirt and stepped around my desk. "So, chocolate?"

He stood up, and I realized he wasn't wearing his security shirt anymore. He was wearing a cotton sport shirt that was pale yellow. Too bad. I liked him better in uniform. In his sport shirt he could pass for a lawyer, and I really hated lawyers tonight. "I know a great dessert place. My treat," he said.

He picked up my purse and handed it to me. "You okay with walking or you want to take a cab? It's about twenty minutes on foot."

"Walking is fine." Maybe being out in the fresh air would wipe the red out of my eyes.

Van said nothing, but he opened my door for me and followed me out.

Neither of us said anything for the first ten minutes. Why was I here with him? All I wanted to do was go home and cry. Or call Max.

But I couldn't go home. What if Blaine was there with Emma?

Banished from my own home. Stupid tears welled up again, and Van put a handkerchief in my hand.

And still he said nothing, just giving me my space and keeping me company.

He was probably worried I was going to throw myself off a bridge into the Charles River. Fat chance of that. No man was worth that.

I blew my nose into his handkerchief, and wondered if there was anything less attractive to a guy than a woman blowing snot. Probably not. Van didn't seem to care, but then again, we were hardly in a sexual-vibe kind of relationship.

I slanted a look at Van. He was humming quietly to himself and had his hands shoved in his pockets. "Why'd you come up to my office?"

He shrugged. "You said you'd get a drink with me, so I was coming to collect."

I narrowed my eyes. "It wasn't because you saw Noah leave and figured he'd just destroyed my heart and my soul and totally humiliated me?"

He shot me an indecipherable look. "Is that what happened?"

"No."

He lifted a brow.

"Okay, fine. Yes, that's what happened." I waited for him to tell me I should have listened to him and pretended I'd already left.

"Bummer."

I frowned. "So I should have listened to you, huh? Sent him away?"

"Might as well get it over with. At least now you know."

Interesting point. "How'd you find my office?"

"I have a map of the building."

Oh. Made sense. He had keys and a map. Could go anywhere. I slanted another look at him, glad it was Van who had that kind of access, and not some crazy.

"We're here." He stopped in front of a little shop with gold curlicue letters on the window.

"Après?" French for *after*. Fitting name for a dessert place.

"Yep." He followed me as the waitress escorted us to the table and seated us by the window, where we could look out on the street.

Even though it was Monday night at ten thirty, the place was still pretty crowded. A lot of people in suits and dressed up, but a few in jeans as well. And there was the most delectable scent of chocolate wrapping around me. Not just chocolate. Pure, heavenly, rich chocolate, settling in my pores, healing my wounds. I inhaled deeply. "Wow."

He grinned. "Thought this might do."

After the waitress brought over a dessert tray and we'd selected an assortment of six different trial desserts, I settled back and looked around while I waited for our food. My mouth was actually watering as I studied the other tables.

"So is it back to Max, then?"

I let my gaze wander back to Van. "I don't know."

He nodded.

At that moment I realized how very little I knew about Van. Our entire relationship was based on my stopping at his booth and spewing about whatever nightmare was bugging me at the time. Van, with his security job, was so far away from the world of lawyers and big business, he'd always been an oasis for me.

But being out with him? It was different. Almost a little awkward. "So, Van, you have a girlfriend?" At his startled look, I added belatedly, "Or boyfriend?" *Damn.* I hadn't meant to let that slip out like that. I'd always thought he might be gay, and now I'd just totally offended him by assuming he was heterosexual. "Sorry."

He looked amused again. "Neither. I'm single."

Which didn't answer the question of which he would prefer. And from the sparkle in his eye, I could tell he'd done that on purpose. Not that his personal life mattered to me. "Um . . . thanks for coming to get me tonight."

His amusement faded, and his eyes got all concerned. "You seem better now, but I was pretty worried about you when I first got into your office."

I bit my lip to keep from crying again. "Yeah, well, I was a little shaken up."

A waitress set a mug of hot chocolate topped with whipped cream in front of each of us. I grabbed the cinnamon stick and swirled it while I tried not to feel embarrassed.

"Want to talk about it?"

I put the end of the stick in my mouth and sucked off the chocolate. *Mmm.* I could feel the sugar improving my mood already. "I thought the fact that we'd known each other for twenty years meant that I could trust him to treat me well. I was wrong."

He nodded.

"Do you realize that he was the first guy I've ever slept with that early in a relationship? I never have sex until there's major commitment." If he was unsettled by the topic of my sex life, he didn't show it. And since he'd already guessed that I'd slept with Noah, and since he knew I'd broken up with Max only three weeks ago, it wasn't as if I were giving him new knowledge. "I'm an idiot."

"Well, how was it?"

I looked at him. "What?"

"How was it? The sex?"

I rolled my eyes. "That's such a guy question."

He shrugged. "You didn't get the emotional commitment out of it that you were hoping for, so I was curious whether there were any redeeming aspects. Great sex might not make up for having to hide under your desk, but it's still something." He wrapped his hands around the mug. "So?"

I giggled and stared at my drink. I could feel my cheeks heating up. "Yeah, well, it was . . . um . . . you know . . . I guess it was good."

"Good or great?"

I pretended I was talking to my hot chocolate. "It was great." I looked up in time to see him grin and wink.

"There you go. See? Something good came of it. Great sex." He nodded. "Always a good thing."

I couldn't help it. I laughed. "You're such a guy."

"Guilty as charged." He sat back as our assortment of desserts arrived, all of them chocolate, all of them horribly decadent. For a moment I felt guilty; then I watched Van take a bite and changed my mind. They looked too good to hold off.

Besides, I'd been dumped. That was totally worthy of food.

"How's the job going? Haven't heard much about that lately."

I rolled my eyes. "I'm on probation."

He looked startled. "Why?"

Fortified by the most amazing chocolate I'd ever eaten, I filled him in on my miserable week, even adding the entire discussion with Hildy. "Moral of the story? Stay far, far away from lawyers of any kind. Noah is also a lawyer. Did I tell you that?"

"You think it's a lawyer thing? All lawyers are miserable SOBs who will heartlessly destroy everything in their path?"

"Yep." I pointed a spoonful of chocolate mousse at him. "That's why there is hope for you. You're not a lawyer."

He studied me. "So if I were, you wouldn't be here eating chocolate with me?"

"No way." At the flicker on his face, I tried to explain. "See, the thing is, you're normal. You have a normal job. You make a normal income. You don't live in a world where appearances, money, and family connections are all that matter. I was raised in this elitist world where everyone judges me—and finds me lacking, I might add—and I'm sick of it. But with you . . . well, none of that exists." I struggled to find my words. "You're more down-to-earth. I feel like you don't judge people on such a superficial level. You know a person's character is more important than what they do for a living or who they know."

He took his time chewing his piece of four-layer chocolate liqueur cake. When he finally swallowed, he said, "I think I'm honored."

I nodded. "Damn right." In that moment, I imagined what it would be like if I took Van to my sister's wedding. Introduced him as the security guard from my building. Can you imagine? My parents would freak.

Not that I'd ever use him. But dating all these guys whom my parents approved of wasn't exactly finding me true happiness, was it?

Van slipped our waitress his credit card before I could stop him, and shook off my cash. "My treat. When I get dumped next time, you can take me out." He grinned. "Feeling better?"

Interesting. "Actually, I am." And he hadn't given me all sorts of TLC or gone off on all the reasons why I didn't need men, or tell me to find someone new. He'd just been there as a friend, listened, bought me food. "Thanks."

"No problem."

Van spent the rest of the evening trying to get the details out of me about what made sex with Noah so good. I was embarrassed and laughing all the way home.

And then spent the night awake in bed pondering that very question. And not liking what I came up with. Sex with Noah had been great partially because of how much I'd liked him. Okay, it had also been because he was an excellent lover and I'd enjoyed the decadent feeling of sleeping with someone before I should.

Then I thought of my discussions with Van. I'd spilled all my innermost secrets to a guy I barely knew. How totally embarrassing. Note to self: Chocolate loosens my tongue even more than alcohol. Chocolate and a broken heart, when mixed with a friendly face—bad combo for someone not interested in sharing her secrets with the world.

I was totally avoiding him for the next week. Like my list of people to avoid wasn't long enough already.

* * *

I woke up at five in the morning to be out of the house before Blaine and Emma got up. No way could I deal with that misery.

I was in the middle of washing my hair when I heard the door to the bathroom click. I froze. "Who's there?"

"Me. Just brushing my teeth."

Emma. God, how I wanted to tell her about my horrible night with Noah. My second thoughts about Max. My conversation with Hildy. I missed her so much. "Em?"

"Yeah?"

"Do you want to go out to breakfast?"

"Today?"

"Yes." I just wanted to be back to where we were.

"I'll check with Blaine. Give me a sec."

"Wait!" I stuck my head out. Emma had her hand on the door, and she was wearing one of her little black nighties. "I don't want Blaine to come. Just us."

Emma paused, then shook her head. "I can't do that to him. We're a couple now."

I felt my jaw drop open. "But you've known him for a week."

Her eyes lit up. "I know! Can you believe it? We totally click. Imagine, me with a lawyer. Who'd have thought? My parents are thrilled. They totally adore him. We're going away this weekend with them to their place in Maine. How about that, huh?"

She looked so happy, I almost didn't want to shove her toothbrush up her nose and ruin the moment. "Great. Have fun."

Emma frowned. "You aren't still mad about it, are you? I mean, you're with Noah and all."

"Yeah." Pride kept me from admitting anything else.

"And to be honest, Blaine's not your type. He's too easy-going. You're too high-maintenance. He'd never give you all the support you need."

I blinked. "I'm high-maintenance?"

"Sure you are. You get all wigged about your family, work, lawyer stuff. Max had to work overtime to keep you stable. Blaine's not into that. We have fun."

Okay, so this was really doing loads to help my mood. "Forget breakfast."

"You sure?"

"Very."

Her eyes narrowed. "Don't be selfish, Shannon. I deserve to be happy."

"You're always happy! You don't have a care in the world! You have no bills, no sense of responsibility when it comes to work ethics, you sleep with whoever, date whoever, and generally flit through life so you don't ever have to deal with anything."

She walked over to me and glared. "Take that back."

"Don't you even get it? We always swore that our friendship was more important than a man, and you've chosen Blaine over me because you have fun with him. Fun? You'll break up with him in two weeks, and I'll be stuck dealing with the repercussions because I work with him. He's already a jerk to me at work, and when you dump him it's going to be even worse. And until you dump him, I have to trip over his underwear in the hall, which sucks."

Her eyes glittered. "Maybe I won't dump him in two weeks. Maybe he's the one."

My stomach thudded to my toes. I had no response to

that, except that it hurt. It really hurt, deep in my core, the same place that Noah had bruised. Not because I wanted Blaine anymore, because I didn't. Never really had, actually. He'd been more of a prize that I could have claimed to help me with my family and my work situations.

But Emma finding the one? That left me alone. *Alone.*

I wanted to congratulate her and giggle with her over breakfast, hearing all the juicy details, but I couldn't. I simply didn't have the emotional capacity at the moment. Not to mention that she didn't have time for one-on-one Shannon/Emma time. "Have fun this weekend."

She looked wary. "Thanks. You too. Hanging with Noah?"

"Yeah, probably."

"We should double-date sometime. Once you get to know Blaine, you'll like him."

Double-date? "Sure. Sounds good."

"How about tonight?"

Thank heavens for my job. "Red Sox game."

"Wednesday?"

Guilt shot through me as I thought of my dinner with Phoebe and Dave. "Busy."

She lifted a brow. "Thursday?"

No legit excuse came to mind right away. "I'll have to check with Noah."

She nodded, but I could tell she didn't believe me for a sec. But she thought it was because I was being selfish, not because Noah had dumped me. A delusion I wasn't in the mood to correct. A girl had to have some pride.

I walked into work that morning determined to forget my personal life. I'd focus on my work, do a great job, get off probation, and I was most certainly *not* going to take Hildy up on her offer to go to lunch and talk about my becoming a lawyer.

Yet, when I sat down at my desk and opened my calendar, there was a lunch with Hildy scheduled for a week from Wednesday, courtesy of Isabel. I debated canceling, but then decided not to hurt the one person who actually seemed to care about me. I'd give Hildy the courtesy of a face-to-face rejection of her idea.

I e-mailed my agenda for tonight's Red Sox game to Otto; then I took a stroll past Missy's office. Still dark. I swallowed. My career wouldn't survive the loss of Missy.

So I returned to my office and began a list of how I could take this intern experience to a new level, really blow the lid off the pot for these guys. Make myself invaluable. After stalling out for a while, I made up a questionnaire and sent it to my interns, asking them what would be the most valuable things they could get out of this summer.

Then I walked by Missy's office again.

Same result.

So I returned to my desk and ordered flowers to be delivered to her apartment. How pathetic was I? Twenty-four years old, and groveling at the feet of some law school goddess to please save my career. Tiptoeing by Otto's office, hoping for another chance to prove my competence. Hiding from the lawyer next door. No social life to speak of. The big two-five coming up soon with nothing at all to celebrate.

Something had to give. And soon.

*　*　*

By the next Wednesday, I had settled into a mode of tense anticipation, waiting for the dam to break. Missy hadn't been sighted, but she hadn't officially quit. No crises with the interns. No call from Noah. A couple messages from Max that I hadn't returned. Hadn't seen Van. A couple dinners with Phoebe and Dave—my one oasis in a miserable life. Friends who were lonely with their significant others away, so we could all three share our loneliness.

We actually had a lot of fun together. I hadn't realized how lonely both of them were, and I felt better after commiserating with them. Except when I thought about how completely miserable I was since Noah had broken my heart. Which was only about five times an hour, so really, I was doing fine.

Otto had canceled our Monday meeting due to a schedule conflict and hadn't rescheduled, so I hoped I'd fallen off his radar again. I had no plans of getting back on.

And now I was sitting across from Hildy at lunch, picking at my chicken Caesar salad. So far she hadn't brought up the law school thing, and I decided to preempt her. "Hildy, I decided I'm not going to law school."

"Why?" She didn't look surprised or particularly worried. Which worried me.

"Because I don't want to be a lawyer."

"Why?"

"Because I don't."

She shook her head. "Not good enough. Why?"

"Because I don't like lawyers."

"Any of them?"

Oh, good one, Shannon. "Except you. You're nice."

Hildy took a bite of her baked chicken breast. "Shannon,

if you can clearly articulate legitimate reasons why you don't want to go to law school, I'll leave you alone."

"Fine. I don't like the whole law firm scenario. I don't want to have to worry about politics. I don't want to work those hours."

"All of which you're currently doing for a fraction of the salary."

"Well, yeah." Good point. But I didn't totally like my job. "And I don't want to give in."

She lifted a perfectly shaped brow. "What does that mean?"

I sighed. "My whole family has been pressuring me to go to law school forever. They're ashamed of my job. If I go to law school, then it's like they win."

Hildy thought about that one for a minute, and I thought I had her. Then she said, "Then again, if you really would like to be a lawyer and you choose not to be merely because you don't want them to win, then you lose twice. Don't be a lawyer because they want you to, but don't give up a career you want merely because they also want you to have that career. You're an adult, Shannon; make the choice for yourself." She tilted her head. "You could always not tell them you're going back to school. Then you'd know it was for yourself."

"But I don't want to be a lawyer." I'd been fighting against it my whole life.

But why? Just because I wanted to piss off my family? Surely I wasn't that shallow and immature?

Hildy set an envelope on the table. "Here's the application. Fill it out and give it back to me by Friday." When I protested, she held up her finger to silence me. "You can always change your mind and back out, but if I don't get this to my husband, you won't have a choice to make."

I pursed my lips and stared at the envelope. For a moment the image of me presenting a law degree to my family passed through my mind. Imagine if my parents were actually proud of me? I immediately scowled. Since when did I make choices to please my parents? I made choices to anger them.

I blinked. Was that what I did? No, I made choices to bring me happiness.

Then why are you at a job that makes you miserable?

CHAPTER THIRTEEN

I want my parents to be proud of me for myself.

That thought occurred to me while I was on the way to meet Phoebe and Dave for drinks after work on Thursday night.

If I became a lawyer, then they'd be proud, but it wouldn't be of me. It would be pride for my career.

But if I took them out of the equation entirely, what did I think about being a lawyer? Why had I chosen a career in a law firm?

Dave and Phoebe had strong opinions about my family and my relationship with them. Maybe I'd run it by them tonight.

I found them in a booth near the dance floor. They were sitting across from each other, buried in deep conversation. I smiled as I slid in. I'd succeeded in helping Phoebe and Dave become better friends. It was a good thing. "Hi, guys."

Dave smiled tensely, and Phoebe didn't smile at all.

"What's wrong?"

"We need to talk to you about something."

This didn't sound good. "Go ahead."

"Shannon?" I looked up to find Van standing at the table. I immediately became embarrassed, recalling how I'd spilled my whole miserable sex life to him. "How are you?"

I shrugged and felt my cheeks heat up. "Fine."

"You haven't stopped by the booth since last week."

"Yeah." I'd been sneaking out the back door, actually.

He touched my arm, and I looked at him. "Dance with me."

I glanced at my friends. "Phoebe and Dave were just about to tell me something."

Dave immediately stuck out his hand and introduced himself to Van, and Phoebe did the same. Van returned the favor, and I felt like a dork for not introducing them. "Phoebe and Dave are my best friends."

My best friends exchanged a tense look, and I wondered again what was up. Dave addressed Van. "Can we keep Shannon for a few minutes? We really need to talk to her."

I sort of wanted to dance with Van. I also wanted to know what was going on. And, okay, I admit it, I was still embarrassed for having spilled so many personal details to Van. Seeing him again brought back the humiliation of the whole Noah mistake.

I turned to Van. "Are you going to be here for a while?"

"I think we're here for the night."

"So how about later? Like an hour, maybe?"

He looked at his watch. "You can find me if you want to dance. I'll be around."

I watched him walk off and settle down at a table of six guys and four girls, all of whom looked about my age. They were attractive and looked like they were having fun.

183

Weird, but I'd never thought of Van as having friends. He was Van from security, not Van who had a life. It never occurred to me what he did when he wasn't at work.

And I was a little jealous, watching that girl with the red hair tuck her arm through his and lean on him, laughing. And he was laughing back.

I wasn't jealous of Van. I was jealous that he looked happy. I wanted to feel like that. Maybe I should get a job as a security guard, where I didn't have to deal with all the crap. It would be the ultimate proof that I wasn't trying to impress my family.

"So, Shannon, we need to talk to you."

I refocused on my friends. "What's up?"

Dave and Phoebe exchanged another glance, and they seemed to be having some silent argument about who was going to tell me. I tensed. What did they know? "Is Noah dating someone else?"

Dave blinked, then shook his head. "It's not about Noah."

"Or Max? He's got a new girlfriend?" *Dammit.* That hurt.

Phoebe shook her head rapidly back and forth like she was trying to dislodge a fly from her nose. "No, no, no. Nothing like that." She looked at Dave. "It's about me and Dave."

I frowned. "What about you guys?"

Dave moved his chair to the other side of the table and put his arm around Phoebe's shoulder—*Look at that bonding. Great stuff!*—and faced me. "Phoebe and I have been spending a lot of time together."

"I know. I've been with you."

He shook his head. "Other time."

"And?"

184

Dave looked at Phoebe, then back at me. "We're in love."

I frowned. "What are you talking about?"

"We love each other. I'm going to leave Yvonne and Phoebe is going to leave Zach so we can be together." They shared a smile. "I've been sleeping over at her apartment every night Yvonne is out of town. Her roommate hates me."

I was stunned. "You guys are having an affair?"

Phoebe frowned. "I don't like that word. We're in love. That's what matters."

Oh, God. I slumped in my seat. "You guys are having an affair. You're married," I said to Dave. "And you're engaged." I glared at Phoebe. "Those promises mean nothing to you?"

"Love transcends all that," Dave said.

"Dave! You were just telling me that you and Yvonne were trying to have children! How can you go from that to . . . this?" I waved my hands, unable to articulate exactly what *this* was.

"Fortunately, there are no babies on the way. That would be awkward." He squeezed Phoebe's shoulder and I felt truly sick.

"I can't believe this. You guys are having sex while you're married and engaged to other people."

Phoebe looked offended. "We didn't want to make any major decisions until we were certain it was going to work out." She smiled at Dave so tenderly I wanted to leap across the table and yank them apart, screaming about commitment and honor and marriage vows.

I'd never liked Yvonne, but this was horrible. How could they do this? "I don't understand how this could happen."

"Love happens. You can't always explain it."

I held my hands over my ears. "You're committed to other people. For life!"

Dave's face was tense. "Listen, Shannon, we're not bad people. We didn't intend for this to happen, but it did. You should be happy for us, that we found each other. Some people go their entire lives without finding their true love."

I thought of Yvonne and Zach, still thinking their beloveds were theirs. They had no idea their significant others were having sex with someone else. And these were my friends. People I loved and relied on. Not some weirdo strangers who had no morals. These were people I trusted. "I have to get out of here."

Phoebe grabbed my hand. "Don't go, Shannon. Please. We need your support on this. It's not going to be easy."

"My support?" My voice sounded like an empty echo. "You want me to support adultery?"

Phoebe glared at my word choice, but Dave patted her hand and kept her silent. That hand had been on Phoebe's naked body, and that hand belonged to his wife. I closed my eyes. I couldn't believe this.

Dave nodded. "Since Emma's moving into Blaine's apartment, I was hoping I could stay at your place for a while. Phoebe and I don't want to live together until the divorce is final."

I yanked my hand free of Phoebe's grasp. "Since when is Emma moving in with Blaine?"

"She didn't tell you?"

"No." *Oh, my God.* My head was going to explode.

Dave looked apologetic. "She told us yesterday after we

told her about us. She's the one who suggested I move in with you. I won't be able to afford my own place until the divorce is final."

"You already told Emma?" They'd met Emma through me. And yet I was last to know? And Emma was moving out?

"Since you two aren't hanging out together anymore, we had to do it separately."

"We aren't hanging out anymore? Is that what she told you?" I knew we'd barely spoken for the last ten days, and she'd been spending most nights at Blaine's instead of the two of them shacking up at our place, but I'd still been thinking it was temporary. She was my best friend and we'd work it out, right?

"So, can I move in?"

I stared at them and envisioned the two of them getting it on on the other side of my bedroom wall. "I have to go."

I grabbed my purse and ran for the exit. Didn't even stop when I heard Van calling my name. My entire world was crumbling under my feet, and there was only one person I wanted to see.

I knocked on Max's door at eleven twenty at night, then stepped back and prayed he wasn't with another woman. If he was . . . that was it. I would be unable to cope.

I heard some shuffling inside, and then the door opened. Max was standing there in his boxers, his eyes squinted in sleep and his hair all messed up. He looked confused. "Shannon?"

The tears started to fall and I couldn't talk. I just stood there like an idiot.

Max pulled me into his apartment, wrapped his arms around me and held me while I cried. At some point he picked me up and carried me to the couch, but I barely noticed. Didn't care. All I wanted was to feel someone's arms around me.

And he was happy to oblige.

After a while, when I couldn't cry anymore, I became aware of the fact that I was on his lap and his forearm was resting on my breasts. I sniffled. "Sorry for crying all over you."

He shook his head and kissed my forehead. "You know I'm always here for you. What's wrong?"

I babbled for almost two hours about everything, except for Noah. It didn't seem appropriate. I told him about Hildy's offer, about Phoebe and Dave, about Emma and Blaine, about Otto screaming at me. After a while, I realized that it really was quite an extensive list.

No wonder I felt like shit.

I stopped a moment to consider all that I'd just poured out, and that was when Max kissed me. On the lips.

It was so familiar. So safe.

Nothing like when Noah kissed me. None of the excitement. None of the quivering limbs and trembling muscles. And look where that had gotten me? Nowhere. I was coming home.

I kissed him back and thought about work.

He picked me up and carried me to his bedroom while his tongue played with mine. I kissed him back, hung on to his neck.

The comforter puffed around me when he set me on the bed. "Still using the same detergent, huh?" The familiar scent surrounded me. I sighed and relaxed. No more games. I knew what Max was like. No questions, no guilt, just us.

His hand cupped my breast and his lips found my nipple. I arched under him.

I needed to go find Missy tomorrow. It had been too long since I'd heard from her. I had to find out what was going on. If she was quitting, then so be it. I needed to know, and I needed to do damage control.

Did I want to be a lawyer? It would be cool to be able to walk into M&S and be an equal. And I did know about the law. But I hated everything about lawyers.

Max made a little noise, and I remembered where I was. I dug my fingers into his shoulders and closed my eyes, trying to relish the moment.

I still couldn't believe Dave and Phoebe were having an affair. Was it my fault for introducing them? I shouldn't let Dave move in. Yvonne would think we were having an affair and probably have me killed.

"Shannon?" Max's voice was quiet, and he stopped kissing me. "What's wrong?"

This is what I'd been longing for since I'd broken up with him? I thought of Van's comment about the great sex I'd had with Noah. The one redeeming benefit.

Or was it?

That was what I wanted now. I didn't want this.

"Max."

He tried to kiss me again. "Mmm?"

"Get off. You're crushing me."

He rolled to his side. "I missed you."

I thought I'd missed him, too. Now I was just more confused. "Did you?"

"Yes." He propped himself up on his elbow and cupped my breast with his free hand. "You know we're meant to be together."

I removed his hand and thought of Dave and Phoebe. If they were right, and I'm not saying they were, but if they were right that they were each other's soul mate, then they made a mistake in committing to the wrong person. I looked at Max. Really looked at him. Would I find myself in Phoebe's shoes in three years if I married him?

What if Noah decided he loved me?

Or someone else? Someone who made me feel special and wonderful?

Would I want to leave Max?

"I don't want to get divorced, Max. Ever."

He pinched my nipple and I shoved his hand away from me. "Max! Cut it out."

He sighed and flopped on his back. "Fine. Let's talk."

"Do you want to marry me?"

He closed his eyes and said nothing.

So I smacked his chest with the flat of my hand. Hard. He jerked up and glared at me. I glared back. "Max, I'm trying to be serious here. Do you want to marry me?"

He frowned. "Are you proposing to me?"

"No!" *Heaven help me.* I hadn't meant that at all. "You talk all the time about how you love me and how we're meant for each other. But I'm almost twenty-five and you're twenty-nine, and there's been no marriage talk. Why?"

He spun away from me and climbed off the bed. "Shannon, I'm not ready for marriage."

Something moved in me, but I wasn't sure what it was. Relief? Dismay? "Why not?"

"Because . . ." He ran his hand through his hair. "I guess I don't feel like I know enough to be sure I never want to be with another woman again."

I frowned. "Is that why you were flirting with that woman at the bar?"

He shrugged. "I don't know."

"If I hadn't come in that night, would you have gone home with her?"

Max was silent, and my stomach dropped.

"I take it your silence means you would have at least considered it."

He sat back on the bed and took my hand. "Shannon, I love you. I do. But I'm not ready for marriage. Let's go back to what we had. Dating. Eventually we'll know whether marriage is the right next step for us."

I stared at his hands wrapped around mine. Then I looked at him. "I don't want to do what Dave and Phoebe are doing."

He looked shocked. "I don't either."

"If we were meant to be, we'd know it by now." I pulled my hand away. "I don't want to stay together because it's easy and safe. That's why I came back here tonight. Because I was scared and alone and I needed familiar ground."

"That's why we're great for each other. I'm here for you."

I shook my head. "Max, that's not a reason to get married or even stay with someone. Because something is familiar."

"So that's why we date and don't get engaged. Let's take the time to figure it out."

I didn't need to think anymore. "I already know. I've been hanging on to you for the wrong reasons."

He said nothing, but he didn't stop me when I stood up. "Maybe you're right."

I stopped and looked at him. "What?"

"Maybe you're right." He rubbed his jaw. "I don't know. Maybe we should really try out some other people. Do some comparison shopping."

Comparison shopping? "Yes, go do some shopping, Max."

He nodded. "I think that's a good idea." He looked at me. "And if we both decide there's nothing better out there, then we'll get married."

Yes, that was my dream proposal. *There's nothing better available, darlin', so what the hell? Wanna go for it?* I picked up my blazer and slung it over my arm. "I'll always love you, but . . ." What was there to say? *I love you, but I don't want you?*

He stood up. "I love you too, Shannon. Let's keep in touch, okay?"

"Sure." It was weird. I didn't feel as empty as when I'd arrived at his doorstep, yet technically I was walking away with one more loss than I'd arrived with.

But I'd gained too. Knowledge. Power. Freedom. Answers. I finally knew for absolute certain that Max was not the man for me. No more second-guessing myself. It was over, and I was free.

I felt the best I had in a long time.

My good mood lasted long enough for me to schedule the baby shower and make cute little pink-and-blue invitations. Of course, that was because I'd cloistered myself away for the weekend. Emma stayed away from the apartment, and I didn't answer the phone. Didn't think about Missy or Hildy or work.

I just enjoyed being finally free of Max, and wondering when I'd have Noah-sex again. Not specifically *with* Noah, but now that I'd experienced that level, I wanted nothing less. I rented a couple movies from the adult section and quickly decided *that* wasn't the kind of sex I was looking for.

I needed some new friends. Single friends. Friends who would go out drinking and dancing. A little harmless flirting would be fun. Unfortunately, everyone I knew was in a relationship.

Then I thought of Van and his crew at the bar the other night. Van had friends. He was my age, and a self-proclaimed single guy. And there'd been more guys than girls at his table. Always a good ratio.

Of course, I did owe him a huge apology for blowing him off for the last couple of weeks, and for ditching him at the bar. Maybe I could bring him a six-pack, like Max had, then beg him to let me be his friend?

I almost laughed. How pathetic was that? *Please be my friend.*

Okay, so I was pathetic. The first step was admitting it. The second step was doing something to remedy it.

I looked at the construction paper and other creative supplies I'd spread out on my floor to make the baby shower invitations, and I decided to make Van a card. One that would apologize and make him smile.

He had a cute smile.

CHAPTER FOURTEEN

On Monday, Van's card was sitting on my desk in its home-made tissue paper envelope, but I couldn't give it to him until tonight, when he came on duty. I didn't know his phone number or address.

First things first. I called Missy. Surprisingly enough, she answered. "Hello?"

"Missy. Shannon McCormick. What's up?"

Silence.

"If you don't talk to me, I'll come over there and harass you in person."

"My dad didn't call yet?"

I frowned. "Why would your dad call me?" Missy's dad was managing partner of one of the other very prestigious firms in the city.

"He's going to call Otto and tell him that I'm quitting. But I didn't want to get you in trouble, so he's going to tell Otto it was his fault for being mean. That way Otto will have no one to blame but himself." She sounded petulant and childish, and my heart stopped beating.

If her dad called Otto, I was sunk. Sunk! No way would

Otto accept that it was his fault. He'd spin the blame in my direction so fast it would decapitate me. I needed this job if I wanted to start attending classes at night.

I frowned. But I wasn't going to law school. . . . I needed the job anyway. I had rent, food, bills, and a life to pay for. Especially since I wasn't dating Max anymore, who would have been happy to hand over some cash to tide me over.

On my own. And I was going to make it.

"Anyway, he's going to call you after he's talked to Otto and let you know how it went."

"You weren't going to tell me yourself?"

Missy was silent.

I cursed the effort I'd put in for her. Anyone who didn't have the courage to quit her job herself was never going to make it in this business, and it was just as well she was leaving. She was twenty-three and still had her dad call up and quit for her?

Made me glad I'd rejected all my parents' offers to gild my path into the legal world. I'd hate it if I ended up like Missy. "Don't have your dad call Otto."

"But I want to protect you."

The girl was sweet; I'll grant her that. Not lawyer material. "You'll do more damage if you have your dad making phone calls. I'll take care of it."

"Are you sure?"

Disgusted at your wimpiness, but yes, sure. "Yep."

"Um, Shannon?"

"What?"

"My dad's trying to get me another job for the summer, but he said it would be helpful if I had a reference from this job. Can I put you down?"

Seeing as how I'd just concluded that Missy would not succeed at any place like M&S, her request put me in an awkward situation. "What kind of job?"

"Another law firm. In Boston."

I'd never been faced with this type of dilemma before. One part of me sympathized with Missy, but another part of me was more than a little annoyed for what she had put me through, and what she was going to put me through.

Plus, there was the simple fact that'd she'd never survive in the big Boston law firm environment, and I wouldn't be doing her any favors by getting her hooked up with one. The poor girl would probably end up in counseling. I swallowed. "I'm sorry, Missy, but I can't give you a reference for another big firm. I don't think you'll survive those any more than you could survive this one. But if you want to work somewhere else, like at a nonprofit or something like that, then I'd be happy to help you out."

"Thanks for nothing." And then she hung up on me.

"Ditto," I said into the empty phone. I pictured poor Missy huddled under her desk hiding from a partner who wanted to berate her. . . . Oh, wait, that was me, the desk-hider-underer. For a moment, I let the guilt of dissapointing a perfectly nice, albeit wimpy kid wash over me and settle in my gut.

Then I clamped it down and banished it to the Unacceptable Emotions corner of my soul and started brainstorming on damage control.

Three hours later, I was sitting in front of Otto, my palms sweating, my knees trembling, my memo getting crumbled in my clutching hand. So much for my goal not to get back on Otto's radar.

"You have five minutes."

Gee, I feel so welcome. Wouldn't it be nice if we could outfit him with a straitjacket, pin him to the floor, and then berate him for hours? It could be a tag-team affair that would last for weeks until every member of the firm had had a chance.

"Well?"

Right. Time to do my thing. I handed him the memo. "Here is a list of all the interns. I wanted to give you a report on each one. Some insight on who is tracking in what direction." I had created a bar chart and broken it down by attribute: work ethic, connections (including family, friends, and significant others), knowledge, personality fit in the firm, attitude, and overall impression.

It was damn good, and even Otto would have to be impressed with my detailed exposé of our interns' deepest secrets. Nothing could get by me.

He studied it for a moment. "So this Jessamee is good? That name sounds familiar."

"She's in the office next door."

He frowned, then shook his head. "Nope. Haven't noticed her."

Must be interesting to be so high up on a throne that you didn't even notice the little people scurrying around you. "Well, she's tough, and she knows what she has to do to get ahead. And she'll do it."

Of course, she was also a bitch, but that didn't mean she wasn't going to make a good lawyer.

He flipped the page, and his eyes narrowed. "What's the story with this Missy Stephens?"

I nodded and tried to look concerned, which wasn't too

difficult. "She's a real problem, Mr. Nelson. She comes with great bloodlines—"

"I can see that."

"But she's never going to make it in a firm. Not here, not anywhere."

He frowned. "Why not?"

"She's soft." I felt horrible bad-mouthing Missy like this, but it was true. She wasn't going to make it, and I wasn't about to lose my job over it. "She's been in my office since day one, complaining about people being mean to her. She won't speak up, won't even look anyone in the eye." I shook my head. "She has no commitment to this kind of lifestyle."

Otto rubbed his chin. "That's a problem. Her dad won't be happy if we don't offer her a position." He looked at me. "Do we still do that thing where we make offers on the condition the intern doesn't accept them?"

It was a policy the firm used to employ to make it easier for interns to get jobs elsewhere. It looked good if they could say M&S had offered them a full-time position. I shook my head. "Not after that last one sued us for making an offer and then retracting it when he accepted."

"Damn kids." Otto frowned. "So what do we do?"

I took a deep breath. "I've been working on a little plan, and I think we've dodged a bullet."

He lifted a brow. "Yes?"

"Well, usually, as social director, I protect the interns so they have a great summer and want to come back."

"That's your job."

Gee, thanks for the recognition that I do it well. You're such a warm and fuzzy kind of guy, Otto. "Anyway, once I realized that it would be a nightmare to hire Missy, because we'd have to let her go almost right away, I decided it would be best if she made the decision to drop out herself." Was I good or what? "Anyway, I just got off the phone with her, and she has decided to drop out of the program. Said she could never work at a place that was so tough on people." I shook my head and tried to look disgusted instead of empathic. "I have no idea how she could grow up in that family and not know what the law is like, but she doesn't."

Otto studied me for a long, impassive minute, and my stomach tensed. I couldn't tell. Would he scream at me for being a fool? Or commend me for doing such an excellent job handling the situation?

It was at that minute that I realized I really didn't want to lose my job. I could handle Otto; I knew what it took to succeed. I could be the next Hildy, molding young female attorneys into powerhouses who would crush the male-dominated nature of the firm. And I'd do it for myself. Not for my parents. *Yes!*

Which meant I had a lot to lose if Otto fired me.

He looked back down at the memo. "So what about this fellow Jim Knockman? Looks like he's on the cusp."

Was he kidding? Not even going to respond? Did that mean I was off the hook? Or that he was impressed with me? Or that he was using the rest of my info, and then was going to fire me?

He eyed me. "Well? What about Jim? Should you manage him out of the program too?"

I swallowed. I think that meant he was okay with what I'd done. That managing out of the program was a good thing.

So I'd done it. I was good at my job, and I'd finally proven it to Otto.

I was a success.

Until I screwed up the next thing. Was this really how I wanted to live?

I needed to do some serious thinking.

When I got back to my desk there was a voice mail from Hildy. It was Monday, and she needed the application tomorrow or it would be too late.

So I pulled out the envelope and looked at it.

Then I put it aside and tried to read e-mails.

Then I opened the envelope and read the application.

Then I went on an intern tour to check in with everyone.

When I came back, the application was still sitting there.

There was nothing binding about filling it out, right? I mean, I could always walk away. And I might not even get into school anyway.

Filling it out didn't mean I wanted to be a lawyer. It simply meant I was keeping my options open.

I chewed on my lower lip for a moment; then I retrieved the electric typewriter from Isabel's desk.

Slipped the first page in. Stared at it for a while. Then I started typing.

I went down to the lobby at eight fifteen, and Van was there. I actually felt a little nervous walking up to him, probably because I had something at stake. I wanted his friendship, and I hadn't done much to earn it. "Um, hi."

He looked up from a book he was reading. When he saw

me, he sort of smiled and slid the book under the desk. "Hey."

"So . . . sorry about blowing you off at the bar."

He shrugged. "You have your friends. That's cool."

There was some serious distance here. I know I deserved it, but it still made me feel bad. And seeing as how I was entirely friendless at the moment, I couldn't afford to give up Van too. "Here." I shoved the card at him, along with a jumbo-size Lindt candy bar. You know, the ones that weigh about five pounds.

He stared at it without picking it up. "What's this?"

"For you." I felt sort of stupid now. "I made it for you."

He looked at me with an unreadable expression. "You made me a card?"

"Yeah. It's bad, but whatever."

I felt really nervous when he picked it up and opened the homemade envelope. He smiled at the front of the card. Good. I'd been hoping for a smile there. When he opened it and read what I'd written, I tensed again. I couldn't remember exactly what I'd finally put down, but it was something to the effect of an apology for blowing him off. And inviting him for dessert at Après, my treat, to start our friendship again.

Dumb, I know, but I'd been a little mentally unstable since the second breakup with Max. I'd been feeling sort of weirdly insightful and deep. Wish I remembered exactly what I'd written on there—he was taking an awfully long time to read it. I hope I hadn't signed it "Love, Shannon," or anything stupid like that, out of habit from writing cards to Max. *Oh, God.* That would be so embarrassing.

Van grinned and shut the card, knocking aside any chance of my checking out the signature. "Never got a card like that before."

I shifted. "Yeah, well, there you go." Was I articulate or what? If I became an attorney, it shouldn't be a trial one, since I obviously had no verbal communication skills when under pressure. What was up with that? I usually had no problem smoothing over potentially awkward social situations. That had been a major job requirement for the past three years. I was always at the ready with a polite response or a small innocuous joke. At the very least I was a pro at changing the subject. All the stress must really be getting to me.

"So I have Thursday night off."

I nodded. Why was I so tense? Did it matter if he invited me out or not? I mean, it wasn't like Van was the only guy in the entire city of Boston who might hang out with me. Or maybe he was. Yes, actually, he probably was. *Geez.* Talk about pressure.

"Dessert an option for Thursday?"

"Sure." *Phew.* Relief was a wonderful feeling. "Maybe we could go out too. Like a bar or something?" Too obvious? "I mean, unless you have plans or something. Like with your friends."

He lifted a brow and studied me. Did I feel exposed or what? It was like he was reading my mind. My mind wasn't a place I wanted visitors right now. It was too much of a mess. "How about we go to dinner first and see what happens?"

Dinner? I wasn't sure I had the cash to spring for dinner

too. Dessert at Après would probably cost twenty or thirty bucks a pop. Well, as long as April didn't collect on my share of the engagement gift, I was probably okay. "Sure. Dinner."

He nodded. "Want me to pick you up at your house?"

"At my house?" This was sort of sounding like a date. Or maybe I was wigging out.

"Or we could meet here."

I nodded. "Right."

He touched my arm. "You okay?"

"Depends on your definition." I wiggled my shoulders and let my hands flap to release the tension. "No, seriously, I'm fine. Let's meet here."

He gave me another look that I couldn't read. "What time? Are you working until your usual time? Eleven?"

I smiled. "I don't have an event, so I'll leave early. How about seven?"

Surprise flicked across his features. "Really? That early?"

"Unless you don't want to get together that early. I mean, I can work later, or we don't have to meet, or—"

He set his hand on my arm. "Relax, Shannon. Seven is fine. I'll meet you at your office?"

"Fine."

He gave me a small smile. "And if I'm two hours late and I don't call, worry. I'm probably dead somewhere."

I started to get tense about the Noah jab, but Van shook his head before I could open my mouth. "I didn't mean it like that. I just meant that you can have high expectations with me and not worry you'll be disappointed. Don't let one bad experience burn you."

What was that about? It wasn't like this was a date. And it was way insightful for a guy. Too insightful. "I'm totally over Noah."

He lifted his brow. "Good for you."

I'm not over Noah. Or Blaine. Or anything. I'm an emotional disaster with no friends, except hopefully you. "So, um, I guess I'll see you Thursday."

He nodded. "Thursday."

I suddenly couldn't think of anything to say, so I left. But I did a little jig in the elevator on the way back up to my office. I had one friend after all!

My phone was ringing when I walked into my office. I answered it without checking caller ID. "Shannon McCormick, may I help you?"

It was my mom. "Max came over for dinner tonight, and he said you guys have really broken up. You're going to start dating other people."

Sounded kinda final to have my mom telling me. "Yeah."

"Just tell me one thing. How did you convince him of that? What's wrong with you?"

I ground my teeth. Shouldn't there be a moratorium on harassing phone calls until I was fully recovered and strong enough to cope? "That's two questions. Which do you want me to answer?"

"Don't be smart with me. How could you drive Max away like that? It was bad enough you kept toying with him and all those breakups, but to actually convince him to date other women? What were you thinking? You're going to regret it and want him back, and it's going to be too late."

"Phoebe and Dave are having an affair." Sterling example of the change-the-topic strategy.

My mom was shocked into merciful silence.

"Because they picked the wrong people. I'm not going to make the same mistake. See you later."

I hung up before she could recover her voice. If I went to law school, my mom would be happy with me. But I wanted her to like me for me.

I frowned. But what was me? Was the real me the kind of person who could hang with Van and his security guard friends and be happy? My parents would be horrified, but all I wanted was to have fun. So maybe Emma was right. Maybe my staying at the law firm had been a subconscious effort to keep one toe in the world my parents would like. Same with dating Max, or lusting after Blaine.

Maybe it was time to find the real me, whoever that was. First step, go out with Van and his friends. Second . . . I picked up the completed law school application and studied it. Turn it in or not?

One minute I felt a surge of power and excitement at the thought of being a lawyer. The next minute I hated everything having anything to do with the legal profession.

But I wasn't exactly unbiased. I had pushy lawyer parents, an uptight lawyer brother, a lawyer crush who'd used and dumped me, a pretentious bastard stealing my friend from me, and an SOB boss. Not difficult to figure out where my hostility came from.

But minus those examples . . . I opened a new document on my computer and began a list titled "Good Things about the Law and Profession If You Take away Everything I Hate about It."

1) It's interesting.
2) It's challenging.
3) There are attorneys like Hildy whom I'd like to be friends with.
4) I would no longer be bottom of the barrel.
5) My pay might actually reflect how many hours I was working.
6) I could become a leader instead of a servant.
7) My wardrobe would still work.
8) I would make more money than these insurgent interns—insert gloating sense of satisfaction.
9) I could use my brain for something more interesting than how to delude interns about the true nature of working at M&S.
10) I would know how the firm works before I even started, so I'd be several steps ahead of everyone else.
11) Even though I'd have to go to school at night and work during the day, it's not like I had a social life to give up.
12) It would be fun to go into debt to pay for school. I love a good challenge!

I stopped and reread my list. Sort of dorky, but all positive. I was pleasantly surprised to find that I could actually be mature enough to assess the legal profession without letting my personal baggage prejudice me. Never would have thought it.

The list wasn't enough to get me to go to law school yet, but I was pretty sure it was sufficient to justify my giving the application to Hildy. So I sealed the envelope and marched it down to her office before I could make my other list—the one titled, "Why I Hate Everything about the Legal Profession."

Then I left the building so I couldn't sneak back down to her office in a half hour and retrieve it.

What was the worst that could happen? I could get into school, feel too much pressure, accept, attend, tell my family, be welcomed into the fold, and then spend the rest of my life in a job I hated knowing that I'd sold out.

See? That wasn't so bad.

CHAPTER FIFTEEN

I inspected my reflection in the bathroom mirror. No slut tank top tonight. Blue jeans, a pair of sandals with a decent heel, a cute V-necked T-shirt that was modest enough to keep my breasts from being on display, yet snug enough to acknowledge their existence. Freshly polished toenails and fingernails. Legs shaved, armpits hair free, eyebrows tuned up, hair brushed and released from the bun. My evening makeup applied, including lipstick, which I never wore. I had even put on my trendy chandelier earrings that dangled down and implied a sense of fashion freedom I didn't usually sport.

Yes, I was worthy of a night of fun, with three minutes to spare.

I slung my suit bag over my shoulder, tucked my makeup bag under my arm, and walked back to my office. Blaine was in his office with the door shut. Typical. I barely spoke to him during the day, other than to bicker over Isabel's time. Emma never came to see him at work, but they were obviously still together, because I hadn't laid eyes on her in a week.

I frowned. Okay, so I missed her. So I was lonely. Apparently I wasn't cut out for the no-roommate schtick. Not even Dave or Phoebe had called me.

Oh, sure. It was my fault because I'd been a bitch to all of them. Maybe it was time to make some more cards.

"You look nice."

I stopped in the doorway to my office and felt my cheeks flame at the appreciative expression on Van's face. I was certain he'd never looked at me as a woman before. Or at least never shown it. It felt weird. We didn't have that kind of relationship.

But it also felt good. I mean, Van was a man, and pretty handsome. And a nice guy to boot. Why wouldn't it make a girl feel good to get him to notice her? So I smiled. "Thanks."

He nodded. "I like that outfit a lot better than the one you wore to that bar the other night."

Nice of him to remember. "Yeah, well, that was a mistake, but feel free not to bring it up again." See? This was why we weren't dating. Because we were too honest. A boyfriend would never tell me when I looked bad, or at least he wouldn't if he wanted to stay conscious. It was okay for Van to be honest, though, because he was only a friend. In fact, it was damn good he was honest, because he was replacing Emma and Phoebe and Dave, whom I relied on for honesty.

Van looked sort of cute, actually. He was wearing jeans and black boots, and a light green shirt that matched his eyes. Interesting. I peered closer. I had never noticed his eyes were such a vibrant green. Very cool.

"They're not colored contacts." He sounded amused,

and I felt my cheeks flame again. "They change based on what I'm wearing."

"I like them."

He raised his brow and I felt even more embarrassed. "So, um, dinner, then?" I said.

"How about the North End?"

"I love Italian." I tossed my suit bag over a chair and grabbed my purse from my desk drawer. Apparently I was feeling the importance of developing this friendship with Van, because I felt all nervous and shaky.

We'd just stepped out into the hall when Blaine walked out of his office. He was carrying his briefcase and looked like he was heading out for the evening. He nodded at me; then his eyes paused for a moment on Van, as if he were trying to place him.

How insulting. How could he not recognize Van? I tucked my arm protectively through Van's and smiled sweetly at Blaine. "Blaine, you remember Van Reinhart? Van, this is Blaine Hampton."

Blaine shook his hand, and I could tell he was still struggling to recall. Van put him out of his misery. "I work security downstairs."

"Oh, right." Blaine had the grace to look embarrassed as he shook Van's hand. "Didn't recognize you out of context."

Shut up, Blaine. You're being a prick. "Van and I are going to dinner." Van might be the security guard, but I was proud to be with him.

Blaine raised an eyebrow as he followed us to the elevator, and I shot him a warning look for no snide remarks. I knew he was remembering Dirk and Noah of recent past. Come to think of it, I'd never told Emma that Noah and I weren't an item, so Blaine didn't know either. Last he knew, he'd had breakfast with Noah after running into him in the kitchen in the wee hours of the morning. Probably thought I was a total slut.

The elevator came and we all got on. "So, leaving early tonight, Blaine?"

He nodded. "Emma and I are going to the theater."

Emma at the theater? Couldn't see that one. "That's nice."

He narrowed his eyes at me. "She misses you."

I tightened my grip on Van's arm, and didn't miss his glance at me. "Well, she's the one who appears to have moved out. I'm home every night."

"Go out to lunch with her. She needs you."

I felt my throat tighten, and I focused on the elevator buttons. Hard. "I wouldn't know where to reach her."

"Leave her a note. She goes home during the day when you're not there."

I knew she did. I'd seen evidence of her existence in the toothpaste being moved and the dishes in the kitchen sink. "She could leave me one."

"She thinks you hate her."

I looked at Blaine. "Why would I hate her?"

"Because she's dating me."

Van looked at me sharply, and I didn't let go of his arm. *Great*. So now Van would think I was in love with Blaine, in addition to Noah and Max. "I don't care who she dates."

Blaine raised an eyebrow. "Then you need to tell her that."

I scowled at Blaine. How come he was suddenly the expert on my best friend? They'd been dating for what? Twenty minutes?

He held up his hands. "Do what you want." The elevator doors opened and he stepped out. "Nice to see you, Van."

Van returned the greeting in a far more pleasant manner than I was in the mood for, seeing as how I was still smarting over the fact that Blaine purported to know Emma better than I did. And that I wanted him to be right, that she missed me and we could be friends again.

Van and I walked outside, and I only sort of noticed that the sun was setting and it was a beautiful evening.

"So isn't Blaine the guy you were trying to impress the night you went to that bar? Wearing that shirt?"

"How come you remember things I would prefer to forget?"

He grinned. "I'm a crime fighter. It's my job to remember details."

A laugh worked its way past my bad mood, and I smiled back at him. "It's really inconvenient."

"So am I right?"

I stuck my tongue out at him—yes, I'm mature—and said, "I was trying to woo him so he wouldn't steal my secretary time. I figured if I showed a little skin, he'd start ogling me and I could threaten him into submission." *Yikes.* Had I actually said that aloud?

He laughed. "Didn't work quite the way you planned?"

I rolled my eyes and felt my tension start to dissipate. "Actually, my roommate started sleeping with him. Seeing him in his skivvies at two in the morning wasn't all that conducive to improving our working relationship." I shivered when I remembered the full-frontal incident. "He actually saw me completely naked the first night, when I didn't realize he was there. How am I supposed to work with him now? It's horrible." Van was laughing hard, so I elbowed him. "It's not funny. Every time I see him, all I can think about is that he's seen me naked. How am I supposed to get him to take me seriously?"

"Well, you saw him in his underwear, didn't you? Shouldn't he be the one who's embarrassed?"

I rolled my eyes again. "Men pride themselves on moments like that. Exposing themselves to a woman? A sign of masculinity. I'm sure he told all his little cronies how he'd gotten caught bare chested."

He rubbed his chin and made a pretense of considering my thoughts. "Let's see. If I were working with a woman and she caught me with my pants down . . . I might be a little embarrassed."

"Might?"

He grinned. "Or I might wonder if she thought I was hot."

I groaned. "See? It's so unfair that guys can think like that."

He laughed and slung his arm over my shoulder in a companionable way. "I'm just kidding. I'd be mortally embarrassed and never be able to show my face again. I can't believe how tough you are to show up at work every day."

I eyed him. "I hate sarcasm."

He widened his eyes like an innocent kid. "No sarcasm. I think you're impressive."

I decided to believe him. Not because I actually thought he was telling the truth, but because I needed to hear that.

The rest of the walk to the North End passed quickly. Van had me laughing almost the whole time with his cheerful jokes and good-natured teasing. I realized it had been a while since I'd been around someone who was just having a good time. Except Emma, but I hadn't been around her much lately, had I?

It wasn't until we sat down at dinner that Van changed the direction of the conversation. "Mind if I ask you a personal question?"

"Probably. But go ahead." I picked a piece of salami off the antipasto salad and tried it. Tasted like salami.

"You haven't seemed like your normal self lately. Want to talk about it?"

I rolled my eyes. "Trust me. You don't want to know."

"Sure I do."

"It'll depress you. And me. I get very cranky when I start expounding on the miseries of my life. And then I'll be in a bad mood for the rest of the night and ruin the evening. And since I'm still trying to get you to forgive me for blowing you off, I don't want to screw it up by being moody."

He studied me for a moment, and I could see him contemplating his response. For some reason I was intrigued, and I leaned forward while I waited for his answer.

"Tell you what."

I grinned, even though I didn't know what he was going to say. "What?"

"I'll give you thirteen minutes to sound off about everything that's bugging you. Then I'll put it all in perspective for you. And then we can't talk about any of it for the rest of the night, and I'll put you in a good mood."

I love a man who takes charge. Random thought. "How are you going to put me in a good mood? I'm pretty intractable once I get committed to being miserable."

He gave me a disdainful look that had me laughing. "I'm

214

insulted by your doubt of my abilities." He punched the buttons on his watch. "The clock is ticking. Start talking. You now have twelve minutes and forty-seven seconds."

"You asked for it." I grinned. "Okay, you know about Blaine. Well, Emma now hates me and we aren't talking. My other two best friends, who are married and engaged respectively, told me they're having an affair. My parents pretend I died so they don't have to acknowledge my failures to their friends. An attorney at work wants me to go to law school so I can be a lawyer there. I'm tempted, but I also hate lawyers and the legal profession, and I don't want to do anything to make my parents happy. Oh, and I have to host a baby shower for my brother's pregnant girlfriend this weekend. And then my sister's getting married in a few weeks to her overachieving, perfect fiancé. So I'm the only one letting my family down, and I might even get fired. Did I mention that? I'm on probation." I paused. "Oh, and I broke up with Max permanently—but that's good—and Noah dumped me because he values my parents' loyalty too much to risk losing it by dating me. Oh, and my birthday's coming up and I haven't accomplished anything that I wanted to by the time I turned twenty-five." I frowned. "I think that's the big stuff."

"You weren't kidding. That's a load."

"I know. No wonder I'm sleeping with random men and alienating my friends and on the verge of losing my job." I felt surprisingly relaxed, given that I'd just laid my guts out on the table. It was great to be able to tell Van everything and not worry. He didn't know my family or my friends or anyone at work, so I could be totally honest with him.

"Okay, ready for my spin?"

"Sure." I propped my chin on my hands and waited. "Lay it on me."

"Blaine? Not worth it."

I lifted a brow. "Well, I know that, but he still stole my best friend and my secretary."

"Doesn't matter. He'll pass out of your life shortly and be nothing but a bad memory."

"Are you going to kill him for me?"

"I could have it arranged. Want me to take care of it?"

His face was so deadpan, I wasn't sure if he was serious. "Um . . . Emma might be mad if I had her boyfriend killed."

"Let me know if you change your mind."

"I will." I tipped my head. "Are you serious?"

He changed the subject. "So you still care about Emma?"

"Well, of course. I—"

He handed me his cell phone. "Call her."

"No."

"Leave her a message on your machine at home. She'll check it."

"I can't. She wronged me."

He lifted a brow. "So?"

"So she should apologize first."

"Get over it."

I frowned. "Get over what?"

"That attitude. If you want to be friends with her, call her. If you don't call her, then stop worrying about it."

"So that's your spin? Deal with it or get over it?"

"Yep." He rubbed his jaw. "So, the work thing and the lawyer thing. Forget your parents and do what you want."

I started laughing. "You make it sound so easy."

"It is easy."

"Oh, yeah? If it's so easy, how do I make my parents proud of me without doing what they want?" I was still laughing. He was being so black-and-white that it was ridiculous.

"Be proud of yourself. They'll catch on."

I rolled my eyes. "You're such a guy."

He didn't look offended. "How?"

"Trying to solve a woman's problems. Thinking that it's as simple as mind over matter, when it's not. Life is more complicated than that."

"Only if you make it more complicated."

"It *is* more complicated."

"Is it?" He sat up and leaned toward me. "See, you're a typical woman."

"I'm going to be offended by this, aren't I?"

He paused. "Maybe."

I laughed again. How ridiculous was this discussion? At the same time, I totally wanted to know what he was going to say. "Appreciate the honesty. Why am I a typical woman?"

"Because you overemotionalize everything instead of dealing with it. You miss Emma, so call her. You miss your adulterating friends; call them. You want to be a lawyer; do it. You don't want to be a lawyer; don't." He shrugged. "If you sit here and get all worked up, then you're miserable and the problem doesn't go away."

I had a suspicion there was some element of wisdom in his advice, but I wasn't in the mood to hear it. "What about the fact that I don't know whether I want to be a lawyer? What's your answer to making that one simple?"

He rubbed his chin and looked thoughtful. "Have you made a list?"

"Of the pros and cons? Yep." I grinned, waiting for him to come up with something. I was pretty sure I had him stumped.

"How much do you like your current job?"

"Not much."

"Then what do you have to lose? Go to school. You can always quit."

Damn. "How do you do that?"

"Do what?"

"Make everything sound simple. Because it isn't."

"So you're saying I'm wrong?"

"Absolutely."

"But you're smiling."

I immediately frowned. "So?"

"So, you said that you couldn't tell me what was wrong without it ruining the evening. Well, you're smiling, and your eyes are even laughing."

Was I? "Wow. I'm having fun. First time in a while. How'd you do that?"

He shrugged, but he was sporting that look of smug male satisfaction. "I have a way with the ladies."

"Oh, shut up." I threw an ice cube at him, which ricocheted off his shoulder and landed in the salad of the woman at the next table. When the woman spun around, searching the restaurant, I dove into my salad and tried to smother my giggling. I glanced up to see Van calmly eating his minestrone soup and not looking at all guilty. Unlike me. Of course, I was the one who'd thrown it.

He caught my eye and winked.

I grinned. "Tell me about you. I don't know anything about your life except that you put up with me and that you work at my building. Where do you live? How do you occupy your time when you're not in the lobby?"

He took a spoonful of soup and studied me. Finally he swallowed. "Can't tell you."

"Why not?" That was annoying. I wanted to know about him.

"You won't like me if you know."

"I'm totally offended. I'm not the kind of person to judge."

"You'd judge me."

Well, if that didn't drum up the curiosity. "Are you a male prostitute? Because that's okay. It's lucrative."

He grinned. "Can't tell you."

"Are you a stripper?" I gave him the once-over. "Looks like you have the body for it."

His cheeks turned slightly pink. "Can't tell you."

"So you are a stripper?"

"Can't tell you." He shot me a look. "Why would you think I'm a stripper?"

"Because you got embarrassed when I mentioned it. It's okay. Can I come see you strip? Where do you work?" Van was cute, and pretty built, but I'd never actually considered him to be a male sex symbol. "Will you give me a private show?"

He grinned. "See? That's why I don't like to tell women. Everyone wants a private show."

"So it's true? You're a stripper?" This was certainly interesting. Never met a stripper before. Can you imagine if I took him home to meet my family? Security guard/stripper. Not that I'd ever expose him to my family. I liked him too much to torture him like that. "Do you make good money?"

He was laughing now. "Shannon, I'm not going to tell you, so give it up."

I folded my arms across my chest and pouted. "You know everything about me, and you won't tell me anything?" I knew he wasn't a stripper. Yeah, he was kind of hot and everything, but he didn't have the stripper aura. Besides, he worked the night shift at my building—that wouldn't have been practical for a stripper, right? Apparently he did have a secret, though, and I wanted to know what it was. "Come on, give it up Van."

"Fine. I live in Brookline."

"Where?"

"You're a pain in the butt."

"And you love it." I fished a receipt out of my purse and handed it to him, along with a pen. "Write down your phone number."

He lifted a brow. "Why?"

"So I can call you."

"Why are you going to call me?"

"So I can harass you into revealing your innermost secrets to me. And write your address down so I can stalk you too. Payback for being evasive."

He laughed. "I've always wanted to be stalked by a woman who wears obscene tank tops." He ducked out of range of a flying sugar packet as he jotted down the info, then handed it across the table. Or rather, he tore half of it off, and kept part of the receipt for himself. "What's your number and address?"

"Are you going to stalk me?"

"No. I want to be able to give the information to the police when I have them arrest you."

"Oh, well, that's good. I imagine there are lots of attractive cops that I could fall in love with, sleep with, and then get dumped by. Great idea." I rattled off my info, watching him jot it down.

Van finished writing, then stuffed the receipt in his wallet. "You need some serious therapy."

"Really?" I should probably have been offended, but the way he said it was nice and supportive, not condescending. "Why?"

"Because you're so hard on yourself. So you made a mistake with Noah? That happens. Doesn't make you a slut or pathetic or anything like that. It makes you human."

Something pinged in my heart, but I shoved it aside. "I was kidding about sleeping with the cops."

"Sort of."

I pursed my lips. He was right. I'd been half serious. "So?"

"So lighten up. You're cute, you're funny, and you're smart, and things are going to work out fine for you."

Van thought I was cute? And funny? And smart? I was quite sure there was no one on the planet who'd agree with him. "Will you marry me?"

He grinned. "No."

"Damn. I really need a mate who will feed me those lines and make me feel better."

"Now that you have my phone number, you can call me whenever you need to. I'll be happy to feed your ego."

I tilted my head. "Seriously?"

"Yep. Call me whenever."

"Maybe I will."

Van studied me thoughtfully for a moment. "Some friends of mine are meeting up later tonight. Want to come?"

221

Victory! I had a new group of friends! But I was also a little annoyed. I was having such a good time with Van, I wasn't in the mood to share him. But what if his girlfriend was one of the ones we were meeting up with? Then I had no right to claim him. Not that I did anyway, but I'd have even less right if he was taken. "Do you have a girlfriend?"

He looked surprised. "You already asked me that a couple weeks ago."

"Well, I didn't know if things had changed."

"No." He looked at me so probingly that I focused my gaze on my straw. "Why do you care?"

"I didn't know if you were supposed to meet up with her tonight. I wouldn't want to interfere, you know?"

"I think I'm capable of managing my personal life."

"I'm sure you are." I felt so stupid. "It's not because I want you for my boyfriend, if that's what you're thinking."

"No, I wasn't thinking that."

"Well, good. Because we're friends. And you already told me you didn't want to date me because I was a relationship disaster." It was good to have this discussion. It got everything out in the open. I felt so much better now. *Grr.*

He smiled. "I wouldn't call you a disaster."

"No?" Something caught in my chest. "So you wouldn't be averse to dating me?" *Dammit, Shannon!* Where had that come from? Made me sound like I wanted to date him. "Not that I want to date you. I just . . . well . . . you're the first person to make me feel good in a while, so of course I would want more of that. And you're pretty attractive and stuff, but I need a friend now, not a boyfriend, and besides, you keep secrets from me, so I couldn't date you anyway, and—"

Van put his hand on my arm. "Shannon."

"What?" I stared at his hand.

"Take a deep breath."

Might as well humor him, seeing as how I'd already made a total idiot of myself. I took a deep breath.

"Let's not go out with my friends tonight."

Dammit. I'd screwed up. He was embarrassed to admit he knew me. "I promise I won't attack you."

He laughed and rubbed my arm. "I just realized that my friends might reveal my secret, so it would be best not to have you mingle with them."

Wow. He really did have something he wanted to hide. "Are you married?"

"No."

I frowned. "An escaped criminal living under an alter ego?"

"No. But you have a good imagination."

"So what's so bad that you won't tell me?" I scowled at him. It wasn't fair. He knew all my secrets, and I felt connected to him, but it was a one-way connection. That was why I couldn't date him. What kind of relationship would that be?

"Let it go." His tone was soft, but firm. He wasn't going to discuss it. "How about the movies? Anything you want to see?"

"With you? Tonight?" At his nod, I shrugged. "Sure. As friends."

"As friends."

CHAPTER SIXTEEN

I was still in a brilliant mood when Van dropped me off at my apartment. The movie had been good, we'd gone for dessert afterward, and then he'd walked me home. We hadn't discussed anything else serious, but had had fun. Plain old fun, with no baggage or issues.

Did I need that or what? Van was my new best friend. Loved him!

I discovered Emma sitting at the kitchen table in the dark. Her feet were curled up under her, and she was eating chocolate ice cream out of the container.

"Emma?" My heart leaped at the sight of her.

She ignored me, and my heart fell again.

Fine.

I ignored her right back and helped myself to a glass of water. I made it as far as the hallway; then I turned back and looked at her. She was still sitting there. "Em? Is something wrong?"

"I'm moving out."

I tightened my lips. "Are you moving in with Blaine?"

"Yes."

I took a deep breath. "Are you sure that's the right thing to do? I mean, you barely know him."

She said nothing.

Dammit. I couldn't walk away. I marched back into the kitchen and sat down across from her. "I miss you."

She looked up immediately, but it was too dark to see her eyes. "You do?"

"Of course I do. You're my best friend." I wasn't going to apologize, though. She still owed me an apology for dating Blaine.

She pushed the ice cream across the table. "Want some?"

I grabbed a spoon and dug in.

We ate in silence for a while. Finally I said, "Noah dumped me."

She made a sympathetic noise. "Why?"

"Didn't want my parents to hate him."

"Bastard."

"Yeah." I sighed. "I think I still have a crush on him."

"Of course you do. Just because he acted like a jerk isn't enough to make twenty years of adoration fade."

I couldn't even explain how good it felt to be talking to Emma. She knew me, really knew me and all my baggage. "What do I do?"

"You want him?"

I sucked some ice cream off my spoon. "Well, I hadn't really thought about it. I'd been trying to forget about him. He's a jerk."

"No, he's not."

I sighed. "I know." I'd known Noah for twenty years, and he wasn't a jerk.

"He's confused." Emma tapped the spoon on her nose. "You should make him jealous."

"I'm not going to play games with him. That's one reason why I like him. Because there are no games." What would happen if I showed up with Van at Lindsay's rehearsal dinner? Would that make a difference?

"Talk to your mom. If she's cool with it, then maybe Noah will chill."

I stirred the ice cream so it started to melt. "But do I want a guy who isn't willing to take the heat for me? Who I have to convince?"

"Sometimes relationships are complicated."

I looked up at that comment, then flipped on the light so I could see her face. "What's going on with you? Is everything okay with Blaine?"

"Sure." She sighed. "I just never thought I'd be moving in with a guy this soon, you know? I mean, I'm all about my freedom."

And then some. "Does he want you to get a steady job?"

"No, he doesn't care."

"So that's good. He has to like you the way you are." It simply amazed me that Blaine and Emma were a couple. Could they get any more opposite? I cleared my throat. "You know, you don't have to move in with him. I like having you for a roomie."

"But Dave wanted to move in with you."

Ah, yes, Dave. "If he moved in with me, his wife would think I was having an affair with him and she'd take out a hit on me. Not interested."

Emma smiled. "That's probably true. She was always jealous of you." She snorted. "Guess she was barking up the wrong tree, huh? You weren't the one to sweep Dave away from his true love."

I frowned. I hadn't thought of it that way. Dave and I had been best friends forever. Why *wasn't* I the one to capture his heart? I could have fallen in love with him quite easily, if he'd given me any signals.

"You think Phoebe and Dave will work out? Seems like a weird way to start." Emma looked thoughtful for a moment, then shook her head before continuing. "I'd never date someone who was taken. How would you know he wouldn't do it to you? No way. They have to be single through and through."

Van flashed through my mind, and his comment that he'd never date me. Probably a good idea, seeing as how I still had a foot in Noah's direction and a dagger in Blaine's direction. At least there wasn't anything going in Max's direction anymore, so that was a start.

"Have you talked to them lately?" Emma asked.

"Who? Phoebe and Dave?" That would be an emphatic no. "No."

"Wonder if they've told Yvonne and Zach yet." She grabbed the phone off the wall. "Let's call them."

I took the phone. "Hang on."

"What?"

"Are we good again?"

She paused, then shrugged. "Are we?"

"I was really upset about Blaine." I held up my hand to stop her before she interjected. "Not because I wanted him for myself, though I did realize that he'd help my standing with my family. But because I really don't get along with him, and I was having trouble with him at work. Having him date you would make work come home in a way I didn't want. I felt you put him in front of our friendship, and that hurt. Especially given how you go through guys so quickly. You'd date him, then dump him, and then it would be even more difficult for me."

Emma's face was tight. "You don't have a right to claim certain guys as off-limits."

"I know." I shook my head. "Forget it." *See, Van? It didn't work to talk to her. She didn't understand.*

"I'm not going to dump him. I'm moving in with him."

"I know." I gritted my teeth. Two choices. Fight it out to no resolution, or accept that Emma couldn't acknowledge the effect her decision had on me, and move on. "And I'm happy for you. I want you to be happy."

She narrowed her eyes. "Seriously?"

"Of course. Why wouldn't I want you to be happy?"

"I don't know. Because you think I'm selfish."

True. But what would it solve? I was tired of fighting. "Doesn't matter. You're my friend, and if Blaine makes you happy, fine. Move in with him, and promise me you'll still go to dinner with me on occasion."

She chewed her lower lip. "Of course I'll go to dinner with you."

"Good." I hesitated. "Girls' night?"

"You mean, will I leave Blaine at home sometimes?"

I grimaced. "Yes."

She was quiet for a moment. "I guess that would be fair." *Phew.* I was sure I'd screwed it up.

"But I'd rather bring him along."

Elation vamoosed. "Emma . . ."

"We'll just have to hook you back up with Noah so we

can double-date." She held up her hand to silence me. "You'll like Blaine when you get to know him, but I won't do a threesome. Blaine and Noah got along over breakfast that morning. Why wouldn't they? They're both lawyers, dating best friends. Lots in common."

I grinned. "It's good to have you back."

She smiled. "Isn't April's baby shower this weekend?"

"Yes, why? Are you coming?"

"Of course!" She sat up, her eyes sparkling. "At the party, we'll corner your mom and challenge her about you and Noah dating. Guaranteed she'll flip out with glee at the thought of you and Noah as a couple. She'll probably dial up his cell from the party to tell him to take you out."

I sucked a glob of ice cream off my spoon, a flitter of excitement in my chest. "The idea has merit. . . ."

"Of course it does!"

"But I don't want to get my hopes up." I definitely didn't relish the thought of being dumped by Noah again. Once was plenty.

"Then don't get them up."

I rolled my eyes. "You sound like Van. It's all mind over matter."

"Van? The security guy?"

"Uh-huh. I went out with him tonight."

"Oh, *really?*" Emma leaned forward. "Do tell."

"It's not like that. We're just friends."

"He's a cutie."

"Yeah." I took another scoop of ice cream. "But we've already discussed it. Friends only. Neither of us has any interest in the other on a romantic level. But I'm hoping to meet some of his friends." I recalled our friend discussion.

"He has some secret, though, and he's afraid his friends will reveal it, so I'm banned from meeting them for now."

"A secret, huh? Like maybe he has a huge crush on you?"

"Actually, I think he's a stripper." Well, not really, but it sounded rather exciting, didn't it?

Emma's eyes widened. "Really? Cool."

I nodded. "The antithesis of a lawyer, huh? No wonder I like him."

Emma tilted her head. "Maybe you should date him. Maybe you need a guy who is the opposite of everything your family wants. Something totally in another realm, so you can live for yourself."

"No way. I'm not dating Van."

"Why not?"

"Well . . ." I couldn't think of anything right at that moment. "Because we're going after the Noah thing this weekend."

Emma nodded. "No reason you can't foster two relationships. Keeps your options open."

"No way."

"There's no problem with dating two people at the early stages. It's quite healthy, actually. Takes the pressure off each relationship."

"So are you dating anyone besides Blaine?"

Emma's eyes widened. "No. Can you believe it? I've been monogamous for almost three weeks. It's the weirdest thing ever." Then she grinned. "And the greatest thing ever. I'm in love."

"You're seriously in love? Like really in love? Love with a capital L?"

She nodded. "Pretty unreal, huh?"

Wow. I leaned back in my chair. "That's awesome."

"I think you mean that."

I flinched at the surprise on her face. "Emma, I'm glad you're in love. I'll figure out how to stand him."

"Once you start dating Noah, you'll be good." She pointed her spoon at me. "No more snide remarks about the man I love, though."

"I'll try. Old habits die hard, though."

She nodded. "As long as you try."

"Are you still going to move out?"

Her grin faded. "Yes. August first. But I'll keep paying rent until you find another roommate."

Three and a half weeks left with my best friend. That sucked. I'd dated Max for two years and never felt the need to move in. Why did Emma have to leave? Then again, a lot could happen in three and a half weeks. The flame of love might fade by then. No need to worry about it yet. *See, Van? I can shake it off.*

"So let's figure out the plan for the baby shower." Emma grabbed a paper and pen.

"Aren't you going to Blaine's tonight?"

"Not unless you want me to."

"No."

She nodded. "Then about the party . . ."

I admit it. I succumbed and used my McCormick family connections, and hosted the party at the Firway Club, courtesy of my mom's membership.

The Firway Club is a very old Boston women's club in the Back Bay. Only the elite women of Boston grace their hallowed halls, dining in their expensive restaurant and enjoying their special lectures and guests. Of course, now it's open to men, as all clubs are, but only two have joined.

It's a female haven frequented by all the big names on the corporate Boston front. Lots of deals get negotiated in those rooms, and special out-of-town CEOs are pampered in the six private suites for members' visitors.

The Firway Club represents everything about being a McCormick that I despise, but I decided to host the baby shower there for several reasons. First, the club took over the food, so I had minimal responsibility. Second, it was the type of place April and my mom would deem worthy.

Between you and me, I was pretty sure the founders of the Firway Club would turn over in their graves at the thought of their beautiful antiques hosting a baby shower for an out-of-wedlock baby, but hey, my mom wanted it there, so who was I to argue?

The baby shower day dawned sunny and bright—which wasn't quite enough to rid me of the gunky feeling in my stomach.

"Why did I agree to do this?" I set a giant bouquet of flowers on the coffee table in the lounge of the Firway Club.

"Because even though you purport to hate everything about your family, you want desperately to be accepted. So you hosted this party hoping that you could somehow work your way back into your mom's favor. Same reason you work at M and S. You hope that by being associated with a law firm, it'll be enough to gain your parents' respect, while still creating the façade that you are your own woman."

I scowled at Emma. "Remind me never to invite you to one of these things again."

She kissed my cheek. "You love me, and you missed having me around to tell you the truth. Someday you'll realize I'm right and listen to me."

"Or not."

Emma flopped down in an antique chair with velvet covering. "Guess what I did."

Something about the look in her eyes sent chills down my spine. "What?"

"Well, I've been to coed baby showers a few times. They're all the rage. So I invited the boys of the family to show up at four o'clock." She grinned. "Gives us three hours of girl time, and then the boys can come." She wiggled her eyebrows. "And guess who's coming?"

My heart lurched. "Noah?"

"Yep."

I sank down next to her, my knees suddenly quaky. "I don't want to see him. Our last interaction was so humiliating."

"After we work over your mom, we need to give her access to Noah. This thing needs to be straightened out immediately." She picked a piece of lint off her short black skirt that was almost acceptable by Firway Club standards. "And I'm doing this only for selfish reasons, so you have a honey and will double with Blaine and me, so don't think I like you or anything."

I was having too much difficulty breathing to respond to her wisecrack. Noah? Coming here? I felt a glimmer of hope in my belly, which I immediately banished. No way did I want to go through this again. "Emma, you have to cancel. I don't want to go through this."

Doubt flickered across her face. "But I thought you really cared about Noah."

"I do. I did. But I don't want to open that up again. He made his choice, and—"

"And you deserve to know whether it could really work. You have to know, so when you see Noah and his wife at McCormick family gatherings for the next sixty years, you're comfortable with the fact that it would never have worked for you. No room for doubt. You have to know whether he was using your family as an excuse or whether he's really not interested."

"No, I don't. I can assume it was the family thing and avoid taking the humiliation personally." I liked that plan much better than actually confirming that I was the cause of the rejection.

"Hello? Shannon? Are you here?"

My mom's voice carried from the foyer, and I stood up. "Emma, don't do this."

"Maybe." With that thoroughly unsatisfactory answer, she stood up to face my mom.

"Emma, so good to see you." My mom kissed Emma's cheek, then scanned my outfit. Her lips tightened in obvious dismay, but she said only, "You look nice, Shannon."

"Thanks." My stomach crunched into a knot as her disapproval wafted over me. She was wearing a cream-colored silk pantsuit. Her hair was styled precisely around her face, and her makeup was impeccable.

I'd been so happy with my blue sundress when I'd looked in the mirror this morning, but now I felt like a frump. Even my expensive new sandals didn't help me feel better.

"These flowers shouldn't be here. Let's move them." My mom dropped her Italian purse on the couch and relocated the bouquet I'd just set on the table. "Shannon, why don't you go check with the kitchen and make sure the food is on time? You're good at that sort of thing."

Right. As long as it didn't require taste, I was competent. Plus it kept me in the back room, where I couldn't embarrass her. "Mom . . ." The front door slammed and I heard the buzz of more female voices. Too late.

I turned and walked to the kitchen, leaving Emma and my mom to welcome the guests.

An hour later I was feeling even worse. April and all her friends were the epitome of everything my mom wanted me to be: classy, professional, tittering at the right jokes, and generally being proper and correct.

Even though it was my show, I'd ended up losing my chair when I checked on the food, relegating me to a seat slightly outside the circle. No one even noticed I was back there.

I was a total outsider, and I hated it.

Even Van couldn't put a positive spin on this one. Actually, he probably could. If he were here, I'd most likely be laughing by now, about something that made me feel good.

Van. I need you.

I grabbed my purse and walked outside. Before I could think about it too much, I pulled out my cell phone and the receipt with his number on it and dialed. He answered on the second ring. "Hello?"

I had no idea what to say.

"Is anyone there?"

"Um . . . hi."

He hesitated. "Who is this?"

"Shannon."

"Shannon." He repeated my name softly. "What's wrong?"

"I need your spinning skills."

He chuckled, and it brought a small smile to my lips. "So you admit my talents, then?"

"Never." I leaned against the iron railing surrounding the flower beds in front of the Firway Club. "I'm merely trying to build up your fragile ego."

"Appreciate it. What's my task for today?"

I sighed. "I'm at this baby shower for my brother's girl-friend."

"And you wish you were pregnant with your brother's child?"

I laughed. "No."

"Good. I was going to have to refer you to a specialist if that was the problem."

"So you admit there are limits to your greatness?"

"I just don't want to get sued. No insurance for counseling on those kinds of issues."

"Ah. Smart businessman." I took a deep breath and noticed the flowers behind me smelled sort of nice.

"So what's the problem?"

I chewed my lower lip.

"Shannon?"

"I don't know how to explain it." I kicked a chunk of grass growing up between the cobblestones of the side-walk.

"Does it have anything to do with your parents pretending you're dead so you don't embarrass them?"

"Something like that." I gave the grass another good thwack, but it ignored me and continued its happy existence. "I just feel like such a loser, you know? Everyone here is a professional, and they're shutting me out. I could burst into flames and disintegrate and they wouldn't even notice." Stupid tears welled up in my eyes, and I levered off the gate to walk down the street. No need for anyone from the party to see me like this.

"Stop letting them treat you like that." His voice was soft, though, gentle.

"How?"

"Don't sit in the corner. Don't let them ignore you. Speak up. Add your opinion. Let them see your charming self."

"I'm not charming."

I felt his grin. "You can be if you want to be. You're also funny and interesting, and they'd be shocked if you actually let your personality out."

I rubbed my temple and wished my headache would go away. "So just go in there and pretend they like me?"

"Yep."

"Just like that."

"Yep."

I took a deep breath. "Not sure I can do it."

"What about the interns?"

"What about them?" I sat down on the steps of a nearby condo and wondered what it would be like to live on this street. Two-million-dollar two-bedroom condos.

"Some of them look down on you, right?"

Like Jessamee? "You could say that."

"And you ignore that. You're funny, outgoing, and you

rule the world. You demand respect from the interns and you get it."

Huh. I hadn't thought about it that way.

"How is this any different?"

"Because they're my family."

Van snorted. "Treat them like you treat your interns. Can't hurt to at least give it a try, can it?"

"I guess not." I could always have my little fantasies about them like I did at work—my cathartic release of socially unacceptable responses that kept me sane. I pictured my mom at gunpoint, being forced to wear dirty jeans, old tennis shoes, and a baggy T-shirt to work. Imagine how horrified she'd be! Damn, that would be funny. I giggled.

"I heard that," Van said. "Go do it, and call me later. Let me know how it goes."

"Okay." I stood up, feeling stronger. I could totally do this. There was room for April to hang out the window next to Blaine, wasn't there?

"I'll be going out soon, so take my cell number and call me on that."

I jotted down his number, then gave him mine at his request. "Van?"

"Yes?"

"Thanks."

"No problem. I'm glad you called. Good luck."

Still smiling, I hung up, and spent the entire way back fantasizing about various ways to humiliate everyone in the room. By the time I returned, I was relaxed, amused, and feeling quite sorry for all of the guests. Little did they know what horrible plights I had in store for them.

CHAPTER SEVENTEEN

The sight of the tight circle nearly killed my resolve. Then I imagined all of those beautiful women with horrible dye jobs, and I smiled. I grabbed my basket of baby shower games, pulled a chair up, forced my way between two women who worked with April, and announced my arrival. "Okay, time for games."

The entire group fell silent and stared at me. I pictured Jessamee's head on everyone's neck, and knew I could dominate. "The boys will be coming later, so this is part one."

I held up a sheet of paper. "I have a list of questions for April. Then, when Travis comes later, we'll ask him the same questions and compare answers. See how compatible they'll be in setting rules in the household." I handed out pens and paper to everyone. "I'll ask the first few questions, and then everyone will have to write down a question and ask it. The more embarrassing, the better."

I ignored the shocked look on my mom's face, and read the first question. "April, when you and Travis want to get intimate, will you lock your bedroom door so your kids don't walk in, or will you wait for times when they are all out of the house?"

Her friends shrieked with laughter (yes, my chest swelled with pride), and April's mouth dropped open. My mom looked like she was going to pass out, but how did she think April had gotten pregnant? Emma grinned—that had been her question.

April collected herself. "Given how often we're home, I'd say we'll have to do the locked-door thing and take advantage of the moment. Otherwise we'll be down to once every six months."

The conversation then plunged into a discussion of what kids could do to a couple's sex life, and I grinned. This was going to be all right.

Next question: "How often will you and Travis have sex once you have the baby?"

Everyone burst into agitated discussion, shouting out answers that ranged from "never" to "There's already a baby, so there's no need for sex anymore!" April conjectured once a week, and the crowd immediately set about correcting her naïveté.

I grinned at Emma, and she smiled back. Van was my guardian angel, and as soon as this party was over, I was going to tell him that. Repeatedly.

By the time the boys arrived, the party was rocking. The conversation had deviated into the mothers telling stories of their pregnancies and births, trying to torture poor April. The laugher was contagious, and I was even caught up in it.

And then I saw Noah, and my world froze.

He was wearing beige slacks and a polo. Clean shaven

with a hint of a tan—no doubt from the golf course—he was totally hot. He caught my eye over the crowd, and nodded at me.

I nodded back. Well, that was a good start, wasn't it? He hadn't totally avoided me.

Emma elbowed me, and I followed her glance. Ray was scowling at Noah, and my mom was watching Ray, her eyes sharp. "I don't think we'll have to say anything," Emma whispered. "Go talk to Noah, and that'll be enough to set things off. Your mom is already onto something."

"I can't go talk to Noah," I hissed. "He ditched me, remember?"

"Keep it casual. Make him wonder what you're thinking. Guys are so easy to manipulate." She cocked her eyebrow. "How do you think I got Blaine? By making him wonder whether I liked him. I certainly didn't slobber over him like all the other women do." She nudged me. "Go do it."

I watched Noah lurk in the corner, looking uncomfortable. I thought of our night together, and how I'd liked him for the last twenty years. This was Noah. A good person. He was worth another try, wasn't he? Nothing that risked my pride of course, but I could put out a feeler.

I stood up and clenched my fist. *I can do this.* I stepped over the pile of baby presents and walked over to him. He watched me approach and didn't look away. Just kept his gaze anchored to my face.

Damn. I really wished I could read minds.

I stopped in front of him. "Hi."

"You look nice."

Knock me down with a two-by-four. "What?"

He touched my hair. "I like your hair down."

241

My heart started racing, and I took a step back. "I thought we weren't taking this thing forward."

He tightened his lips. "Right. We're not."

I didn't believe him. Not for a second. He was having second thoughts! God, I wished I could call Van and ask him what to do. Then I frowned. Somehow I didn't think this was something to ask Van about. I had to figure this one out on my own. "What if my family were okay with us dating?"

His gaze was locked on my face. "Did you talk to them?"

"No. But I could." I corrected myself. "We could."

He looked at my lips. "What are you doing tonight?"

"Nothing."

"Let's go out."

Yes. I ordered my hormones to the corner for a time out. "No. I can't do that again. I had an incredible time with you, but I'm not going to put myself out there again until and unless you're willing to see it through." *What are you saying?* my subconscious was screaming at me, but I dug my fingernails into my palms and refused to concede. No way was I going to let him make me feel like dirt again. I pictured him old and gray with another woman on his arm, and knew I had to stay in control.

He took my hand. "I'm sorry, Shannon. I panicked when Ray got hostile with me."

My hand tightened around his despite my orders to the contrary. "It's not enough, Noah. I deserve better."

"I know."

"Hey." Ray stuck his head between us. "What the hell's going on?"

Noah dropped my hand like he'd been burned. "Nothing."

Ray glowered at Noah. "I thought we talked about this."

"We were just chatting. Same as we always do."

Wimp.

My mom appeared on my left side. "What's going on over here?"

I looked at Noah, but he wouldn't meet my gaze anymore. "Nothing, apparently." I took my hand and my pride off to the kitchen and left Noah to fight the battle on his own. I hoped he felt the brunt of my family's anger for once. Wouldn't it be nice for someone else to know what it felt like to be told they were a disappointment?

I glared at the world and marched into the kitchen to check on dessert. That was what I was good at, managing events. That was where I fit. I wasn't even good enough for a family friend to date. I stopped in the doorway to see April sitting at the table crying.

Crying.

Oh, shit.

I glanced over my shoulder at the door that had just swung shut behind me. "I'll get Travis."

"No!" Her head snapped up. "Don't!"

"Um . . . okay." I had no idea what to do. "So I'll leave you alone then."

"Will you stay for a minute?"

Crap. I had no idea how to deal with a hormonal pregnant woman. Especially one who made me feel completely inferior. Then I thought of her reaction to my embarrassing questions at the party. She was at least partly human.

I inched my way across the kitchen and sat down across from her. "Can I get you some water or something?"

She shook her head and blew her nose into a beautiful linen napkin.

"Okay." I looked around the kitchen and tried to think of something to say. "So, the party's going well."

A fresh wail erupted. What was up with April making that kind of noise? I looked toward the door, hoping someone would hear her and rush in to save the animal that was being tortured.

No one arrived. I was on my own.

I reached out and patted her arm. "Um . . . something wrong at work?"

She dragged her head off her arms and looked at me. *Yikes.* Someone needed to be told about waterproof mascara.

"Why won't he marry me?"

Okay, it's totally clichéd, but my mouth actually dropped open. "Travis?"

"Of course, Travis. Who else?"

I decided to forgive the sarcasm, given the nature of our discussion. "I thought you guys didn't want to get married."

"Shannon!" Another wail. The woman had lungs. "I'm going to have a baby and not be married to the father! I love Travis, and he doesn't want to marry me!"

I handed her a paper towel and decided I hated my brother. "You asked him to get married?"

"Of course!" April blew her nose on the paper towel, missing my subtle wiping under my eyes. She looked like a raccoon who'd been punched in the eye. "He isn't ready to commit."

"But he's ready to be a father?"

"No!" She burst into fresh tears. "He doesn't even want the baby. But he loves me, so he's sticking around. I keep thinking that when I have the baby, he'll fall in love with it. But what if he doesn't? What if I end being thirty-one with no husband and an absentee father for my baby? And what if Travis leaves me? I love Travis and I don't want to lose him!"

Well, damn. And I thought my life sucked. "You think talking to him will help? Does he understand how much this means to you?"

"If he doesn't, he's got his head up his ass."

I smiled. "Well, it *is* Travis we're talking about."

April shook her head and looked at me. "What am I going to do, Shannon? Your mom gives me these looks like I'm a total embarrassment to the family because of this whole baby thing. I know that's why she asked you to do the shower. Do you see any of her friends here? None of them. Because she's embarrassed."

Holy cow. I couldn't believe what I was hearing. "April, my mom adores you. She'd trade me for you in a heartbeat."

"Yeah, sure, before I got pregnant."

The least she could have done was deny it.

April looked at me. "But now I'm like you."

So nice to know my ostracism was obvious to everyone.

"Except it's worse because I'm not actually related to your family."

I struggled to stay positive and not smack her face into the cheesecake and walk out. "On the other hand, perhaps that's a good thing. I think there's more room for flexibility if you don't actually have the McCormick name."

When April burst into tears, I realized that might not have been the best thing to say, given how badly she wanted the McCormick name.

"Listen, April, maybe you need to sit down with Travis and really talk to him." I debated how much to say, but hey, she had no qualms about admitting I was a freak, so why should I hold back? If she wanted to marry Travis, then that would make her family, and as family, I was morally obligated to be honest. "Maybe he thinks you don't want to get married. I always assumed you were so into your career that you didn't want to get married or have kids."

April wiped her eyes—much better—and sniffled. "Well, I didn't want to get married or have kids, but now that I'm pregnant, I've changed my mind." She looked at the black mascara all over the napkin, then started scrubbing frantically at her face.

"So you need to make that very clear to Travis."

"I did."

"Then tell him again." I thought of Van, and his advice to just deal with it or move on. "Tell him that he has to marry you. Period."

April shook her head. "You're so naïve, Shannon. I don't want to force someone into marrying me."

Naïve? How was I naïve? I was trying to be helpful. "Travis is probably scared and he needs a kick in the pants." *Hmm . . .* Who did that sound like? *Anyone seen Noah lately?* "And don't worry about my mom. Her approval is overrated anyway."

April finished wiping her face—I'd still recommend a repair trip to the bathroom—and looked at me. "I thought you hated the fact that your mom and dad are embarrassed about your career. I thought you really wanted their approval."

I frowned. That little notion was getting bandied about with increasing frequency these days. Perhaps it was time to do a little self-evaluation. But now was not the time to admit weakness. "So what are you going to do?"

"Cry."

I almost laughed. Who would have thought that little Miss Arrogant would be reduced to a sniveling lump of patheticness? If I didn't feel so bad for her, I'd be enjoying it. As it was, it merely served as more reason for me to hate my parents and their stupid standards, which they'd obviously passed on to their sons. "Well, may I suggest that when you finish crying, you make a stop in the ladies' room to tidy up?"

She put her hands to her face. "Do I look that bad?"

"You look like you've been crying."

She cursed—another surprise—and stood up. "I can't let anyone know I've been crying. You won't tell anyone, will you?"

"I could talk to my mom and Travis if you want. . . ."

"No!" She lowered her voice. "No."

Fine. I was just trying to be helpful.

Two members of the serving staff walked into the kitchen with loads of dirty dishes, and April took that as her cue to bail. I hadn't even stood up to inspect the preparation of the cheesecake when my mom walked into the kitchen. "Shannon."

I looked up to see my mom and Ray standing in the door. *Shit.* "What?"

"Leave Noah alone." Disgust dripped from Ray's words.

Oh, so that's how it was? I was stalking Noah? "Shut up, Ray."

"No, you listen to me. You're putting Noah in a difficult position by pressuring him for this relationship. He values his relationship with the family, and you can't use your crush on him to drive him away. Eventually he'll start to avoid you and skip family gatherings and we'll all lose out."

My mom had her arms folded across her chest, and she was letting Ray talk.

"Is that what Noah said?" I couldn't believe it. It was one thing to be a wimp, but to have him say that kind of thing about me? It made no sense.

"He didn't have to," Ray snapped. "It was obvious how uncomfortable he was coming here today, and then you walked right up to him."

My mom was still silent.

I clenched my fists and glared at Ray. Forget Noah. If he couldn't protect me, I sure wasn't going to protect him. "Maybe the reason he was uncomfortable coming here today is because he slept with me last week, then dumped me on my butt, and he was worried that I might have told someone about how he treated me."

My mom looked shocked, and even Ray was stunned into silence.

"Yes, that's right. Noah and I slept together, and it wasn't me attacking him. It was a two-way endeavor, and if you dare to hold me solely responsible for it, then I'll . . ." I couldn't think of a good threat, other than to say that I'd never attend another family function again, but they'd be thrilled, so it was hardly a good threat.

"Noah slept with you?" Ray's voice was so tight I wondered if his vocal cords would snap.

"Yes, before you and he discussed it. It was already a done deal, and it was because you freaked on him that he blew me off."

Ray cursed, and I echoed the sentiment.

I kept on going. "I appreciate that you like Noah, but just once can't you put me, a blood relative, before all this other crap? Why can't you be upset that Noah took advantage of your sister instead of thinking I seduced Noah?"

"Noah didn't take advantage of you. You said it was mutual." A muscle was twitching in Ray's cheek, and his eyes were flashing. Good thing he wasn't violent or I might be inching toward the pots to get myself a weapon to brain him when he came after me.

"So what? Any normal protective brother would still be responding irrationally and blindly defending his sister's honor." Yeah, in my dreams. My mom still hadn't responded. Perhaps she was going into shock. That would be interesting.

"I gotta get out of here." Ray turned and walked out, leaving me and my mom alone together.

I did a quick check to make sure she didn't have any knives or other weapons within reach. All clear.

A noise from behind me reminded me that the serving staff was still in the room. *Great.* So glad to be humiliated in front of a crowd.

"Shannon, we need to talk."

"Not now. I have a party to run." If I took one minute of grief from my mom, I'd turn on her for making April feel bad. And since April wanted to be miserable alone, I should accommodate her. "Later." I shot a glance at the staff, knowing my mom would never want to air family embarrassments in public.

Her cheeks colored immediately, and her lips clamped shut.

Victory for Shannon. "You can call me later and berate me for being a slut."

"Shannon!" She looked almost faint. How dared I use that word in front of other people?

I walked out of the kitchen and wondered how I was going to make it through the rest of the party.

Noah was hovering by the kitchen door when I pushed open the swinging door.

I glared at him. "Get away from me."

"We need to talk." He grabbed my arm and hauled me around the corner into the coatroom. Seeing as how it was the middle of summer and sunny, we had it to ourselves. "What did you say to Ray in there? He came out of the kitchen looking like he was ready to kill me."

I sighed. This party was really going downhill. "I told him we slept together."

Noah made some noise like a drowning elephant. "Why?"

"Because he said I was stalking you and I needed to leave you alone. Apparently you did nothing to correct his interpretation of the situation, so I felt it was my duty." I folded my arms and dared him to mess with me.

"And your mom was in there?"

"Yep."

"What did she say?"

"Nothing. She's saving it for when we're in private later." As if I'd be answering that phone call.

Noah groaned and rubbed his hands over his eyes. Funny, but I wasn't feeling all that sympathetic to him at the moment. "I'll have to go talk to them," he said.

"And say what?" If he denied we had sex, I was going to see if Van was serious in his offer to have the men in my life killed.

"I don't know. Damage control."

"Are you going to tell them you're in love with me and you want to be with me and they'd better support it because you'll choose me over them if they don't?" Interesting. Not sure how that question came out. Didn't even realize it was forming in my brain. But now that it was out there, I was quite interested in the answer, even though I was willing to wager quite a bit that I could guess his response.

He stared at me.

I waited.

He stared.

Hmm . . . I waved my hand slowly across his face. Blank stare. I hadn't realized Noah was one of those men who was allergic to the word *love*. *Note to self: Next time I consider falling for a guy, ask him his opinion about the word* love.

He caught my wrist in his hand. Guess he was conscious after all.

"I'm not ready for that," he said.

"Me neither." I twisted my hand free, not really wanting to feel his touch at the moment. "However, I would be willing to tell my family to back off so we could have a chance to figure out what we want from each other."

"That's because—"

"Don't you dare say it's because my family doesn't like me already so I have nothing to lose, or I'll kick you in the nuts. I swear I will." Yes, I was such a charmer, wasn't I? Well, sorry, but I was about at the end of my coping capacity for the day.

"I wasn't going to say that."

"Then what were you going to say?"

He hesitated. "You're strong. You've been fighting the pressure of your family for your whole life. I'm not used to that."

Damn right I was strong. A force to be reckoned with. "Flattery will get you nowhere."

He stroked my cheek. "Give me a couple weeks to work on Ray and to talk to your parents."

A disobedient flutter jumped in my belly. How pathetic was I? One nice gesture and I was ready to forgive him. "I don't . . ."

He kissed me.

CHAPTER EIGHTEEN

His lips were soft and warm, his tongue demanding and hot. My traitorous body responded, and I pressed myself against him. All the same feelings as before erupted in my body: the longing for him, the years of adoration, the passion and heat. His arms crushed me against him, and my breasts pressed against his chest.

It felt like exactly where I belonged.

My eyes drifted shut as he trailed his lips over my neck, across my collarbone, and over my chest, pushing aside my neckline to access my breasts.

God, did he have my number or what?

His hands slid up under my dress and clamped onto my bottom, his thumb flicking under the strap of my thong. He made no pretense of trying to camouflage his interest in the situation, pressing the front of his pelvis into my stomach.

I felt cool air on my back and suddenly my breasts were almost exposed. My nipples cried out for his tongue, and were graciously rewarded.

"Good Lord! You guys need to get a room!"

I flung Noah off me to find Emma standing in the doorway, looking extremely amused. "Em!"

"What exactly do you think would have happened if your mom had walked in here?" Emma gestured to me. "I don't think she's as comfortable with your nakedness as I am, as your roommate and all."

I looked down to see my breasts waving to the audience. "Crap." I pulled my straps back over my shoulders, then found myself spun around while Noah zipped me back up.

How gentlemanly of him.

He pulled my dress back down and fixed my hair. How cute was that? I grinned at Emma, who smiled back.

"Sorry about that," Noah said to me. "I didn't mean for that to happen."

I beamed at him. "It's a sign that you can't live without me. You might as well admit it and figure out a way around my family. I won't wait forever for you."

Noah didn't roll his eyes or even groan with disgust. He simply looked thoughtful. "Can you give me a couple weeks?"

"To talk to Ray and my parents?"

He met my gaze. "Yes."

Sweet.

"But I won't go behind their backs. I have to talk to them first."

If I felt like being doting, I could call him traditional, like in the old days when a suitor asked the father's permission before proposing. If I felt like being bitter, I could call him a wuss with screwed-up priorities and leave him stranded in the coatroom alone until his nether regions came back under his control.

But seeing as how my hormones had flared up and were interfering with rational thought, I decided to give him a break. "Go talk to them. I won't wait, but if I'm still available when you come around, then so be it."

I saw Emma's nod ever so slightly. Couldn't let him hold all the cards, could I? Okay, so maybe even with someone you've known for twenty years, you needed to play a few games. I hate games. But for self-preservation, I'd indulge. "See you later."

I left him in the coatroom with his erection. Sometimes there are advantages to being a woman.

I called Van on my way home. Emma left to go over to Blaine's, so I was on my own. Van answered on the first ring. "What happened?"

"Too long to discuss over the phone. Got dinner plans?" What a glorious evening. Noah had the hots for me, even if he was a wimp. April was feeling the pain of being rejected by my family—though I felt a little bad about that, it also made me feel better. (Somehow it was nice to know I wasn't the only one who fell short of my parents' expectations.) Emma and I were reconciled, and I'd managed to be entertaining.

Of course, I was even more annoyed by my family, but hey, you can't have everything.

"Actually, I'm at dinner right now with some friends," Van said.

"Oh." I already knew he wasn't going to invite me along for that one.

"How about if I stop by your place later? Would ten thirty be too late?"

I looked at my watch. It wasn't even six o'clock yet. That was one long dinner. Not that it was my business what Van did with his time. "Yeah, that's fine."

I picked up some Chinese takeout on the way home, and let myself into my apartment.

Dave was sitting on the couch watching television. A vase of roses was on the coffee table, along with a box from my favorite bakery. "Shannon." He sat up quickly and turned off the television. "How are you?"

I looked at the four duffel bags on the floor in the corner. "Passing through?"

"I brought you roses."

"I noticed." I hadn't seen Dave since his declaration of adultery for a woman other than me.

"And a double-fudge cake."

My mouth watered. "I figured that's what was in there."

"So, you want some?"

I held up my Chinese food. "I have to eat dinner first." I walked into the kitchen and ended the conversation.

Dave sat down at the kitchen table and waited for me to dish up. "Can I please stay here?"

"Does Yvonne know you're here?"

"Yes."

Oh, great. Guess I'd better get a German shepherd and a personal bodyguard to check my car for bombs. "Dave! She's going to think I'm the one having an affair with you."

"I'm not having an affair."

"Oh, no?" I sat down across from him and opened my moo shu pork. "What would you call it? A good friendship?"

"I love Phoebe."

"And what about Yvonne? I thought you loved her?"

Dave shrugged and tried to help himself to a piece of pork. I smacked his hand and brandished my fork at him. He retreated to his side of the table. "I do love her. Just not in the way I love Phoebe. I've never felt this way before."

I sighed and chewed for a minute.

Dave waited in silence. Smart guy.

"I don't understand, Dave. How could you walk away from your marriage? You're the king of fidelity." I shook my head. "Having you leave your spouse is an indication that everything holy and sacred about marriage is a farce."

Dave was quiet for a while before he spoke. "I can't explain it, Shannon. All I know is that Phoebe is my soul mate. I married the wrong person."

I married the wrong person. Words to strike fear into the heart of single women everywhere. What if I married the wrong person and he left? Or I met my true love after I had someone else's ring on my finger?

Chilling.

"I'm not a bad person."

I didn't answer.

"I made a mistake. I was twenty-one when I married Yvonne. Too young."

"How does Yvonne feel about this? Does she agree you guys shouldn't be together?"

Dave had the grace to look pained. "No."

I took a mouthful of noodles and studied Dave. "So were you having doubts before you fell for Phoebe?" My Phoebe. I introduced them and made sure they were friends. So was I an accomplice to adultery? Nice.

Dave rubbed his chin and shot another longing glance at my food.

Good. I hope you're hungry.

"I think I'd been fighting those doubts for a long time. That's why I agreed to try to have kids. I figured that maybe that would fill the gap."

I stared at him. "That's so stupid."

"I know. Can you imagine if Yvonne was pregnant?" He rubbed his eyes. "I was so close to mucking everything up."

"So close? Looks to me like you already did."

Dave dropped his hand. "Can you give me a break? I need you."

Dammit. I didn't want to be needed. "Dave, this is hard for me. I don't agree with what you two are doing."

"Do you believe in love? True love?"

Sometimes I did. Other times, not so much. "Generally, yes."

"Then nothing else matters. It's about love. We love each other. I didn't realize how much was missing from my relationship with Yvonne until I found Phoebe. She feels the same way about Zach."

I felt deflated. Even the Chinese food didn't taste good anymore. "Did Phoebe break up with Zach?"

"She went out to Chicago this weekend."

"Has she called?"

Dave shook his head.

"Doesn't that make you nervous? What if he changes her mind?"

The twitch under Dave's right eye told me he'd already considered that possibility. In fact, now that I examined him closer, he looked extremely tense. Nothing like the Dave I knew so well. "Are you okay?"

He shrugged. "I feel guilty."

Well, good. If he felt guilty then maybe I wouldn't have to be so hard on him.

"And I'm worried about how it will all work out." He shook his head. "I never meant to hurt Yvonne. I still love her, and I feel horrible. She hasn't gone to work in three days. I stayed around to make sure she was okay, but she kicked me out tonight. Doesn't want my help."

For the first time in my life, I felt a bond with Yvonne. Maybe Noah and Dave were conjoined twins divided at birth.

I frowned. Did Noah feel about me the way Dave felt about Yvonne? Only partially interested in me, so that even if we got together, he'd leave as soon as something better came along? I didn't like that idea. If it was true love between us, then wouldn't he be clamoring for my love instead of having to have his arm twisted?

"So can I stay here?"

"Emma still lives here."

"I'll sleep on the couch."

"Dave . . ."

"Please." He leaned forward and took my hand. "I need a friend."

Should've thought of that before you violated your marriage vows and made Phoebe do the same. "Fine. You can stay for a couple nights. But you can't move in. Yvonne seriously wouldn't have any problem having me killed."

"I told her it wasn't you."

"And I'm sure she believes every word out of your mouth these days." I wasn't exaggerating. Yvonne scared the hell out of me. She was extremely protective of what she considered hers, and I'd gotten more than one harassing phone call from her when she found out Dave had spent time with me.

Although, as it turned out, it looked like Yvonne was right to be concerned about Dave's female friends.

Go with your gut. That's what they say. Yvonne should have gone with hers and chained Dave to their bed.

I sighed. "You can sleep in Emma's room tonight. She's staying at Blaine's."

"Thanks."

I felt guilty at the relief that consumed Dave's features. What kind of a person was I to turn down a friend in need, even if I didn't agree with what he'd done? "You can stay as long as you want."

He grinned and gave me a hug. "I love you, Shannon."

"Yeah, yeah." I pushed him off me. "How about that cake? I could use some chocolate. I've never harbored a fugitive before."

Dave and I were halfway through part two of the *Lord of the Rings* trilogy when my buzzer sounded. I glanced at the clock. Ten fifteen. Van.

I jumped up and hit the buzzer. "Hello?"

"Is Dave there?" The tearful voice sounded suspiciously familiar.

"Phoebe?"

Dave leaped up. "Phoebe's here?"

I buzzed her in and watched the change that came over Dave. The tense lines left his face, his eyes were bright, and he was smiling.

Okay, so maybe that looked a little bit like true love. I'd never seen his eyes go that sparkly when he was talking about Yvonne. His expression was usually more shuttered, like he was afraid she'd leap out of the woodwork and catch him being a bad boy hanging out with his friend Shannon.

On the plus side, with Dave dating Phoebe, I was no longer persona non grata in Dave's life. So that was good, right?

I opened the door to my apartment and walked into the kitchen to dispose of the cake dishes.

I heard the door open, a murmured greeting between them, and then the distinct sound of sloppy kissing.

It was one thing to let Dave stay here and still be an advocate of fidelity. It was something else entirely to have my adulterous friends using my apartment as a sex haven. Rules were going to need to be established.

After they got through with their dog-in-heat greeting. I had no interest in going out there and observing that.

"Shannon?" I turned in time to be attacked by a desperate hug from Phoebe. "Thank you so much for letting Dave stay here. You are the best. I'm so sorry."

I rolled my eyes and patted Phoebe's back. I didn't feel like I was the best at the moment. I actually felt really weird and awkward.

Dave grinned at me from the door. He did look happy. "So, Phoebe, how did it go?"

She let go of me and turned to Dave. "It was awful. Awful." Tears trickled down her face, and her lower lip started to tremble.

He held out his arms and she flung herself into them.

They stood like that for a long while, holding each other, Dave whispering little things into her ear while he stroked her hair and kissed the top of her head.

Dammit. I wanted someone to hold me like that!

I wondered if there were any married men in my building. Maybe I could woo them away from their wives. . . .

The buzzer rang again, and I squeezed past the pretzel of love and hit the intercom. "Hello?"

"It's Van."

I looked at my friends. Yes, Van's timing was great, wasn't it? "Come on up."

By the time Van made it to my apartment, Phoebe and Dave had migrated to the couch, where they were all snuggled up and whispering. I had just decided to send them to Emma's bedroom when Van walked into the apartment, courtesy of the door I'd left open.

He was wearing shorts and sneakers and a T-shirt. The baseball hat looked totally cute on him. He was sporty and athletic, but not at all like Noah. Better than Noah. "Hey."

He grinned at me. "You look cute."

I forgot I was still wearing the dress from the engagement party. The same dress that had been around my waist while Noah was sucking on my breasts in the coatroom. Suddenly I felt extremely sluttish and embarrassed. I wondered what Van would think of me if he knew what I'd been doing.

"What's up with the blush?"

Curse Van and his perceptiveness. "I'm not used to you commenting on my appearance." Which was true too. And it sounded better than, *I was thinking about how my nipples had been between another guy's teeth only a few hours ago.* I grabbed his wrist and tugged him toward the living room. "I have surprise guests. Sorry."

He didn't look bothered by the news. "No problem."

Why was I annoyed at his complacence? It wasn't as if I wanted him to want to be alone with me. I mean, sure, I was beginning to consider him my special friend, but that didn't mean that he should be averse to sharing me with others, just because I was starting to feel that way.

I cleared my throat, but it did nothing to get Dave's and Phoebe's lips detached from each other. "Hey! I have company!"

They broke apart, their eyes all misty and dreamy. As I said, I had to admit I'd never seen either of them look that happy. Not that it made what they'd done all right, but it did complicate things a bit for me. "You guys remember Van from the bar. Van, this is Phoebe and Dave."

They exchanged greetings; then an awkward silence descended over the room. It was too obvious that Dave and Phoebe wanted to be left alone to grope each other.

Against all my morals, I found myself saying, "Maybe you guys would want to be alone. Emma's room is open. She's staying at Blaine's tonight."

They didn't move. Finally Dave said, "That won't make you feel awkward?"

"Well, of course, but not as awkward as having to watch you two make out on my couch while I have company."

They exchanged glances; then Dave stood up and pulled Phoebe to her feet. "We won't have sex."

Van grinned, and I shuddered. "I would really prefer not to hear the details, okay? Just go in there and keep it quiet."

"Can I stay over?" Phoebe asked.

Yeesh. I felt like the mother of teenagers. "Fine, but please don't make it a habit. This whole thing is still weird for me." How was I supposed to sleep while Phoebe and Dave made little love noises on the other side of the wall? I mean, sure, I could observe that they both seemed happy, but I wasn't exactly feeling all warm and snuggly with the whole concept just yet.

Phoebe grinned and they ran off to the bedroom, slamming the door with extra zeal.

"Let me guess. Your friends who are having the affair?"

I frowned. "Does it make me a bad person that I'm letting Dave stay here? He left his wife and Phoebe broke up with her fiancé this weekend, so it's in the open, but I'm feeling really strange about it."

Van rubbed my shoulder. "Friendship is important. I think you're doing the right thing, but I also think it's fine to be uncomfortable."

I was glad Van appreciated that there was something odd about it. If he thought leaving spouses for other people was ordinary and fine, then it would worry me that he might think it was okay for him.

Not that it would matter to me. He was my friend the way Dave was. If Van left his wife someday, it wouldn't be me he was leaving. "Want some cake? Dave brought it to bribe me."

"Sure."

I set Van up with some cake, then plopped myself next to him on the couch. I sat sideways facing him, my bare feet shoved under the cushion he was sitting on.

"Who are the flowers from?" Van asked the question so casually I was almost suspicious.

"Dave. More bribery."

He nodded. "So how was the engagement party? Fill me in."

I gave Dave a blow-by-blow of the affair, including the April fiasco, but omitting the Noah thing. For some reason, I felt weird telling him about it. When I finished, Van cut himself a second piece of cake. "Sounds like you handled it well."

"Thanks to your advice. I've already decided to declare you my official savior."

He grinned and held up a forkful of cake. "Want a bite?"

Oh, wow. This was intimate. "Sure." He slipped the cake into my mouth, careful not to jab me with the prongs. I tried not to think that his lips had been on that same metal only moments before. It was practically like kissing. But not.

He said nothing, but his eyes became a little darker.

I felt like mine were too.

"So . . ."

"What?" I watched him scoop another piece of cake onto his fork and wondered if he'd feed me again.

"What's the status of Noah? And Blaine? And Max? And any other men I might not know the name of?" He put the cake in my mouth and drew the fork out slowly. "What's your status, Shannon?"

My stomach fluttered. What did he mean by *that?*

CHAPTER NINETEEN

"My status? You mean, like, am I dating any of them?" My mouth felt dry all of a sudden.

Van studied my face. "Not just that. Are you still hung up on them?"

Does kissing Noah a few hours ago count? "Nothing is going on with any of them."

He was looking at me really intently, and I met his gaze. "What if Noah comes knocking at your door? Are you going to go back to him?"

Ah . . . Of course I was. So why didn't I want to admit it? I finally shrugged. "Depends."

"On what?"

"If he's begging. If I'm not interested in someone else by then. If I decide that being with him won't put me in Dave's situation." I hugged my arms around my legs and rested my chin on my knees. "I won't get married until I know it's right. I'm not going through divorce, and I'm not going to marry a guy who thinks there is someone better out there."

Van nodded slightly. "And you're not sure where Noah fits in?"

I felt a fuzz on my shins and realized I needed to shave. How totally embarrassing. "I'm beginning to think that Noah isn't enough." I grabbed a blanket and laid it across my legs. "If it was right, really right, then he would have been committed from the first minute, you know?"

"What about you? Were you committed to him from the first minute?"

I pursed my lips and rocked back and forth. "I think it's difficult to separate twenty years of a childhood crush from the reality of an adult relationship."

"So . . ."

I looked at him. "So, I'm unsure." It was incredible how much I didn't want to admit all this to Van, but I had no choice. I couldn't lie to him, could I? No. We didn't have that type of relationship.

He picked up my hand and started playing with my fingers.

Wow. Talk about butterflies in my belly. And these weren't platonic butterflies that came out to play when I was with my girlfriends. These were hot, sexy, majorly hormonal butterflies. "So tell me your secret, Van. What do you do in your spare time? Are you really a stripper?" I tried to tease the answer out of him.

He brought my fingers to his lips and kissed the tip of each one. "It's not the right time to tell you."

"Why not?" I watched his lips play with my fingers and wondered whether anyone had ever passed out from fingertip kisses, because I was certainly teetering on the edge. *Noah who?*

"Because you'll hate me."

I tried to think about his words. "I seriously doubt I could hate you."

"When I believe that, I'll tell you. I don't want to be judged."

What kind of person did he think I was, that I'd hate and judge him because of something he did with his life? "Van."

"Mmm . . ."

"I need honesty in a relationship."

He lifted his gaze to mine. "Do we have a relationship?"

My heart was beating fast. "Of sorts."

He gave the palm of my hand a long kiss, then released it. "I'm not interested in being anyone's second choice."

What could I say to that? He was right. "And I couldn't choose someone who isn't being honest."

His eyes were dark. "Then I guess we're at an impasse."

I didn't want an impasse! I wanted a kiss! *Oh, wow.* Did that make me a total slut, kissing two men within the same six hours, and liking them both? "I guess."

"I should go." He stood up.

"You can stay. Watch a movie. As friends."

He eyed my thigh, exposed where my dress had slid up above the blanket. "I'm not in the mood for that kind of an evening."

On a whim, I shifted so my dress went even higher. Van's eyes glittered and he caught his breath. My stomach flipped, and I knew we'd crossed a border tonight. How did we go back? Did we want to? There wasn't space for Noah and Van in my bed, and I didn't even know if either of them wanted to be there.

So I stood up and let my dress fall back down. I echoed the regret in Van's eyes. Then again, he was a guy and I was a woman. Just because he liked the sight of my thigh didn't mean he'd want to date me or anything like that. It meant he was a man. "Yes, you should probably go."

He nodded. "You should know that I'm not going to be working security for the next three weeks."

I blinked. No Van? No casual visits? "Why not?"

"Part of my secret life. You can call me, though. I'll be around."

I frowned. "But where will you be?"

He kissed my cheek. "I'll see you later."

Van let himself out, leaving me standing in my living room. Alone. So alone. My friends were having sex in the bedroom vacated by my other friend who was having sex. My relationship with my new best friend had taken a turn that might ruin our friendship, and even Noah couldn't make a move until he got permission. And since Max was complete history, I had no options there either.

Damn.

I had absolutely no one to turn to.

Which meant there was only one option: make myself sick eating the rest of the cake.

Jessamee flung my office door open and marched inside. "He doesn't even know my name."

I set down my coffee and wiped the spillage off my blouse. *Thank you, Jessamee, for scaring the crap out of me.* "Who doesn't?"

"Otto Nelson!"

You should be grateful, you little snot. "So?"

"So, I want him to know my name and advocate for me for a job. I say hello to him every day and he ignores me."

She folded her arms across her chest. "It's your fault. We've all been blackballed by our association with you."

My gaze snapped to her face. *"What?"* *Stay calm. Stay professional.*

"All the interns. How can we succeed when the person in charge of us is on probation? We've been discussing it for days, and I got nominated to come talk to you."

I folded my hands under the table and ground my fingernails into the palm of my hand. "And what is your proposal?"

"Quit."

I had to close my eyes for a full five seconds before I could risk a response. When I did, my jaw ached with the effort of staying externally serene. "I hate to disappoint you, Jessamee, but I'm not in trouble with Otto. He treats everyone like that." I shrugged in what I hoped was a casual, relaxed fashion. "I'm not the plague. I'm respected and you're in good hands."

Jessamee narrowed her eyes. "I don't believe you."

The little witch. If I were an attorney, she'd never speak to me like that. But no, because I was the social director she thought she could trounce all over me. I was so damned tired of being undervalued because of my job title! I stood up, placed my palms on my desk, and leaned forward. "Ms. Bouchillion, you will do well to remember several things if you want to be a lawyer. First of all, the support staff is critical to your success. I suggest you learn how to respect them. Second, the reason Otto hasn't noticed you is because I've been working overtime to make sure you and all the other interns are flying beneath his radar. He doesn't think highly of people. Period. If you get noticed by him, it will *not* be in a positive way. As an intern, you won't survive getting on Otto's bad side. I know that, and that's why I protect you."

Jessamee walked over to the desk and faced me straight on. "You're wrong."

I narrowed my eyes. "About what?"

"Otto doesn't hate everyone who walks across his path. Only the people who screw up." She paused for emphasis. *Nice touch.* "I won't screw up. Give me an assignment working with him."

"No." My brain was crashing against my skull. Had anyone's brain ever actually spontaneously combusted? I tried to picture Jessamee hanging out my window with staples in her feet, but even that didn't lower my blood pressure.

She leaned closer. "Yes."

I narrowed my eyes. "And what happens if I give you an assignment with him and he fires you?"

"It won't happen."

"And what if it does?"

"It won't."

I grabbed a yellow notepad and a pen and shoved it at her. "Write and sign a statement that you are begging me to be assigned to Otto, and that if it goes belly-up, you hold only yourself responsible. Add that I'm advising against this course of action, so you can't claim I didn't warn you." Maybe it was overkill, but I knew my job wasn't exactly secure.

Jessamee grabbed the notepad and wrote. Then she signed her name with a flourish and handed it back. "Now what?"

"I'll get back to you."

"When?"

I shot her my most hostile look. "When I do." Yes, sweet Auntie Shannon wasn't exactly fulfilling job requirements right now, was she?

"Fine."

"Fine." I sat back down and turned to my computer, dismissing her.

She waited for a moment; then she stomped out.

I typed for another three minutes, and then I dropped my face into my hands. *I can't deal with this anymore.*

"Shannon?"

I snapped upright and smiled at Hildy. "Hi."

"Are you free for lunch?"

I groaned. I was not in the mood. I needed lunch away from the firm. "Um . . ."

"My husband wants to interview you for law school."

"Seriously?"

She grinned. "Yep. Meet him at Bertucci's at eleven. He'll be waiting in the foyer. His name is Frank Moss."

I nodded. Given my morning, the lure of law school was pulling strong. "I'll be there."

The prospect of my lunch date kept a smile on my face the rest of the morning, even after I had to practically promise my soul to Kathy Michaels to get her to hand me some of Otto's work for Jessamee. Misgivings were running rampant when I gave Jessamee the assignment, but I had no choice.

Besides, Jessamee was tough. If anyone could deal with Otto, it was her. Who knew? Maybe she'd survive and become the next female partner.

Yet when I walked away, I couldn't help but think I

should have tried harder to dissuade Jessamee. I felt like I had failed in my job.

Frank Moss spotted me instantly when I walked into Bertucci's five minutes early. "Shannon McCormick? Frank Moss."

"Hi, Mr. Moss." He pumped my hand with enthusiasm, and I felt cheered by the warmth in his gaze. What did I expect? He was married to Hildy, wasn't he?

"Call me Frank." He led the way to the table and jumped into his seat, his ruddy complexion and bald head making him seem even more approachable and chipper. "So, obviously there's a bit of a problem because you haven't taken the LSAT."

"Yes, I understand that. I can postpone my application until next year—"

"No, no. That's not necessary." He opened his briefcase and laid my transcript from undergrad school on the table. "I like this. Good stuff."

"Thanks." I wondered where he'd gotten that. I hadn't submitted it.

He folded his arms across the table. "So why do you want to go to law school?"

Great question. I didn't suppose having the authority to trounce Jessamee would count, huh? "My parents are both lawyers, as are two of my brothers. It's a family thing." No need to elaborate that those reasons were exactly why I *didn't* want to become an attorney.

He nodded and jotted down some notes. "Any reason why you didn't go straight into law school?"

"Because I wanted to make sure I was doing it for the right reason, and not merely because it's in my genes."

"What's your right reason, then? I assume you've found one, given that you're here."

"Because . . ." *Um* . . . "I'm interested in the law."

"What part?"

Shit. He was onto me. Weren't these the same questions I'd been asking myself? The same questions I didn't have answers for yet? "It's challenging. I like to use my brain."

"Lots of jobs are challenging. What is it specifically about law?"

There was sweat dripping down my back. *Nice.* "I think law is interesting. I like reading cases. I like the power."

"Power? What kind of power?"

Power to trounce people who previously looked down on you. "The power of knowledge." *Good ad-lib.* I rocked. "The power to help protect the rights that America was founded upon."

He nodded and wrote something down.

I got a nod. Sweet. I was going to survive this interview.

Ten days later, I woke up on my birthday morning in a bad mood.

Since the interview, life had settled into a bit of a routine. Dave and Phoebe shared Emma's room every night (I'd relented on my no staying over policy. They were just so darn happy together that I couldn't say no.), and Emma and I had met for lunch a number of times. It was good to have my friends around again, and I began to understand the bond Dave and Phoebe had. Not that I agreed with what they'd done, but I did understand.

Which scared the crap out of me. I didn't want to make that same mistake.

Jessamee had been giving me the cold shoulder and had given me minimal response when I asked how it was going with Otto. Several attorneys had pulled me aside privately to question my assignment of Jessamee to work with Otto, and I could tell that my reputation was getting murky.

So I crossed my fingers and hoped that Hildy's husband came through. Maybe I'd even go to the day program and cut out of my job early. I called him and left him a message to that effect. He didn't call back.

My mom hadn't tried to get in touch with me since the party. Neither had Ray.

I wasn't sure how to feel about that. My mom had never given me the silent treatment before. Had I finally crossed the invisible line?

Not even a call from Emma saying she was taking me to dinner could fix my mood. By the time she came by my office at five o'clock—Emma didn't allow me to work late on my birthday—I just wanted to go home and sulk.

My own mom hadn't even called to wish me a happy birthday. Or Dad. Or Noah. Or Ray. Travis had phoned, but I was so mad at him for refusing to marry April that it hadn't exactly been a warm and fuzzy conversation.

Emma bounded into my office, wearing a hot-pink mini and a black tank top. "Ready?"

"Can we skip?"

Blaine appeared behind Emma. "Nope. Birthdays are for celebrating."

I stared. "You're coming too?"

Emma nodded. "It's time that the two most important people in my life became friends."

I gave Blaine a half smile. "Great." I supposed Emma was right. She didn't seem to be tiring of him.

He gave me a relaxed smile. "Well, come on, birthday girl. We have plans."

Birthday girl? Never thought Blaine was the type to call anyone a birthday girl. Emma must have seriously loosened him up.

Emma tossed me some clothes. "You can't go out for your birthday in a suit. I brought some clothes."

Ugh. "You didn't bring the black tank top I put through the garbage disposal, did you?"

She grinned as I reached into the bag and held it up. "You're kidding!"

"There's a blouse to wear over it. It's too classic not to wear. With all those holes in it, it's positively obscene. You have to go for it." She shoved Blaine out of the office. "Give us five minutes to change."

She shut the door behind her and wiggled her eyebrows. "You ready for a makeover?"

"Definitely not." But I couldn't help but grin. How could I not be amused at the thought of wearing that tank top from hell?

She held up a makeup kit. "Too bad. Let's go!"

Fifteen minutes later I was laughing. I was wearing the black tank top under a see-through blouse that Emma had bought for me. It was daring, yet modest enough that you couldn't tell just how much flesh the torn shirt revealed. It actually looked somewhat fashionable. I was impressed, as I was with Emma's makeup job. Combined with my stilettos and my tight black jeans, it made me feeling pretty good. Not as slutty as the bar night with Blaine, but definitely sexy.

And fun. I was having fun.

Blaine winked when we opened the door. "Nice." No sarcasm there at all.

I grinned. "Thanks."

Emma held up a blindfold. "Ready?"

"You can't blindfold me."

"Of course we can. It's a surprise. Come on." She fastened the handkerchief around my eyes; then each of them took an arm. "Trust us."

"Do I have a choice?"

"Nope. But don't worry. This will be your best birthday ever." Emma whispered. "Lots of hot sex."

"Emma!" But I couldn't help the swirl of excitement in my belly. Had she gotten Noah to come?

CHAPTER TWENTY

There were cars rushing by, and I could hear the chatter of commuters as they rushed to the train station.

"Watch your head." A hand pressed on the top of my hair as I climbed into a car.

Emma helped me with my seat belt, and then she and Blaine settled on either side of me.

"Where are we going?"

"It's a surprise." Emma shifted. "So what's going on with Van? He's pretty cute. Dave and Phoebe said he came over the other night."

I let my head flop back. "He is cute."

"And?"

"And what?"

"Any interest there?"

"On his part or mine?"

"Yours." Emma jerked, and it felt like she'd kicked something.

"I think I could totally go for him, but he's not interested because of my baggage with Noah. Plus he has some major secret that he's not telling me, so I'm not into that." I rubbed my chin. "I guess the answer is, I have no idea. Doesn't matter anyway. He hasn't called me."

"What if he did? What if he asked you out on a real date? What if he wanted to kiss you? Would you?"

"Of course, but that doesn't mean that it's smart or that he would want to."

Emma tucked her hand through mine. "How about Dave and Phoebe?"

"They're good. Happy. It's weird for me, but I'm glad for them."

"And April? How do you feel about April?"

I frowned. "What's with all the questions?" Then I heard a giggle. *Oh, crap. She wouldn't have.* I yanked my blindfold down and found myself in the back of a huge limousine that was full of people I knew.

Including Van. Who was sitting directly across from me with an indecipherable look on his face.

Double damn. What had I said?

"Surprise!" Everyone was laughing hysterically, and someone shoved a glass of champagne into my hand.

Dave and Phoebe were there, and April (no Travis), Lindsay and her fiancé, Dr. Perfect.

And Van.

And no Noah. Or Ray. Or my parents. I bit my lower lip and tried not to notice.

A rousing rendition of "Happy Birthday" filled the limo, and they all agreed it was hysterical to hear me talk about everyone in the limo. April kicked Lindsay. "I can't believe you giggled! We could have gone through all of us!"

Thank God they hadn't. What if I'd said something embarrassing? The whole Van thing was bad enough.

Then he smiled at me, and I felt better. Maybe my birthday was going to be all right after all.

Emma had reserved a private function room at my favorite Italian restaurant in the North End. Gino Randazzo, the owner, crushed me in a bear hug the moment I walked in, and his whole staff serenaded me.

I grinned a goofy smile and felt embarrassed. And happy.

I threw my arm around Emma's shoulder as we walked back to our room. "Thanks."

She grinned. "Just have fun. And don't worry about the cost. April and Lindsay are paying for the whole thing."

My smile faltered. "Really?"

"Yep. They wanted you to have a great birthday and knew that not all of us have a ton of money. That's their gift as your family."

Wow. I didn't know what to say. What about the black-sheep thing?

I sat down in a chair decorated with balloons and streamers, and Van sat down next to me. April grabbed the chair on the other side, and I smiled. *How about that, huh?* April choosing to sit next to me. Being dismissed by my family had given us a common bond.

"Happy birthday."

I turned to find Van smiling at me. One hand was across the back of my chair and he was leaning toward me. He smelled good, like soap and the woods. "Thanks." I tilted my head. "Where have you been for the last week and a half? I thought you hated me." It had been so weird leaving work at the end of the day and knowing I wasn't going to see Van in the lobby.

He grinned. "Did you miss me?"

"Yes."

His smile faded. "You did?"

"Of course I did. Obviously you didn't miss me."

"I was busy."

I noticed he didn't deny not missing me. "Doing what?" He shrugged and I rolled my eyes. "Give me a break, Van. Don't even tell me it's more of this secret you have."

"It is."

How aggravating was that? "You know all about me, and yet you don't trust me?" I pushed his arm off my chair. "This is why it would never work between us even if you were interested. I need total honesty in my relationships, and even my friendships."

His eyes flashed and he wrapped his hand around my arm. "We need to talk. Come here." He stood up and pulled me to my feet, ignoring my protests when he dragged me out of the room into a hallway.

My back against the wall, he flanked my shoulders with his hands flat on the wall and glared at me. "Listen, Shannon, I think we've developed a pretty strong friendship, haven't we?"

"Yes." Van was tall, wasn't he? I hadn't quite realized it before.

"As a friend, I expect you to respect my privacy when I ask for it. I will tell you eventually, but not now. Don't dwell on it or take offense."

I lifted my chin. "I've seen what happens when people aren't honest with each other. It destroys relationships. I've been totally honest with you, even when I've shared some things that really don't make me look good. But I trusted you not to judge me. It's completely offensive that you think I'm so shallow that I'll judge you based on some secret."

He cursed under his breath. "Shannon, I appreciate your trust in me and I won't let you down. But our relationship is so new I don't want to push you away."

"It's not that new! I think we're pretty close, actually."

His eyes flickered. "Not close enough. Yet."

Something caught in my throat. "What do you mean?"

"I won't be a second choice. I'll wait until I'm first in line."

I swallowed and my heart started pounding. All I could think about was the cake-feeding episode. Was that what he was talking about? "First in what line?"

He ran his thumb over my lower lip. "I think you know what I'm talking about."

What was up with the trembling in my legs? "You're just trying to take advantage of what I said in the limo."

"That you'd kiss me if I kissed you?"

"I didn't say that. I'd never kiss you." I stared at his lips. "At least until you were honest with me."

"And I won't kiss you until there are no more shadows from other guys around."

What guys? I couldn't think of anyone but him. "No one else is here tonight. Just you."

His eyes darkened and his gaze fastened on my lips.

Oh, wow. Kiss me, Van.

"What about Noah?"

"What about him?"

"If he were here tonight, would you be with him?"

I would have thought "yes" would be the answer that jumped to my mind, but instead, "I don't know" was what popped in there. Since when did Noah not occupy the top place in my life?

"Too slow." Van's voice was dangerously soft.

I met his gaze. "I was thinking."

He lifted a brow. "And?"

"I was thinking that I was expecting my answer to be that I'd be with Noah, but that wasn't what came to my mind."

"What came to your mind?" He leaned closer, looming over me like some protective warrior.

"I don't know."

"You don't know what came to your mind, or you don't know what you'd do if both of us were here?"

"The latter."

"Not enough."

"Well, until I feel commitment from you, I'm not going to cross that line. Secrets, Van."

He bent his head until his lips were only a fraction of an inch from mine. "In due time." And then he brushed his lips across mine, soft, tender, and fleeting.

And I wanted more.

I grabbed the front of his shirt. "Kiss me again."

His eyes said no, but his lips disobeyed. He kissed each corner of my mouth, then caught my lips in a kiss that made my body quiver. Warm heat imbued my body at the gentle exploration of his tongue, and I clung to his shirt with a desperation I couldn't understand. It was different from Noah: hot and passionate, but also pure and complete, with a sense of rightness that was honest, not built on years.

"Shannon!" Emma's voice carried from the other room. "Noah's on the phone! He wants to wish you a happy birthday."

Crap.

Van stopped kissing me, but he didn't move away. He kept his gaze on my face and sucked my soul from my body with his eyes. I couldn't look away.

Emma walked around the corner, then stopped. "Whoops. Never mind."

Van caught her arm as she turned back into the other room. "She'll take the call."

I closed my eyes. Noah had to call me now? When I opened them, Van's face had become shuttered. He touched his thumb to my lips. "My point exactly," he said. "I don't want to play this game."

Then he left me in the hall with Emma and the phone.

"Emma . . ."

She held up the phone. Right. Noah could hear me. Sighing, I grabbed her phone. "This is Shannon."

Noah's deep voice filled my ear. "Happy birthday, Shannon."

"Thanks." Emma started to leave, so I waved her to stay. "Are you coming?" *Please say no.* Ack! What was I thinking? I wanted Noah there . . . didn't I?

"I can't. I'm in LA for business. I was hoping to get back tonight, but there's no way. I'm here at least another two days. But I wanted you to know I would be there if I were in town."

My stomach fluttered. "You would? Did you talk to my family?" Was this it? The moment of commitment?

"I'm in negotiations with Ray. Gotta deal with him before I hit up your parents."

Negotiations? What was there to negotiate? *I'll sleep with your sister but only on the even days of the month?* "Whatever."

284

"No, don't go. I'm really going to try to figure this out. I want this to work between us. I really do."

"Fine. Give me a call when you have the details of the contract hammered out." I hung up the phone and handed it back to Emma.

She grimaced. "I'm really sorry about interrupting. I had no idea you and Van would be out here kissing."

"Me either." I leaned against the wall and let my head flop back against the plaster. "What am I doing?"

"You're stringing two guys along, which is great. Now that I'm with only one guy, we need someone out there to do the double-duty thing." Emma tugged on my hair. "Don't worry so much about it. It'll work out."

I looked at her. "But I'm confused. I mean, Noah's the one I want, so why did I kiss Van? And enjoy it?" And I'd really enjoyed it. The mere recollection of his lips on mine sent goose bumps cascading down my arms.

"I don't know." Emma tucked her arm through mine. "But let's go in there and find out."

Against my better judgment, I returned to the party. It would have been a better plan to go into hibernation until I figured things out, so I couldn't muck anything up, but I was the guest of honor, wasn't I?

Van had returned to the seat next to mine—that was a good sign, wasn't it?—and was chatting with Lindsay. April was listening to a discussion between Phoebe and Dave, and she didn't look happy.

She looked like I usually felt at McCormick family gatherings: alone, unhappy, and an outsider.

So I sat down in my seat, set a hand on Van's shoulder—I felt the need to bond even if he was engaged in another conversation—and faced April. "How are you doing, April?"

She turned to me and shrugged. "Fine."

Should I ask about Travis? Was that topic open for discussion, or had her confession been a momentary bonding? "How's the pregnancy going? Feeling all right?"

"Usually. I think I've been pretty lucky." She twisted her napkin in her lap. "What's up with you and Noah?"

Out of the corner of my eye, I saw Van look in our direction. I ignored him and faced April. "I don't think anything is going to happen with him."

"Why not?"

Was Van still listening? "Because I don't want a man who has to debate whether I'm worthwhile to pursue. After twenty years, if he doesn't know he really wants me, then it's not enough. Don't you think?"

April nodded. "That's what I was trying to tell you about Travis. If he doesn't want me on his own, what do I have to gain by forcing him into marriage?" She nodded at Dave and Phoebe. "If I do, I might end up like Dave's wife."

"I'll never let that happen to me."

"How do you know? I mean, we can do our best, but it might still happen." Her eyes got teary again. "I don't know what to do."

Hormonal Pregnant Woman appeared again, but this time I didn't feel panicked. I felt like I understood her. "Have you talked to Travis?"

She nodded. "He gets mad and storms out."

"Guilt."

"What?"

"For his whole life, when Travis feels bad about something, he gets angry instead of dealing with it. If he's getting angry, that's a good sign. It means he cares a lot, so all hope isn't lost."

A glimmer flashed in her eyes. "You think?"

"Yep."

"What about your mom? Would she accept me then?"

I frowned. I couldn't really provide happy news on that front. "Honestly, I've never figured out how to win my mom's approval, so I can't help you there."

April studied me. "Too bad."

"Yeah." I held up a wineglass. "Cheers to being McCormick family rejects."

She lifted her water glass and smiled. "Cheers."

As I sipped my wine and looked out at the table, I felt the best I had in a while. There was the distinct possibility of friendship with April, I was thoroughly reconciled with Emma, Phoebe, and Dave, and both Noah and Van seemed interested in me.

Maybe my life wasn't so terrible.

Five days later, either Noah had been in a plane crash on his way home, or he'd decided not to call me.

I wasn't sure which reason I preferred.

It was almost five o'clock on Wednesday, and I was about ready to head out to a reception at the New England Aquarium for the firm when Isabel appeared in my doorway. Her face was tight and tense.

"What's wrong?"

"Otto needs to see you now."

I frowned. "Can't it wait until tomorrow? I have to leave now to get over to the aquarium to make sure the food is all set." Okay, so I was also hoping to avoid Otto. Who needed to see him last thing before going home? He'd give me nightmares all night long.

Then again, knowing I had a meeting looming with him would be equally stressful.

"Kathy said now."

"Are you sure?" My gut sank a little bit. What could be so important? Somehow I doubted he was consumed with a burning need to give me a raise or compliment me about something.

"Now."

Crap. "Can you do me a favor? Will you go over to the aquarium and get things rolling in case this takes a while?" Translation: in case Otto needed an hour to bawl me out.

Isabel's eyes widened. "You want me to go run the event?"

"Just till I get there. You know what's going on more than anyone else does." Because Blaine had slacked off a bit and actually let Isabel help me. Was it because of Emma or merely a reduced workload? Either way, I wasn't going to question it.

"Okay." Isabel looked excited. "I'll head over now."

It was weird to see her that fired up. It reminded me of how I had been when I started here. And it made me realize that I hadn't felt that way in a while. Probably still recovering from the dog-track episode.

I pushed my chair back. Might as well get it over with.

Otto's door was shut when I knocked on it. "Come in."

Darn it. My wish that he'd dropped to the ground in a coma hadn't come true. I pushed open the door and stepped inside.

"Sit down, Shannon."

I sat and folded my hands in my lap to hide their trembling. "What can I do for you?"

"I ran into Brett Stephens at a bar association meeting this afternoon."

Brett Stephens? Who was he?

"He clarified some things for me."

I frowned. I had no idea what he was talking about.

"You told me his daughter left the firm because you managed her out because she was a poor investment."

Stephens? Missy's last name was Stephens. I'd bet any amount of money Brett was her all-powerful attorney father who had been planning to call Otto and tell him off. "Mr. Nelson—"

He held up his hand to silence me. "Apparently she left because of the dog-track night."

I gritted my teeth. "Mr. Nelson—"

"She told him that I was a bastard whom she could never work for, because of how I'd treated you." His face was red, and sweat was dripping down his temples. "Apparently, she didn't understand that it was you who screwed up, not me. Isn't that your job, to make things clear for the interns?"

I dug my fingernails into my hand, frantically thumbing through my options. What was the best method of damage control?

"And then, on top of that, you lied to me to explain why she'd left."

"She wasn't a good fit for the firm, Mr. Nelson. I wasn't making that up."

"But you lied."

Crap. "I—"

He flipped a yellow legal pad across the desk. "You've been having interns sign documents that you aren't responsible for the bad situations you put them in?"

Jessamee. *Traitor.* That notebook had been in my desk drawer. She'd ratted and someone had searched my desk. Unbelievable. "I can explain that. . . ."

"I don't want an explanation. Lying to interns, lying to me, making poor choices for outings, and having interns sign contracts to indemnify you." He scowled. "Lying to me."

Didn't suppose it would be in my best interest to point out that he'd already mentioned that one. "Sir, there are explanations for all of that."

"Do you realize the interns have given you a vote of no confidence?"

"What?"

"Ms. Bouchillion brought me the memo. They feel that association with you is hampering their career opportunities."

That little witch. After all I'd done to help her when I'd really wanted to lay her out with a slap shot to the head.

"This firm is built on an impeccable reputation. We simply can't have people representing us in a poor light. You're in charge of the interns, so you are the face of the firm to the people who are our future." He shook his head. "Your behavior is beyond redemption."

What about yours?

"Ms. McCormick, you are fired for behavior unbecoming to the firm."

Fired? As in *fired?* As in, no job? "Mr. Nelson, please give me a chance to explain."

"Kathy? Can you please come in?" His secretary walked

in as if she'd been hovering next to the door waiting to be summoned. Had she known my future when she'd called Isabel? Sent me in here with no warnings? "Please escort Ms. McCormick to her office to collect her personal belongings. Would you like me to have security accompany you?"

Kathy looked at me. "I think we'll be fine."

"Mr. Nelson, please let me explain."

Kathy took my arm. "Come on, Shannon. It's over."

"But it can't be." How could this happen? I thought I'd worked my way off probation? That he'd started to see what I brought to the firm?

Otto sat back down at his desk and turned his back on me. Dismissed. "Mr. Nelson, please . . ."

"Shannon." Kathy tugged on my arm. "Come outside with me for a minute."

"But . . ."

"Come on."

I took one last glance at Otto's back; then I followed Kathy out of the office. She didn't stop walking when we got out there, but escorted me down the hall. Back to my office. "Kathy, there has to be something I can do."

"There isn't. Have some pride and don't make him have to call security."

That was my choice? Walk out with dignity or be dumped on my butt? No appeal? Tears were battling at the back of my eyes, but there was no way in hell I was going to let them out. We passed many attorneys, one of whom asked me what time the aquarium festivities started. I muttered some answer and forged ahead.

Too many people around. I had to leave. Get out with some dignity.

I made it to my office and grabbed my purse. "Can I come back later for my pictures?" I had to get out. *Get out, get out, get out.*

"No. Take your stuff now." She nodded at the corner. "There's a box."

The box hadn't been there when I left. Someone had delivered it—a cardboard moving box. Such a statement of premeditated finality. It even had my name written on the side.

Kathy shut my office door and started pulling photographs off my desk and setting them in the box.

I bit my lower lip and ordered my tears to subside. No way was I going to fall apart in public. No way. *Keep it together, Shannon.*

Kathy and I worked together for twenty minutes packing up my office. She checked every piece of paper I packed to make sure there was no firm information going home with me. I'd never felt like such a crook.

She rode the elevator downstairs with me, and walked me out to the sidewalk. It was too early for Van to be on duty, but it didn't stop me from looking over at the desk to see.

No Van.

Kathy held out her hand. "Your keys."

My keys. To my office. My firm. I fished them out of my purse and handed them to her.

"Good luck, Shannon. You know there are people here who will give you a reference."

I said nothing. What was there to say?

She gave me a sympathetic smile and then walked away, leaving me standing on the corner with my box. Three years of bloodsucking service, reduced to one small box.

Fired from a job that wasn't even worthy of me, according to my family. My family. What were they going to say?

The rehearsal dinner for Lindsay's wedding was two days away. How the hell was I going to manage that?

Forget it.

I wasn't going.

Tears sprung out of my eyes, and this time I couldn't stop them. I couldn't cope, and there was only one person I wanted to talk to.

I pulled out my cell phone and dialed Van's number, praying for him to answer.

CHAPTER TWENTY-ONE

No answer at his house.

So I called his cell.

No answer.

So I hung up and dialed again.

This time he answered on the fourth ring, sounding breathless. "Hello?"

All I could do was cry.

"Who is this?"

Fresh sobs burst free.

"Shannon?"

"I got fired." Well, that was what I was trying to say. It came out sounding like unintelligible gibberish.

"Where are you?"

Wow. He'd understood. His talents never ceased to amaze me. "On the sidewalk outside my building."

"Stay there. I'll be there in ten minutes."

Stay here? "I can't. Everyone will see me." At that moment the bus I'd reserved for the aquarium pulled up. "I have to leave." I grabbed my box and stumbled down the street. I'd never realized how difficult it was to navigate city streets at rush hour when being blinded by tears.

I flipped off a cab honking at me and made it across the street unscathed. Unfortunately. A few good tread marks on my head might do wonders for my mental outlook.

"Where are you going?"

It sounded like Van was on the highway now. "I don't know. Somewhere away." I stopped in front of Mrs. Fields cookies. Chocolate. "I'm getting cookies."

"Good. But where are you?"

"I don't know." He cursed and I yelled at him. "Don't swear at me!"

"I wasn't swearing at you. With you."

Oh. That was better.

"Where are you?"

God, was he a pest or what? I looked at the street signs and reported my location. Van gave me directions for where to meet him a couple blocks over, and I hung up.

I ordered three dozen cookies and began to devour them while I waited for Van to arrive. I sat on the curb with my bag of cookies and my box and my red, puffy eyes, watching cars drive by. I had no idea what kind of a vehicle Van drove, so I was embarrassed by leaping up on three different occasions and practically diving into the passenger seat of cars that slowed down to make a turn.

One woman even shrieked and powered her window shut, nearly taking off my head.

By the time the navy-blue SUV pulled to a stop in front of me, I refused to get up or acknowledge it.

"Shannon!"

I looked up to see the passenger door of the SUV open and Van leaning across the seat. He was wearing an old T-shirt and a pair of cutoff sweats and a baseball hat. Even though his sunglasses obscured his eyes, I knew he wasn't laughing at me. I stood up and let the fresh tears flow. "Van."

He slammed his truck into park despite the annoyed honking of the car behind him—my hero, willing to brave the wrath of a Boston driver—and jumped out.

He had me enveloped in a massive hug before I had a chance to move. I smashed my face into his shoulder and let him protect me. Did it feel good or what to have his arms around me? So good I bawled even harder.

I felt his lips on the top of my head, and I cried more.

He made comforting noises and rubbed my back. He didn't tell me to stop crying or to shape up; he just held me while I poured it all out.

After what felt like three hours, I had no more tears left. I wondered if his arms were cramping from holding me.

Van put his lips against my ear. "Can you make it to the car?"

I could do that, couldn't I? It was only a few feet away. "Probably."

He chuckled and guided me to the SUV, keeping his arms securely around me. He helped me get in—the narrow skirt that went with my suit wasn't exactly conducive to climbing into an SUV that didn't have running boards. He fastened my seat belt as if I were a little child and then kissed me, definitely not like a little child.

"I'll get your stuff."

My box ended up the backseat, my cookies on my lap, Van in the driver's seat, and then we were off. To where? I didn't know, and I didn't care. I let my head flop back against the seat and closed my eyes.

When he took my hand and held it, I smiled.

We didn't talk until I felt the truck bump up over a curb. I opened my eyes to find myself in a quiet suburban neighborhood, pulling into the driveway of a cute little one-story house painted white, with black shutters and a well-kept small front lawn. "You live here?"

"Yep." He pulled into the garage and shut off the car. "I hope it's okay to come here. You didn't seem to be in the mood to offer an opinion."

"No, it's fine." I sure didn't want to go home, where I would run into Dave and Phoebe and have to answer questions. Questions. How did one respond to "How was work today?" after you'd been fired?

He grabbed the cookies. "Let's go in."

I followed him into the house. The first room we entered was a kitchen. It was clean and neat, not bad for a bachelor. "You have roommates?"

"Nope." He set the cookies on the counter. "Want something to eat?"

"The two dozen cookies filled me up."

He grinned. "Two dozen?"

"Yeah." I tore off my blazer. "Do you have something I could change into? I'm not in the mood to be wearing work clothes."

"Sure. Be right back." He jogged out of the room.

He hadn't asked me what happened, giving me my

space until I was ready to talk about it. How did he know the right approach to take? How had he sensed I didn't want to recap it yet?

Van reappeared holding a T-shirt, a pair of sweats, and some socks. "I'm afraid they're going to be huge on you."

"Better than the suit. Thanks." I followed his directions to the bathroom, where I shed the prison garments and pulled on Van's clothes. I took an extra minute to hold them to my face and inhale before I put them on. They smelled like Van, and it felt so good. I needed some comfort, and Van's clothes were like my snuggle blanket.

I was laughing when I opened the door. "Am I a sex goddess or what?" The crotch of the sweats was nearly at my knees, and the shirt hung past my thighs.

Van was lounging against the kitchen door frame, his arms folded across his chest. "Never realized my clothes were so sexy."

His eyes were serious, and the laughter died in my throat.

"Can I ask you a question?" he asked.

I nodded.

"Was I the first one you called?"

"Yes."

He looked thoughtful. "So you didn't call Noah?"

I frowned. "I guess I didn't."

"Why not?"

"Because I wanted you." I cleared my throat. "I mean, I wanted you with me. You were the one I needed." *Damn.* I'd forgotten my manners. "Thank you for coming to get me. I really appreciate it."

He waved it off and walked over to me, stopping about

six inches away. He hands were at his sides, his gaze fixed on mine. "I want to kiss you."

I swallowed. "You do?"

He shook his head. "No, that's not what I meant."

Hope faded.

"I want to make love to you."

My body sprang to alertness and my hormones went into formation. "You do?"

"Yes."

"But . . ."

He held out his hands and waited.

Oh, God. Did I want this? Was I ready to commit to him? To leave Noah behind forever? To take Van and my friendship to a place we could never return from?

Yes.

Without a doubt, I knew this was what I wanted. What I'd wanted for ages.

So I put my hands in his.

"Your hands are shaking."

I licked my lips. "I'm nervous."

"Why?"

I shrugged. "I don't know."

He tugged me toward him and I followed. His left hand settled on my hip, and he laid his right hand sort of along my cheek and under my chin.

This was it. This wasn't going to be like the stolen kiss at my birthday. This was going to be the whole nine yards. I caught my breath and lifted my face to his.

His lips touched mine, and my world exploded. Sounds corny, but come on. How else can you describe the moment when you know your life will never be the same, that you are forever changed all the way down to your soul?

He crushed me against him, and I clung to his shoulders. His lips were everywhere, sucking my essence from my body. He nibbled on my ear, my collarbone, manhandling my lips with a kiss so passionate and possessive I wanted to crumble.

Breaking the kiss, he flanked my face with his hands, his touch gentle and tender. "Shannon."

Look at that face. It's the face of the man I could love. "Make love to me."

"What about Noah?" he asked.

What about him? "He's nothing in comparison to you."

"What if he walked in that door ready to declare himself to you for eternity? What then?"

I smiled. "I wouldn't care. I want you."

He grinned. "You didn't hesitate."

"Didn't have to think about it." *Come on, Van. Take me to your bedroom and make love to me until I collapse.* I laced my fingers behind his head and pulled him close. "Van Reinhart, I want you to make love to me right now."

His eyes danced. "Who am I to disappoint such a sexy woman?" He led me down the hall and pushed open the door to his bedroom. I had a vague sense of it being decorated in some shades of blue or something, but all I could really focus on was the king-size bed with a very inviting navy comforter.

He stopped me right next to the bed and turned me to face him. "I've been fantasizing about this moment for a long time."

"Really?" *Nice squeaky voice.*

"Swear." He knelt in front of me and pulled my shirt up to expose my stomach. The instant his tongue started circling my belly button, my legs collapsed. Van caught me and guided me to the bed. "You okay?"

"Yes." How breathless was my voice? "Keep doing that."

He grinned and trailed his lips over my stomach. "Like this?"

"That'll do." I flopped down on my back, stretched my arms over my head, and arched my back like some feline in heat. Not surprisingly, I felt like purring.

"How about this?" He moved upward, tracing the outline of each rib, his fingers flicking at the bottom edge of my bra.

"It suffices." I barely managed a coherent response on that one. I was squirming under him, my muscles contracting on their own. "Feel free to experiment more."

Hallelujah for the front-clasp bra. Van made quick work of it, and when his mouth closed down on my left nipple, my entire body jerked. About eighty times. I'd never heard of sexually induced convulsions, but it was apparent I was making history.

My other breast clamored for attention, and he showed his impartiality. Between his hands and his lips and his tongue, both my breasts were happy, but other parts of me were getting restless, parts that had never been this vocal.

I tried to talk, but failed utterly. It's hard to speak when you can't catch your breath. So I engaged in the universal language of love and tried to pull his shirt over his head. He laughed and helped me, returning to my side when my shirt and bra had joined his shirt at the far end of the bed.

Van cupped my breasts. "Gorgeous."

For once in my life I was really glad I had a big chest. To make Van happy today, I was more than willing to suffer saggy boobs and back pain when I was fifty.

"The night you wore that tank top . . ."

"You had to bring that up, didn't you?" *Oh, wow.* Teeth on nipples was something else.

"I wanted to lock you in a closet so no other guy could see you."

"Really?" How sweet was that? "I had no idea."

Conversation paused for a moment while he made his way down my belly with his tongue. No need to talk. The conversation would keep. My raging need for his body against mine wouldn't.

"As good as you look in these, they need to come off." Van tugged at my sweatpants and I showed my appreciation of such a good idea by trying to assist him in removing my pants. Oddly enough, I removed his instead of mine. I wasn't quite sure how that happened, but seeing as how he managed quite well on his own to disrobe me, I decided not to worry about it.

He stretched out on the bed, and I was wrapped up in his arms and legs, skin meshing with skin, kissing him so frantically I felt as if my head were going to spin off. It was then that it happened.

I knew.

That I loved him.

That I couldn't live without him.

That never again would I be the same.

That if he didn't want to spend the rest of his life with me, I would crumble into a pile of dust.

That if he did love me, then I could get through anything. Being fired, rejected by my family, anything. He was my strength, my core, my joy, and my glory, and for some stupid reason, I'd been fighting it.

Never claimed to be smart.

I realized suddenly that Van had stopped kissing me and was staring at me.

Did I have food in my teeth or something? Surely his need for me was stronger than that? "What?"

He touched my cheek with the back of his hand. "I can't believe I'm here with you." His voice was so full of tender wonder that it brought tears to the backs of my eyes. With that kind of comment, it certainly seemed to be a distinct possibility that he too was feeling the love.

"I can't either. It's perfect. Wonderful." I kissed him. "It's like everything that's gone wrong in my life has suddenly been turned right. Without all of that misery, I wouldn't be here with you, and that makes it all worthwhile."

He lifted his brow. "You mean that?"

"Of course." I was really digging this mushy stuff, but here was this hot naked guy whom I was completely in love with lying on top of me. Certain opportunities simply had to be taken advantage of. "Make love to me. Now."

He grinned and rolled me on my back. "Not yet." Then he made it very clear what he had in mind to fill the time.

And I had to say, I wasn't opposed. Not one bit. I even joined in the fun a bit to show what talent I had with my mouth on his more interesting body parts. I am proud to say that I did womankind proud. And you know what? I have to admit I'd never enjoyed that before. Not ever.

But with Van, it was empowering to have him quivering under my touch. I wanted to give him as much pleasure as he was giving me. My first experience as a selfless lover. Amazing what true love could do.

"Hang on." Van groaned the words as he rolled away from me.

I followed him and grabbed the condom packet out of his hand. "Let me." I pushed him onto his back and tore open the foil. "I've never done this before. Which side is up?"

His face was twisted in torturous agony as he turned it over. I unrolled it and gave a few extra-loving touches to keep him from falling asleep.

The moment things were in place, he grabbed my hips and flipped me onto my back. Was he taking charge, exerting his power? I was okay with that. It was obvious who was the one in control. Because I loved him, I'd let him think he held the upper hand.

He hooked my ankles over his shoulders and slid inside. Instant explosion of everything: joy, love, and an unbelievable sensation of completeness. Fastest orgasm I'd ever had. Good thing, because Van hit a speed record too.

We were both laughing when he collapsed next to me. Laughing and trembling and enjoying the ongoing spasmodic jerks of our bodies experiencing aftershocks.

Van wrapped his arms around me and hauled me against him. "You belong here. In my bed. With me."

Couldn't say I disagreed with the man.

CHAPTER TWENTY-TWO

I was wearing Van's T-shirt and shorts while I watched him cook breakfast the next morning. Cereal was fine with me, but he'd insisted that our first morning together had to be memorable. To him, memorable meant a feast that would settle right on my hips, but I didn't care.

I had a feeling Van wouldn't kick me out if I added a few more dimples to my lush supply of cellulite.

He looked at me as he scrambled the eggs. "So, you want to talk about your job?"

"I think you look incredibly sexy in boxers." That was all he was wearing, and he carried it well. I'd never been with a guy whom I wanted to jump while he was whipping his fork through a bunch of yolks. Must be that true-love thing. With bed-head and heavy stubble, he was so cute I wanted to die. I couldn't believe he'd picked me.

"Does this mean you don't want to talk about work? Not that I mind having you ogle my body."

I sighed and rested my chin on my hands. "I got fired. Culmination of everything that's been going wrong there lately."

"You going to sue for gender discrimination? Wrongful discharge?"

I laughed. "What are you, an ambulance-chasing lawyer?"

"No." He turned back to the stove and dumped the eggs into the frying pan. "What are you going to do then?"

I watched his back muscles flex as he cooked the eggs. "Hildy coerced me into applying to law school."

He looked at me sharply. "I thought you hated lawyers."

"I do." I rubbed under my eye and wished I had makeup. "But do I hate them because of my family or because I really hate them?"

"But either way, you hate them."

"I suppose." I stretched my arms, happy and content. It was amazing to feel this way after losing my job. Which just showed the power of love and great sex. "The question is, if I became one of them, would I stop hating them, or hate them more?"

"Maybe you shouldn't hate them. Have you ever considered not judging them all by the McCormick family standards? That maybe some of them are all right?"

"Hildy's nice."

"Anyone else?"

I rolled my eyes. "I'm really not in the mood to think charitable thoughts about the legal profession right now."

Van nodded. "What are you going to do for a job? Are you going to apply to another firm to be social director?"

"I don't know."

"Or go to law school?" His question held a thread of hope that brought me up sharply.

"You want me to go to law school?" Warning bells clanged in my head and tension closed around my gut.

"No, no, no." He dropped his spatula and squatted in front of me. "I want you to be happy. If you went to law school, then maybe some of the conflict with your family would disappear and you'd feel better. That's it. I don't care what you do."

My family.

Two big, fat, ugly words.

"I think I'm going to throw up."

My darling Van got a worried look on his face. "What's wrong? Was it the coffee? I know I tend to make it industrial strength."

I touched his face, but I was too tense to smile. "I have to go to my sister's rehearsal dinner tomorrow night. How am I supposed to tell them I got fired? They'll be disgusted that I couldn't even keep a job that wasn't good enough for me. Could I be more of a failure than that?" I could envision the look of total disappointment on my mom's face, then her quick glance around to make sure no one else heard the truth about her daughter. That would be it. "They'll have me killed."

Van chuckled. "They're not going to have you killed. "

"Yes, they will. The only thing that kept me alive before was the fact that I was working in a law firm, so they could tell people I worked there and then knock me out with a sledgehammer before I could say that my job was as social director, not as a lawyer." I slumped in my chair and didn't tell him they'd also kept me alive because I'd been dating Max. As wonderful as Van was, he wouldn't be a reason for my parents to spare me. "Did I tell you they had my grandma knocked off? I know I'm next."

"Shannon!"

I clutched his arms. "You said you could arrange a hit. Can you have my whole family killed off and make it look like an accident? It wouldn't be murder. Self-defense ahead of time."

He was laughing now. "I don't have any underworld connections, sorry."

"Stop laughing! It's not funny! You have no idea what my family is like."

His smile faded. "I talked to April a bit at your birthday. I have a pretty good idea, actually."

"Then tell me how I'm going to deal with them on Friday without putting my life at risk."

"Want me to come?"

I stared at him. "You want to come?"

"Unless you don't want me to." His face closed off slightly. "I'm sure Noah will be there."

How could he *possibly* wonder where he stood in my life? I threw my arms around him and buried my head in his neck. "That would be the best thing ever if you came with me."

His arms tightened around me. "Thanks."

"For what?" My voice was muffled by his shoulder.

"For responding that way."

I pulled back and looked at him. "Van, no matter what's wrong in my life, it's better when I'm with you. I want you there with me. Screw my parents."

He lifted a brow. "You want to bring a security guard boyfriend to the party to offend your parents?"

Boyfriend? "You're my boyfriend?"

"Well, I sure as hell hope so, after last night."

I grinned. Was my smile actually hitting my ears? Sure felt like it. "Cool."

He cocked his head. "You don't care whether I'm a security guard, do you?"

"Or a stripper." I teased, then I kissed him. "I know that's your secret. When are you going to dance for me?" A slight cloud drifted into my bliss. I'd forgotten about his secret. How could he hold back on me now?

His face darkened. "Not yet."

"Van!" I stomped my foot and scowled. "That's so unfair. And it hurts me that you won't trust me."

"When I tell you, you'll understand." Then he kissed me, and I thought I heard him whisper under his breath, "I hope."

Yeah, I hoped so too. And when we finished christening the kitchen floor with our lovemaking, I was going to tell him exactly what I thought about secrets between lovers.

In the meantime, suddenly I wasn't feeling so nervous about the rehearsal dinner. My pillar of strength was going to be on my arm. With him by side, I could get through anything.

Except a car bomb set by my family under my Jetta. We'd take Van's truck to the party. Problem solved.

For now.

The moment I walked into the church for the rehearsal, I knew it had been a mistake to tell Van to meet us at the restaurant. I couldn't do this alone.

I stood at the back of the church, watching my family

mill around the front of the chapel. They were all there. I was the last one present. I noticed April sitting off by herself right away. Travis was hanging with Ray by the altar.

And, surprise, surprise, Noah was talking to my mom and dad. Sucking up. *Shit*. I forgot about Noah. I'd have to tell him about Van. Actually, that might be kind of satisfying. *See what happens when you take a wonderful woman for granted? You lose her.*

Maybe I should leave. No one seemed to care that I was there.

I looked at April again, sitting by herself.

Or I could join her, so we could be ostracized together. It was unbelievable to think that April might become my soul mate in my family. Maybe I should offer to finally pay my share of Lindsay's gift, seeing as how she'd never collected.

Or not. It wasn't as if I had an income at the moment.

Which I wasn't going to tell anyone. Why should I? It was my business.

Relieved at my incredibly wise and self-protective decision, I walked farther into the church and sneaked down the side aisle. No one noticed me as I slid in beside April. "How's it going?"

She started and whipped around. Then her face softened. "I never knew how hard it was to be you."

Ah, yes. That sounded complimentary. "It's not so bad." I leaned back and folded my arms. "So how are we going to sabotage the rehearsal? Any ideas?"

April gave me a half smile. "None that are legal."

I couldn't believe how sad she looked. It almost made

me forget my own problems. "Maybe being around this wedding will make Travis realize he wants it too."

"Maybe." There was no hope in her voice.

What a bastard. How could Travis do this to her? "Did you guys ever talk about marriage before you got pregnant?"

April sighed. "A little. But we always concluded there was no reason to get married, since we didn't want to have kids."

"What about love? Commitment? Taking care of each other when you're old and decrepit?"

"You don't need marriage for that."

Well, I guess not, but still. "Technically you don't need marriage for kids either."

"I know. That's what Travis says."

"So maybe you could be happy like that?"

She looked at me. "Except that when I became pregnant, I realized I wanted everything I'd thought I didn't. Kids, a marriage, a family."

Oh. Guess that could be a problem. "I don't blame you."

"Travis is pissed because he feels like I turned the tables on him. We had this understanding, and now I want to change it."

I fiddled with my hair and had an idea that made my stomach turn. "Why don't you ask my mom for help?"

April shot me a shocked look. "You're kidding."

"Well, you said she's ostracizing you because of the out-of-wedlock thing."

She narrowed her eyes. "Appreciate your bringing it up."

"Oh, come on, April, don't get offended. I simply meant

311

that you and she want the same thing: to have you and Travis get married. If she knows you want it too, then maybe she'll work on Travis, or at least understand that it's not your fault." The words weren't even out of my mouth when I was hit with a wave of regret at no longer having April be an outcast with me at family gatherings. Nice mature attitude.

Given the black look April gave me, I astutely realized she wasn't bowled over with my idea. "How many times do I have to tell you? The marriage will fail if I have to force him into it. He has to want it."

"Maybe you shouldn't be so moral and upright. Force the jerk into it. With any luck he'll have a change of heart, like you did. At worst, you'll get alimony."

"I don't need his money." Her voice dripped with disgust.

"Sorry. I was trying to be helpful. At least I'm sitting here with you."

She shot me a look. "Would you be sitting here with me if you didn't have to?"

"Yes. Would you be sitting with me?"

She had the grace to look embarrassed. We both knew the answer and had lived it for the last few years when she was happy with Travis and not pregnant. She and Noah were the same: willing to trade me to be in my family's bosom.

Funny how my bond with April didn't feel quite so special at the moment.

"Now I would."

I looked at April. "What?"

"If I worked everything out with your family, I'd still sit

with you." She smiled. "You're all right, Shannon McCormick."

I felt myself smile back. Maybe there was the start of a friendship here after all.

"Shannon! Where have you been?" My mom snapped her fingers. "We've been waiting for you."

"I've been here."

"Well, come over here." My mom hesitated. "You too, April."

"We're pariahs," I whispered to April, who smiled.

Lindsay had asked April and me to be bridesmaids, in addition to three of her friends and Geoff's two sisters. It was a nice gesture, I guess.

I was leaning against the pew listening to the minister's instructions when I felt someone looking at me. I glanced up to see Noah studying me. When he caught my gaze, he shot me a smile.

I ignored him.

"What are you doing?"

I turned to find Ray leaning over my shoulder. "What?"

"Noah smiled at you."

"Oh, for God's sake, Ray, I've known him for twenty years. It's not like we're going to pretend we don't even know each other." Too bad I was going to have to end it with Noah. I'd love to have it work out just to torture Ray. "What's your deal, anyway? Why is the concept of me and Noah so offensive to you?"

"Mom! Ray and Shannon are fighting." Lindsay's pouty whine invaded my mind, and I was instantly embarrassed. The last thing I needed was that kind of attention.

I moved away from Ray. "Sorry." I muttered my apology to no one in particular, and the minister swiftly resumed his instructions while my mom eyed us.

As did Noah. When he saw me looking at him, he lifted his brow. What was that supposed to mean?

By the end of the rehearsal, I was spun so tight I was certain my head would snap right off. I'd endured a few remarks about my job and I felt some really weird vibes going on between Ray, Noah, and my mom. I had the distinct impression they'd discussed me, and I didn't like the feeling. Especially since no one seemed inclined to enlighten me.

And Travis wasn't touching April. He stood stiffly next to her while she folded her arms across her chest.

Undercurrents of tension were running rampant, and I expected an explosion at any second.

I was thrilled to get back out to my car, and yes, I did resist the urge to check under it for a bomb. But only just. Not that I knew what a bomb would look like, but still. I was thankful my dependable old Jetta started without excessive fireworks, and I spun off toward the very posh and trendy downtown restaurant for the dinner.

When I pulled into the parking lot, I saw my mom and dad walking with Ray and Noah. My dad had his arm around Noah's shoulder and they were all laughing about something. Travis and April were in his car yelling at each other, and Lindsay and Geoff were fawning over each other, looking like the spread in some bridal magazine. The caption would read, "The happy couple at their rehearsal dinner."

I couldn't deal. I closed my eyes and leaned back

against the headrest. How was I going to avoid the topic of my job tonight? They were going to find out. I knew they were. Then Noah would laugh and be glad that he'd never pursued me.

A light knock on the window interrupted my pity session. When I saw Van peering at me, I grinned and unlocked the door. "I'm so glad you're here."

"Night's going that well, huh?"

I'd never seen him dressed up, and he looked great. His suit fit his body to perfection, showing off his gorgeous physique. "Can you abduct me so I can't go to the dinner?"

He grinned and distracted me with a very hot kiss that had my nether regions longing for his kitchen floor again. "Ready?"

"I think my legs are jelly."

"Good." He grabbed my hand and pulled me to my feet. "Come on. We'll make fun of everyone behind their backs."

"I like your style."

Van stepped back from me and inspected my outfit. It was the same black dress I'd worn to Lindsay's engagement party. It was what I felt the best in, and I needed that comfort. "You look gorgeous."

Points for the dress. "Thanks."

He pulled me against him and made it clear exactly how much he liked me in that dress, but in a perfectly respectable way. Unlike Noah, who'd nearly undressed me in front of everyone.

Van might be a security guard, but he had a hell of a lot more class than Noah.

"What's going on here?" April's amused voice danced in my ears.

Total embarrassment. I pulled away from Van, but he hauled me back against him, throwing his arm around my shoulder and making it very clear he was with me.

Such a change from Noah. Any wonder I loved this guy? "This is my . . . boyfriend, Van Reinhart. Van, this is my brother Travis and his . . . better half. You remember April from my birthday party." April shot me a grateful look. No doubt she wasn't high on the *girlfriend* label at the moment. *Fiancée* or *wife* would be much better, especially now that she was beginning to show.

Van's arm tightened around me when I said *boyfriend*, and a warm glow settled in my belly.

"Nice to meet you."

Everyone shook hands in a very dignified fashion, but it was apparent that April and Travis were nearly overflowing with questions about Van and his boyfriend status. Probably because he was so gorgeous in his beautiful suit, they couldn't understand how I could have landed him.

We strolled inside with April and Travis, engaging in polite conversation, Van's arm still securely around me. When we reached the foyer, he stopped and nodded at April and Travis. "We'll catch up."

April shot me a look that said we'd be making a trip to the ladies' room in short order so I could fill her in.

Van turned me toward him. "What did your family say when you told them you got fired?"

I made a pretense of flicking some dust off his jacket. As if there'd be dust on it. He was dressed impeccably. "Haven't told them."

"Why not?"

"I'm a wimp." I straightened his already straight tie. "Why

do I need to expose myself to that? I'll send them all an e-mail after the wedding, and then hide from them for a while." I finally looked up. "What do you think?"

There was no mistaking the disappointment in his eyes. "You should face them. The first step in making them accept you for who you are is to be proud of yourself."

"Be proud? I got fired."

"You're an amazing woman, and it takes more than a job or a lack thereof to change that."

I love you. The words were so close to slipping out, but I squelched them. It was too early for pronouncements of love, especially when he was still hiding things from me. "I'll think about it. That's all I can say."

He nodded. "I'll back you up either way."

I considered that. Did he mean he'd tell my family they were wrong if they started to condemn me? Once he witnessed the McCormick money, power, and influence, would he be so willing to throw away their favor to defend me?

The thought was too overwhelming to ponder.

"Okay, let's go in." I put my arm through his. "Don't leave my side, okay?"

He lifted the back of my hand to his lips. "I promise."

Even Van on my arm couldn't squelch the dread that settled in my gut as we walked inside.

CHAPTER TWENTY-THREE

By the time we arrived, everyone was seated. The only two spots were at the end of a long table. My mom and dad were at the opposite end with Lindsay and Geoff.

I took the chair at the foot of the table, and Van sat on my left. Unfortunately, since my dad was sitting at the head of the table, I had to look directly at him. At least my mom was on the left side, so she was less visible. I doubted she could even see Van from where she was sitting, and relief surged through me.

Then guilt, as I realized I was worried about my mom and dad's reaction when they learned what Van did for a living. Not that I was ashamed of Van, but I didn't know if I had the strength to handle more disdain—or even worse, what if they made Van feel bad?

Then I'd feel terrible and—

"Who is this?" Ray asked. *Great*. He and Noah were in the two seats closest to us. I'd been so busy watching my parents I'd missed that little detail.

I could see Noah studying Van. Probably trying to remember why he looked familiar, and wondering why he was there with me. Then I saw a smug tilt to his lips, and I realized he thought I'd arranged a date to make him jealous. *Fat chance of that.* "Van, this is my brother Ray and a family friend, Noah Quinlan." I looked at Ray and Noah. "This is Van Reinhart, my boyfriend."

Ray's face reflected shock, and Noah looked annoyed. "Your boyfriend? As of when?"

Van set his hand over mine, which was sitting on the table, in a masculine display of ownership. "We've been friends for a long time, and we finally realized it wasn't enough." He smiled at me. "I've been waiting for her for a long time."

My cheeks tingled and I grinned stupidly.

Noah scowled, and Ray looked stunned. "Really?" Ray asked. "You're really a couple? This isn't a farce to make me think you don't want Noah anymore?"

I tried to kick him under the table, but succeeded only in smashing my toes into something really hard. Like the table leg. *Crap.* Hurt like a mother.

Van's face tightened. "It's real."

Only two words, but he said them with such finality that I couldn't imagine anyone would question him.

Ray apparently agreed, because he relaxed and grinned a huge smile. "Welcome to the family, Van. Glad to have you."

Noah said nothing, but his eyes were glittering. *Too damn bad.*

"Can we have everyone's attention, please?" My dad tapped his water glass and everyone stopped talking. "Lindsay's mom and I would like to make a toast."

My mom stood up next to my dad, and I heard Van curse

and suck in his breath. He leaned back in his chair and looked absolutely horrified. I touched his arm. "What's wrong?"

"That's your mom?"

"Yes. Why?"

He cursed again and looked like he was trying to disappear into his chair.

My dad continued with his toast. "We'd like to welcome Geoff to the family. You are a great addition to the McCormick family, and I will proudly claim you as my son-in-law."

I glanced at April, who appeared to be on the verge of tears.

My mom lifted her glass. "And we're looking forward to our first grandchild."

April brightened.

My mom continued. "With two doctors as parents, the child is sure to be a credit to his genes. So get busy!"

Good God. Was she kidding? I looked at April's shocked face and wanted to throw a plate at my mom. It was a total and complete dismissal that there was already another grandchild on the way. Even Travis looked surprised.

That couldn't have been intentional, could it? My mom wouldn't be that harsh.

Everyone lifted their glasses and my parents sat down. I tried to catch April's eyes, but she was staring at her lap and chewing on her lower lip.

Van sat up again and leaned toward me. "Maybe I should leave."

"What?" I stared at him. "You can't leave."

"I'm not sure I belong. All the doctors and lawyers."

So sweet. I put my hand on his arm. "Van, you tell me I should be proud of myself. Same goes for you."

"I heard you got fired."

The conversation at our end of the table stopped instantly as everyone turned to stare at Noah, who was looking at me. "What did you say?"

Noah jerked his head at Van. "I heard you two talking in the lobby about the fact that you got fired. What happened?"

Bastard.

"Who got fired?" My mom's voice penetrated the crowd, and Van shrank back in his chair.

What was his problem? She wasn't *that* scary.

April was looking at me with empathy in her eyes.

I lifted my gaze to my parents, who were both looking horrified. "I got fired." I lifted my chin. "Two days ago."

"Oh, *Shannon.*" Like she couldn't believe I'd done something so stupid. "What did you do?"

"Who's your date?" April said suddenly. "Is this your new boyfriend?"

That woman was absolutely my new best friend. "Yes." I gestured to Van. "I'd like you guys to meet Van Reinhart, my boyfriend." The word was rolling quite easily off my tongue now. *Boyfriend. Boyfriend. Boyfriend. Van is my boyfriend.*

Van looked embarrassed and nodded, still leaning back in his chair so no one on his side of the table could see him.

"What do you do, Van?" my dad asked.

I tensed, and Van looked more than a little concerned.

"He's a security guard," Noah said, triumph ringing clear. "That's where I know him from. He works the night shift in Shannon's building."

I lifted my chin. "Yes, he does."

My dad looked like he was going to pass out, and even April looked startled. My mom, on the other hand, wouldn't be put off. She pushed back her chair and walked around the table to get a look at this lowly security guard who was dating her loser daughter. With any luck, she'd decide we were both so low on the totem pole that we weren't worth worrying about.

She came to a stop behind Noah and Ray; then her gaze narrowed. "I know you."

Van muttered something and looked desperate.

My mom leaned closer. "You work at my firm, don't you?"

I sat up. Her firm? Her law firm? "Do you work day security there?" That was his secret? That he had two jobs?

"Yeah."

But my mom was shaking her head. "No, I've seen you in meetings, haven't I?" She pursed her lips. "Do you work for my firm?"

Van stopped squirming suddenly and sat up. He took my hand in his and turned his back on my mom. "Shannon, I didn't want to tell you until it was too late for you to back out."

My heart felt achy and heavy. "Tell me what?"

"I've been going to law school during the day for the last few years. I've been working security at night to pay for it." He swallowed. "I interned at your mom's firm. Just took the bar exam a couple weeks ago. You know, when I disappeared for three weeks? I was grinding it out studying." He tightened his grip on my hand. "I'm going to be working there starting in the fall."

"No fucking way."

"I didn't know she was your mom."

I pulled my hand away from his, my head spinning. "Why didn't you tell me?"

"Because I was afraid you'd judge me for being a lawyer. As soon as you told me you loved me, I was going to tell you, I swear."

Of all the things to hide from me. "You know how I feel about lawyers."

"That's why I couldn't tell you." He jerked his head at Noah. "After he blew you off, I thought for sure I'd never have a chance if you knew what I did."

My dad roared. "Noah blew her off? What does that mean?"

Ray scowled. "They slept together."

"What?" My dad's face got so red and twisted he looked like Otto's twin.

I felt sick. Betrayed. Utterly betrayed.

And then I saw Noah's smug face, and I hated him with everything I possessed. "Don't you dare look at me like that," I shouted. "You used me, and somehow you got my mom and Ray to think it was my fault. You don't deserve your place of royalty in this family." I was on my feet now and I shrugged out of Van's grasp. "You"—I pointed at my mom—"should be disgusted with yourself. Just because I'm not some fancy lawyer, you take Noah's side. You're disgusting, and I can't believe I've spent my life trying to win your favor."

"Shannon. Sit down."

I lowered my finger, but instead of sitting down I leaned in closer toward my mom. "And it's not just me. Even April is your victim." April sucked in her breath and I waved in her direction. "You treat her like a leper because she's pregnant and unmarried. But it's your own damned son who won't marry her! April wants to be a wife and a mother, as well as a superstar professional, and your own stupid son is too self-centered to even consider sacrificing a moment of his precious freedom for a woman who loves him and his own damn child!" I was screaming now, and I didn't care. "And it's your fault! You're so obsessed with work and success that you've made Travis and Ray the way they are, picking career over family and what's important!"

I grabbed my purse off the chair, fighting back tears. I would never let them see me cry. "I know you've been looking for the chance to disown me, but I'm taking it away from you. As of now, I'm no longer a McCormick. I'm simply too ashamed to admit I'm related to you." I glared at the room. "I hope you all rot in hell."

I walked out with as much dignity as I could muster. Which was probably negligible, but hey, I was about out of dignity these days.

Van caught up to me at the front door. "We have to talk."

I peeled his hand off my arm. "How could you lie to me? To find out like that, in front of everyone?"

"I know, I'm sorry." He tried to grab my hand, but I pulled away. "I was too afraid to lose you. Our relationship was so tenuous, with all these other guys in the picture, I couldn't afford to give you a reason not to come to me."

"So you lied?"

"I omitted. And I was going to tell you as soon as I felt we were secure."

"How do I know you didn't use me to get into my family? I

thought you had no idea who my family was, and that's why I trusted you. Because you wouldn't have ulterior motives."

"I didn't know who they were!"

"As if there are that many McCormick lawyers around." I felt so empty. "What else did you lie about?"

"Nothing! Shannon—"

I held up my hand. "Not tonight, Van." I pulled my keys out. "I have to go."

"Can I follow you home?"

"No." I couldn't even look at him. The one person whom I'd totally trusted. "I thought you were like me, Van. A regular person. And you're one of them."

He narrowed his gaze. "Is that why you liked me? Because you thought I was a nobody?"

"No!"

"You're a reverse snob, as bad as your mother."

I wanted to slap him. "I am not my mother."

"Yes, you are. You judge people by their careers exactly the way she does, but you hate anyone professional and respond to those who you feel are nobodies." He moved closer. "You didn't even like April until she was on your mom's bad side. Wake up, Shannon. Until you do, you're going to look in the mirror and see your mom's face, all the parts of it you don't like."

I stared at him. "I hate you."

"Too bad. Because I love you." He kissed me hard and fast, then walked out.

I didn't go after him.

When I got home, Dave, Phoebe, and Emma were in the middle of making chocolate chip cookies. I tried to duck past them into my bedroom, but Emma stopped me. "Shannon! Your letter from the law school came."

I froze. My letter? I slowly turned toward them. I must have looked awful, because the moment I was facing them, each got a horrified expression on their face.

"What's wrong?"

"What happened to you?"

"Are you okay?"

I ignored them. When was I going to learn to wear water-proof mascara? "What does it say?"

Emma held it out. "I didn't open it."

"Open it." My hands were shaking too much to function. They'd been shaking the whole way home, and I'd almost crashed into a fire hydrant when I'd missed a sharp turn.

She tore the end off and unfolded the letter inside. Dave and Phoebe leaned over her shoulder, and the three of them read it together. Then they looked at each other.

"What?" The anticipation was killing me.

"You got in."

"I got in?"

They nodded. "To the day program."

"Holy shit."

Emma tossed the letter to Phoebe. "You look terrible. Come here." She pulled me into the kitchen and settled me on a chair. "Put your head between your knees."

"I'm not going to faint." I did as she directed anyway, in case the buzzing in my ears and the spots dancing in front of my eyes were indicative of anything dangerous.

I got into law school.

Me. A lawyer. What sense did that make?

Phoebe stuck a spoonful of cookie dough into my hand. "Eat."

It's not easy to eat cookie dough upside down, but I managed, being the incredibly talented glutton that I am.

"Are you going to go to school?" Dave asked.

"What about work?" Emma said. "I thought you were going to go to night school and keep your job during the day so you wouldn't have to ask your parents for money?"

I sat up slowly and looked at them. "I got fired." *Ow.* The words still stabbed me through the heart.

Emma grinned and clapped me on the back. "Welcome to the club. How does it feel?"

"Crappy." I scowled at her. "Getting fired from a career isn't the same as you getting fired from one of your experimental jobs."

"It wasn't a career. It was a life-sucking job that was destroying you." Emma looked very pleased. Probably figured I wouldn't harass her the next time she was fired.

Ha.

Phoebe licked one of the beaters. "The timing is perfect. You don't have a job, so go to school full-time."

"Yeah." I filled my spoon and nibbled on the cookie dough.

"So it's fate," Emma announced. "You were destined to go to law school and become a lawyer."

"Yeah." I chewed a chocolate chip.

"Are you going to tell your parents or let them figure it out on their own?" Phoebe answered her own question. "Don't tell them, so you can't convince yourself you're going to school to make them happy."

"I agree," Emma said. "Someday they'll figure it out and

you can laugh at them. Isn't this funny how you're going to be a lawyer after all this? Total crack-up."

I looked at Dave, who hadn't said anything. He was scooping cookie dough onto the baking sheet. "Dave?"

He finished loading up the sheet and stuck it in the oven. Then he leaned against the counter and folded his arms across his chest. "What happened tonight?"

How did he know? "I disowned my family." It didn't sum up all the anguish of the night, but it covered it on a high level. "And Van lied to me."

"Talk."

I looked at Emma and Phoebe, who nodded.

Did I want to talk? "I'd rather not."

Dave went to the fridge, pulled out a bottle of white wine, popped the cork, and served all of us. Then he set a plate of hot cookies in the middle of the table, pulled up a chair, and sat down. "We've got warm cookies, wine, and all night. Talk."

Talk about Van? Noah? My job? My family? April?

Phoebe put the box of tissues in front of me before the tears even arrived. "Let it all out, honey. We're here."

I looked around the table. "Do you realize this is the first time in forever the four of us have been together?"

Emma nodded. "It's a sign that we were meant to be here tonight for you. Talk, girlfriend."

I sighed and picked up cookie. "I have no idea where to start."

"Why'd you get fired?"

That. I sighed. "It was a conspiracy."

"Of course it was," Emma said. "By who?"

328

"Mutinous interns." *Little rabid varmints.* "Insane old men."

And there it began, the process of my unloading all that had been crushing me lately. My friends listened and nodded. We drank and ate. I blew my nose and went through an entire box of tissues. By the time I finished, we'd had to make another batch of cookies to sustain us. "There you have it. My life."

Dave rubbed his chin, playing with Phoebe's hair with his other hand. I wanted someone to play with my hair! I wanted someone to love me so much they'd give up everything for me!

But no, the guy I loved had lied. Not exactly comparable assets.

"I'm glad you told your family off," Emma said. "It's about time someone had the nerve to stand up to them."

"What about law school?" Dave asked.

"It seems like the logical answer. I could always quit if I wanted to." I sighed. "But it doesn't feel right."

"Does anything?"

Van. He'd felt right. Except he wasn't who I'd thought he was.

"What will you do if you don't go to law school?" Emma asked.

I shook my head. "Nothing. I should go. I mean, what else is there to do, right? It's not as if I liked my job that much. I don't want to go to another firm and deal with the same thing. They'll be more mutinous interns and psychotic old men wherever I go." I ground my palms into my eyelids. "I can't believe I got fired."

"Get over it," Emma said. "It's not a big deal. Everyone gets fired at some point in their life."

I glared at her. "This is my first time, so I'm going to feel sorry for myself. It sucks."

"How does it suck? You hated your job anyway, and you didn't have the courage to quit. I think it's great." Emma picked up another cookie and shoved it into her mouth. "Quit bellyaching and grow up."

"Grow up? Coming from the woman who can't hold down a job or pay for her own expenses."

"Hey!" Phoebe banged her fist on the table. "Don't start that again!"

"Fine." I folded my arms across my chest. "Sorry."

"Sorry," Emma replied.

Dave sat up. "What do you like about your job?"

"My old job?"

"Yes."

I sighed. "I guess I liked putting on events and being social. I liked being in charge. I liked entertaining others. I liked Hildy."

"And what didn't you like?"

"The atmosphere of a law firm. Having to tread so carefully around the egos. Knowing I was considered auxiliary and not critical."

Dave finished jotting down what I'd said and spun the paper in front of me. "What does it say to you?"

I studied the list. "That I like events and hate the law firm part."

"Then why are you considering a career where you give up the events part and take on the law firm part?"

I frowned. Not a bad point. "You think I should become

an events manager? Work for an events firm or something?"

"Do you?"

I trailed my hair around my index finger, and a slow burn of interest began to churn inside me. "Maybe." I studied the list. "Maybe."

CHAPTER TWENTY-FOUR

I spent the day going through the want ads in the *Boston Globe* and on the Internet. I found seventeen events positions and applied for all of them. And you know what? For the first time in a long time, I was excited about my professional future, or at least the possibilities.

The law school acceptance letter was open on my desk. Every so often I picked it up and read it again.

Shannon McCormick, attorney-at-law.

It had some appeal, I supposed.

But not enough. I smiled and set it aside.

"You think it was blowing up at your family that finally gave you the courage to walk away from anything law related?"

I looked up to find Emma lounging in my doorway. "Maybe."

"You know I'm right, that you were at the law firm as a subconscious concession to your parents' desire for you to be an attorney, don't you?"

I leaned back in my chair. "It's possible, I guess."

Emma nodded at the newspaper on my bed. "You're

finally going to leave all things law behind. How does it feel?"

I smiled. "Good."

"Then it's the right decision." She hesitated, then levered herself away from the door frame and sat down on my bed. "It's four thirty."

"So?"

"We need to leave for the wedding by five."

I turned back to my computer and resumed typing. "I'm not going."

"I am."

"I don't care."

"So is Blaine, and Dave and Phoebe. We're all going."

I ground my teeth. "So?"

"I think you should go."

"Forget it." I spun around to face her. "How can I? I made a total fool of myself yesterday. Plus I disowned them. If I show up today, they'll think I want to be back in the bosom of my family, as if I was ever there." The thought was chilling. I couldn't bear to make them feel smug.

"Depends on your reentry."

"How so?" Okay, so maybe I was a little intrigued.

"It's all in the presentation. Go to the wedding on your own terms. You want them to accept you? Then you have to accept them, as well as yourself."

"What are you, a psychiatrist?"

"Nope." She got up and retrieved my bridesmaid gown from the closet. "You'll never forgive yourself if you don't mend the relationship with your family. You have to go."

"I don't have a date."

"Then return Van's phone call. He's called, what, a hundred times today?"

I looked at the flowers on my desk that he'd sent earlier this afternoon. "He isn't who I thought he was."

"Maybe he's better."

"Because he's a lawyer who lied to me to get to my family?"

"Because he loves you so much he couldn't bear to risk losing you."

I stuck my tongue out at her. "Since when did you become a romantic?"

"Since I fell in love."

That surprised me. "You're really in love with Blaine? Like really and truly?"

She grinned. "Yep. It's awesome."

"But he's not your type. He's a lawyer and he wears suits. Short hair, polished shoes. Not rebelling against anything."

"Go figure. Guess love transcends anything, huh?" She walked to the door. "Love could transcend a little deception done for love, don't you think?"

"He's like everyone else, choosing my family over me."

"How?"

"He didn't defend me when I had my meltdown. If he loved me, he'd be willing to trade my family for me. But instead he's going to work for my mom's firm." I shook my head. "That's why I thought he was safe. As a security guard, he had no stake in my family. But now? He does. And if I went out with him, he'd always have to be treading that line between me and my family. His career will be in my mom's hands. Do you really think I'll come first?" I shook my head. "No way, Emma. I'm not going through another Noah."

She pursed her lips. "I understand."

"You do?" I didn't want her to understand. I wanted her to tell me I was wrong, that Van would never put my family before me.

"Yes. Don't invite him. But I think you need to come to the wedding. We're leaving in a half hour, and we're taking you with us. You'll look stupid going down the aisle in sweatpants with unwashed hair, so I suggest you head to the shower now, because you will be coming with us." She smiled sweetly. "Blaine is way stronger than you, so don't think you can fight it."

After she left, I sat at my computer for another five minutes, thinking and writing some notes.

Then I walked to the bathroom to take a shower.

I walked into the back of the church four minutes before the service was supposed to begin. My mom was flitting around straightening boutonnieres, my dad was in the corner looking overcome by the occasion, and the bridesmaids were clustered in the corner.

I walked over to the sea of blue taffeta and stood on the outside while they fawned over my sister.

It was April who noticed me. I waited for the hostility of last night to flare up in her eyes, and I tensed as she walked over to me. I considered making a break for it, but my mom was in the doorway and I didn't want to mess with her. April was the lesser of two evils.

She stopped in front of me. "You had no right to announce my personal life to your entire family."

"I know. I'm sorry." I was. "I lost it."

"Travis was pissed."

I grimaced.

"Your mom apologized."

"What?" Surely I'd heard wrong. Still had shampoo in my ears or something.

She smiled. "Your mom apologized. She said she hadn't been aware of how she was treating me until you brought it up. Then she boxed Travis's ears and told him he was unworthy of me."

"Really?" My mom going after a favored son? Unheard-of.

Her smiled widened. "How about that?"

"So you're back in her favor?"

"Uh-huh."

A thought dawned on me. "And you're associating with me in front of them?" My throat got all thick and clogged.

"You saved me." She slung her arm over my shoulder. "You're stuck with me now, sis."

I spun around to face her. "Sis?"

She grinned. "Yeah."

"Are you kidding? But . . . you said he was pissed? And that you didn't want to marry him if he was forced into it?"

April looked gorgeously happy as she shrugged. "He convinced me he really wanted to get married. He has to clean the house and do all the laundry and cooking for the next six months to prove it, but when he agreed to that, I knew he was serious." She rolled her eyes. "These boys are so wimpy. He was terrified of being a father, of figuring out to balance family and work. When I told him I was afraid too, it was like everything got better, because we could find our answers together and admit our fears to each other." She caught Travis's eye across the room and smiled at him. "It won't be easy, but we'll make it."

Some of the heaviness left my shoulders, and I was happy for her. Real happiness, not that mixed stuff that was laced with jealousy and resentment. This was a much better feeling.

I tensed and turned around. Sure enough, my mom was watching me. The procession started before she could approach me, but I knew I was still going to have to deal with her.

I avoided every member of my family until we were sitting down for dinner. I was at the table with the bridal party, which included Ray and Noah. My parents were at another table, luckily.

How could Lindsay have seated me next to Noah? I nodded at him as he sat down. "Where's Van?"

I ignored the empty seat next to me. "Not here."

"Didn't survive last night, huh?"

"What do you care?"

He slung his arm over the back of my chair and leaned toward me. "Seeing you with him last night made me realize what a mistake I'd made not fighting for you. I talked to Ray and your parents, and told them I wasn't going to stay away from you."

I glanced at Ray, who was watching us, but his expression wasn't hostile. It was resigned.

"Shannon, look at me."

I returned my gaze to Noah. "I know you were with Van on the rebound because I hurt you, and I'm sorry for that. I was wrong. You were right, but I'm here now." He took my hand. "Give me another chance."

"Shannon."

I looked up to find my mom and dad standing over us. I

swallowed and pulled my hand out of Noah's. "Hi." My brain kicked on then, and I grabbed for my purse and fished my acceptance letter out of it. I handed it to my mom and waited.

She unfolded it and they both read it. The most amazing glow of happiness lit up my mom's face. "Oh, Shannon. I can't believe it. You're going to law school."

My dad beamed and clapped me on the shoulder. "Well done."

"I'm turning it down."

They stared at me, their faces turning to stone.

"I need to follow my own dream." I swallowed deeply and became aware that the entire table was listening. Probably because they'd all been at the rehearsal dinner last night. "I'm going to find a job in event planning. Not doing events for a law firm. Events for the sake of doing events. It's what I like, and it's what I'm good at." My words stuck in my throat, and I had to take a sip of water before continuing. "I'm going to live for myself. I hope you can be happy for me and proud of me, but if you can't, I'm not going to try to please you anymore, and I'm not going to worry about it."

Noah squeezed my knee, and I wanted to punch him. Interesting. Not the reaction I would have expected from myself.

My mom and dad looked at each other, then back at me. It was my mom who spoke. "We're sorry, Shannon. I had no idea how you felt."

I lifted my chin and tried not to care about what she thought about me.

"We wanted you to be a success."

"I was."

My mom raised her eyebrow.

"Except for the getting-fired thing," I admitted. "Other than that, I was great at my job, and I'll be great at my next one."

"And you'll try not to get fired?"

I rolled my eyes. "See what you think of me? How insulting is that?"

Sweating discomfort with this kind of intimacy, my dad patted my shoulder. "Whatever you want to do is okay."

My mom looked rather ill, but she echoed his sentiment. "You are more important than your job."

"Really?" It wasn't much, but it was a start. "You won't pressure me anymore to be a lawyer or get a graduate degree?"

"What about event management? An MBA in marketing might be helpful."

"Mom."

She grimaced. "I'm sorry." She knelt down and took my hand, staring intently into my eyes. "Shannon McCormick, you listen to me, because I'm saying this only once. I love you and I'm proud of you. If I pressure you to accomplish more, it's only because I know you're so talented you can do anything you want. But it's not my place to push my dreams onto you." She fiddled with my bracelet. "My parents wanted me to take over their business. You know what it was?"

I shook my head. My mom never talked about her parents, who had died long ago.

"They owned a restaurant. It had been in the family for three generations. As their only child, I was expected to take over. I became a lawyer instead, left town, and never went back." She tightened her grip. "I never realized I was doing the same thing to you."

My mom had a history? A family? Sensitivity? Stunned didn't begin to describe how I felt.

"I'm so sorry, Shannon. Please know that I will do everything in my power not to repeat the past, but if I do, say something. Don't sit there being miserable until you can't take it anymore and you walk away forever, like I did. Tell me."

"You're not easy to tell things like that to."

She met my gaze. "Somehow, I think you're strong enough to handle it."

Yes, I guessed I was. "Okay."

She smiled and tucked a stray hair behind my ear. "Just don't do it at a party in front of other people screaming at the top of your lungs, okay?"

I grinned. "Maybe. I'll try. Remind me if I forget, okay?"

"Funny girl." She squeezed my hands. "I love you."

Was that the first time she'd said those words to me in my adult life? I was pretty sure it was. I wasn't sure I even knew how to say them back, but I decided to try, because we'd probably never have another moment like this again. "I love you, too, Mom."

"What about me?"

I grinned up at my dad. "You too."

He nodded gruffly. "Same here."

"Excuse me." We turned toward the stage, where the bandleader was speaking into the microphone. "Before we start the dinner music, we have a guest who would like to say something."

Lindsay muttered something about unauthorized speakers, and then Van walked up to the microphone and I forgot everything else.

"Hello." His voice cracked and he cleared his throat. "This won't take long."

My heart was racing, and I didn't know why. Nothing he could say would change my mind.

"Celeste McCormick, could you come up here, please?"

My mom? He wanted my mom? He was going to beg my mom's forgiveness for being associated with me? No wonder I hated him.

Her heels tapping smartly on the gorgeous wood floor, my mom walked up to the stage and stood next to Van. "Yes?"

He faced her. "I have received an offer for employment at your law firm, have I not?"

"Yes." My mom looked the part of the gorgeous, sophisticated lawyer, and Van looked like he belonged on her arm. He was a lawyer through and through.

"I apologize, but I must officially decline the position."

I sat up.

My mom looked shocked. "Why?"

"Because I love your daughter. I think it could lead to a conflict of interest if I were working for her mom. I choose her over you."

Noah cursed next to me, and April clapped. All I could do was stare.

A slow smile spread over my mom's face and she looked at me. "A good choice."

Van waved at the audience. "That's all. Thanks."

He followed my mom off the stage and walked over to me. "Hi."

"You . . ."

"I love you. It doesn't matter what law firm I work at." He tugged me to my feet. "I'll spend the rest of my life apologizing to you if that's what it'll take to get you to forgive me."

"Van . . ." To say I was overwhelmed would be a massive understatement. He'd turned down a job at the most prestigious firm in the city. For me. *For me.*

"Forgive me. Love me. Be mine."

I grinned and felt the last weight float away from my shoulders. "We're both unemployed now. We'll have to live off bread crumbs."

"I still have my stripping business. Maybe you could join. We could have a couples act. We'd be all the rage."

I entwined my fingers through his. "We should practice a lot in private first."

He smiled. "Agreed."

It was time to put my heart out there. He'd earned it, and it was worth the risk. "Van . . ."

"What?"

"I love you."

His face lit up.

"But it will take lots of great sex before I'll forgive you."

"In that case, I hope you never forgive me so I have to spend my life trying."

I grinned. "That was the best wedding speech I've ever heard." And then some. I was hooked, big-time.

And this time, just maybe, I was finally headed in the right direction with my life.

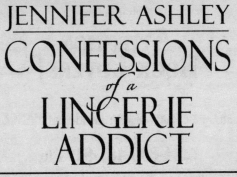

JENNIFER ASHLEY
CONFESSIONS
of a
LINGERIE
ADDICT

The fixation began on New Year's Day: Silky, expensive slips from New York and Italy. Camisoles and thongs from Beverly Hills. Before, Brenda Scott would have blushed to be caught dead in them. Now, she's ditched the shy and mousy persona that got her dumped by her rich and perfect fiancé, and she is sexy. Underneath her sensible clothes, Brenda is the woman she wants to be.

After all, why can't she be wild and crazy? Nick, the sexy stranger she met on New Year's, already seems to think she is. Of course, he didn't know the old Brenda. How long before Nick strips it all away and finds the truth beneath? And would that be a bad thing?
